Martin Hyde, The Duke's Messenger

John Masefield

Table of Contents

Martin Hyde, The Duke's Messenger..1

John Masefield..1

CHAPTER I. I LEAVE HOME..2

CHAPTER II. I LEAVE HOME AGAIN..12

CHAPTER III. I LEAVE HOME A THIRD TIME...........................17

CHAPTER IV. I LEAVE HOME FOR THE LAST TIME...................21

CHAPTER V. I GO TO SEA...31

CHAPTER VI. THE SEA! THE SEA!..40

CHAPTER VII. LAND RATS AND WATER RATS.........................48

CHAPTER VIII. I MEET MY FRIEND..54

CHAPTER IX. I SEE MORE OF MY FRIEND..............................60

CHAPTER X. SOUNDS IN THE NIGHT.....................................67

CHAPTER XI. AURELIA..75

CHAPTER XII. BRAVE CAPTAIN BARLOW................................83

CHAPTER XIII. IT BREEZES UP..91

CHAPTER XIV. A DRINK OF SHERBET.....................................98

CHAPTER XV. THE ROAD TO LYME...104

CHAPTER XVI. THE LANDING...109

CHAPTER XVII. A VOICE AT DAWN...114

CHAPTER XVIII. I SPEAK WITH AURELIA.................................120

CHAPTER XIX. I MEET THE CLUB MEN....................................127

CHAPTER XX. THE SQUIRE'S HOUSE......................................132

CHAPTER XXI. MY FRIEND AURELIA AND HER UNCLE.............139

CHAPTER XXII. THE PRIEST'S HOLE.......................................146

CHAPTER XXIII. FREE..152

CHAPTER XXIV. THE END...158

Martin Hyde, The Duke's Messenger

John Masefield

- CHAPTER I. I LEAVE HOME
- CHAPTER II. I LEAVE HOME AGAIN
- CHAPTER III. I LEAVE HOME A THIRD TIME
- CHAPTER IV. I LEAVE HOME FOR THE LAST TIME
- CHAPTER V. I GO TO SEA
- CHAPTER VI. THE SEA! THE SEA!
- CHAPTER VII. LAND RATS AND WATER RATS
- CHAPTER VIII. I MEET MY FRIEND
- CHAPTER IX. I SEE MORE OF MY FRIEND
- CHAPTER X. SOUNDS IN THE NIGHT
- CHAPTER XI. AURELIA
- CHAPTER XII. BRAVE CAPTAIN BARLOW
- CHAPTER XIII. IT BREEZES UP
- CHAPTER XIV. A DRINK OF SHERBET
- CHAPTER XV. THE ROAD TO LYME
- CHAPTER XVI. THE LANDING
- CHAPTER XVII. A VOICE AT DAWN
- CHAPTER XVIII. I SPEAK WITH AURELIA
- CHAPTER XIX. I MEET THE CLUB MEN
- CHAPTER XX. THE SQUIRE'S HOUSE
- CHAPTER XXI. MY FRIEND AURELIA AND HER UNCLE
- CHAPTER XXII. THE PRIEST'S HOLE
- CHAPTER XXIII. FREE
- CHAPTER XXIV. THE END

CHAPTER I. I LEAVE HOME

I was born at Oulton, in Suffolk, in the year 1672. I know not the day of my birth, but it was in March, a day or two after the Dutch war began. I know this, because my father, who was the clergyman at Oulton, once told me that in the night of my birth a horseman called upon him, at the rectory, to ask the way to Lowestoft. He was riding from London with letters for the Admiral, he said; but had missed his way somewhere beyond Beccles. He was mud from head to foot (it had been a wet March) but he would not stay to dry himself. He reined in at the door, just as I was born, as though he were some ghost, bringing my life in his saddle bags. Then he shook up his horse, through the mud, towards Lowestoft, so that the splashing of the horse's hoofs must have been the first sound heard by me. The Admiral was gone when he reached Lowestoft, poor man, so all his trouble was wasted. War wastes more energy, I suppose, than any other form of folly. I know that on the East Coast, during all the years of my childhood, this Dutch war wasted the energies of thousands. The villages had to drill men, each village according to its size, to make an army in case the Dutch should land. Long after the war was over, they drilled thus. I remember them on the field outside the church, drilling after Sunday service, firing at a stump of a tree. Once some wag rang the alarm−bell at night, to fetch them out of their beds. Then there were the smugglers; they, too, were caused by the war. After the fighting there was a bitter feeling against the Dutch. Dutch goods were taxed heavily (spice, I remember, was made very dear thus) to pay for the war. The smugglers began then to land their goods secretly, all along the coast, so that they might avoid the payment of the duty. The farmers were their friends; for they liked to have their gin cheap. Indeed, they used to say that in an agueish place like the fens, gin was a necessity, if one would avoid fever. Often, at night, in the winter, when I was walking home from Lowestoft school, I would see the farmers riding to the rendezvous in the dark, with their horses' hoofs all wrapped up in sacks, to make no noise.

I lived for twelve years at Oulton. I learned how to handle a boat there, how to swim, how to skate, how to find the eggs of the many wild fowl in the reeds. In those days the Broad country was a very wild land, half of it swamp. My father gave me a coracle on my tenth birthday. In this little boat I used to explore the country for many miles, pushing up creeks among the reeds, then watching, in the pools (far out of the world it seemed) for ruffs or wild duck. I was a hardy boy, much older than my years, like so many only children. I used to go away, sometimes, for two or three days together, with my friend John Halmer, Captain Halmer's son, taking some bread, with a blanket or two, as my ship's stores. We used to paddle far up the Waveney to an island hidden in reeds. We were the only persons who knew of that island. We were like little kings there. We built a rough sort of tent–hut there every summer. Then we would pass the time there deliciously, now bathing, now fishing, but always living on what we caught. John, who was a wild lad, much older than I, used to go among the gipsies in their great winter camp at Oulton. He learned many strange tricks from them. He was a good camp–companion. I think that the last two years of my life at Oulton were the happiest years of my life. I have never cared for dry or hilly countries since. Wherever I have been in the world, I have always longed for the Broads, where the rivers wander among reeds for miles, losing themselves in thickets of reeds. I have always thought tenderly of the flat land, where windmills or churches are the only landmarks, standing up above the mist, in the loneliness of the fens. But when I was nearly thirteen years old (just after the death of Charles the Second) my father died, leaving me an orphan. My uncle, Gabriel Hyde, a man about town, was my only relative. The vicar of Lowestoft wrote to him, on my behalf. A fortnight later (the ways were always very foul in the winter) my uncle's man came to fetch me to London. There was a sale of my father's furniture. His books were sent off to his college at Cambridge by the Lowestoft carrier. Then the valet took me by wherry to Norwich, where we caught a weekly coach to town. That was the last time I ever sailed on the Waveney as a boy, that journey to Norwich. When I next saw the Broads, I was a man of thirty–five. I remember how strangely small the country seemed to me when I saw it after my wanderings. But this is away from my tale. All that I remember of the coach–ride was my arrival late at night at the London inn, a dark house full of smells, from which the valet led me to my uncle's house.

I lay awake, that first night, much puzzled by the noise, fearing that London would be all streets, a dismal place. When I fell asleep, I was waked continually by chiming bells. In the morning, early, I was roused by the musical calling made by milkmen on their rounds, with that morning's milk for sale. At breakfast my uncle told me not to go into the street without Ephraim, his man; for without a guide, he said, I should get lost. He warned me that there were people in London who made a living by seizing children ("kidnapping" or "trepanning" them, as it was called) to sell to merchant–captains bound for the plantations. "So be very careful, Martin," he said. "Do not talk to strangers." He went for his morning walk after this, telling me that I might run out to play in the garden.

Martin Hyde, The Duke's Messenger

I went out of doors feeling that London must be a very terrible place, if the folk there went about counting all who met them as possible enemies. I was homesick for the Broads, where everybody, even bad men, like the worst of the smugglers, was friendly to me. I hated all this noisy city, so full of dirty jumbled houses. I longed to be in my coracle on the Waveney, paddling along among the reeds, chucking pebbles at the water-rats. But when I went out into the garden I found that even London held something for me, not so good as the Broads, perhaps, but pleasant in its way.

Now before I go further, I must tell you that my uncle's house was one of the old houses in Billingsgate. It stood in a narrow, crowded lane, at the western end of Thames Street, close to the river. Few of the houses thereabouts were old; for the fire of London had nearly destroyed that part of the city, but my uncle's house, with a few more in the same lane, being built of brick, had escaped. The bricks of some of the houses were scorched black. I remember, also, at the corner house, three doors from my uncle's house, the melted end of a water pipe, hanging from the roof like a long leaden icicle, just as it had run from the heat eighteen years before. I used to long for that icicle: it would have made such fine bullets for my sling. I have said that Fish Lane, where my uncle lived, was narrow. It was very narrow. The upper stories of the houses opposite could be touched from my bed-room window with an eight-foot fishing rod. If one leaned well out, one could see right into their upper rooms. You could even hear the people talking in them.

At the back of the house there was a garden of potherbs. It sloped down to the river-bank, where there were stairs to the water. The stairs were covered in, so as to form a boat-house, in which (as I learned afterwards) my uncle's skiffs were kept. You may be sure that I lost no time in getting down to the water, after I had breakfasted with my uncle, on the morning after my arrival.

A low stone parapet, topped by iron rails, shut off the garden from the beach. Just beyond the parapet, within slingshot, as I soon proved, was the famous Pool of London, full of ships of all sorts, some with flags flying. The mild spring sun (it was early in April) made the sight glorious. There must have been a hundred ships there, all marshalled in ranks, at double-moorings, head to flood. Boats full of merchandise were pulling to the wharves by the Custom House. Men were working aloft on the yards, bending or unbending sails. In some ships the sails hung loose, drying in the sun. In others, the men were singing out as they walked round the capstan, hoisting goods from the hold. One of the ships close to me was a beautiful little Spanish schooner, with her name La Reina in big gold letters on her transom. She was evidently one of those very fast fruit boats, from the Canary Islands, of which I had heard the seamen at Oulton speak. She was discharging oranges into a lighter, when I first saw her. The sweet, heavy smell of the bruised peels scented the river for many yards.

I was looking at this schooner, wishing that I could pass an hour in her hold, among those delicious boxes, when a bearded man came on deck from her cabin. He looked at the shore, straight at myself as I thought, raising his hand swiftly as though to beckon me to him. A boat pushed out instantly, in answer to the hand, from the garden next to the one in which I stood. The waterman, pulling to the schooner, talked with the man for a moment, evidently settling the amount of his fare. After the haggling, my gentleman climbed into the boat by a little rope–ladder at the stern. Then the boatman pulled away upstream, going on the last of the flood, within twenty yards of where I stood.

I had watched them idly, attracted, in the beginning, by that sudden raising of the hand. But as they passed me, there came a sudden puff of wind, strong enough to flurry the water into wrinkles. It lifted the gentleman's hat, so that he saved it only by a violent snatch which made the boat rock. As he jammed the hat down he broke or displaced some string or clip near his ears. At any rate his beard came adrift on the side nearest to me. The man was wearing a false beard. He remedied the matter at once, very cleverly, so that I may have been the only witness; but I saw that the boatman was in the man's secret, whatever it was. He pulled hard on his starboard oar, bringing the boat partly across the current, thus screening him from everybody except the workers in the ships. It must have seemed to all who saw him that he was merely pulling to another arch of London Bridge.

I was not sure of the man's face. It seemed handsome; that was all that I could say of it. But I was fascinated by the mystery. I wondered why he was wearing a false beard. I wondered what he was doing in the schooner. I imagined all sorts of romantic plots in which he was taking part. I watched his boat go through the Bridge with the feeling that I was sharing in all sorts of adventures already. There was a fall of water at the Bridge which made the river dangerous there even on a flood tide. I could see that the waves there would be quite enough for such a boat without the most tender handling. I watched to see how they would pass through. Both men stood up, facing forwards, each taking an oar. They worked her through, out of sight, in a very clever fashion; which set me wondering again what this handsome gentleman might be, who worked a boat so well.

Martin Hyde, The Duke's Messenger

I hung about at the end of the garden until dinner time, hoping that they would return. I watched every boat which came downstream, finding a great pleasure in the watermen's skill, for indeed the water at the Bridge was frightful; only a strong nerve could venture on it. But the boat did not come back, though one or two other boats brought people, or goods, to the stairs of the garden beside me. I could not see into the garden; that party wall was too high.

I did not go indoors again till Ephraim came to fetch me, saying that it was time I washed my hands for dinner. I went to my room; but instead of washing my hands, I leaned out of the window to watch a dancing bear which was sidling about in the lane, just below, while his keeper made a noise on the panpipes. A little crowd of idlers was gathered round the bear. Some of them were laughing at the bear, some at his keeper. I saw two boys sneaking about among the company; they were evil-looking little ruffians, with that hard look in the eyes which always marks the thoroughly wicked. As I watched, one of them slipped his hand into a man's pocket, then withdrew it, passing something swiftly to his companion, who walked unconcernedly away. I ran out of doors at once, to the man who had been robbed.

"Sir," I said, when he had drawn away from the little crowd. "Have you not been robbed of something?"

He turned to look down on me, searching his pockets with both hands. It gave me a start to see him, for he was the bearded man who had passed me in the boat that morning. You may be sure that I took a good note of him. He was a handsome, melancholy-looking man, with a beard designed to make him look fairer than he really was.

"Robbed of something?" he repeated in a quiet voice. "Yes, I have been robbed of something." It seemed to me that he turned pale, when he found that he had been robbed. "Did you see it?" he asked. "Don't point. Just describe him to me. No. Don't look round, boy. Tell me without looking round."

"Sir," I said, "do you see two little boys moving about among the people there?"

"Yes," he said.

"It's the boy with the bit of broken pipe in his hat who has the, whatever it was, sir, I'm sure. I saw it all."

"I see," he said. "That's the coveter. Let this be a warning to you, boy, never to stop in a crowd to watch these street–performers. Where were you, when you saw it?"

"Up above there, sir. In that house."

"In Mr.Hyde's house. Do you live there?"

"Yes, sir."

"Since when? Not for long, surely?"

"No, sir. Only since yesterday. I'm Mr. Hyde's nephew."

"Ah! Indeed. And that is your room up there?"

"Yes, sir."

"Where do you come from then? You've not been in town before. What is your father?"

"My father's dead, sir. I come from Oulton. My father was rector there."

"Ah," he said quietly. "Now give this penny to the bear–ward."

While I was giving the penny to the keeper, the strange man edged among the lookers–on, apparently watching the bear's antics, till he was just behind the pickpocket's accomplice. Watching his time, he seized the boy from behind by both wrists.

"This boy's a pickpocket," he cried aloud. "Stop that other boy. He's an accomplice." The other boy, who had just taken a purse, started to run, letting the booty drop. A boatman who was going towards the river, tripped him up with an oar so that he fell heavily. He lay still where he had fallen (all the wind was knocked out of him) so that he was easily secured. The boy who had been seized by the bearded man made no attempt to get away. He was too firmly held. Both boys were then marched off to the nearest constable where (after a strict search), they were locked into a cellar till the morrow. The crowd deserted the bear–ward when the cry of pickpockets was raised. They followed my mysterious friend to the constable's house, hoping, no doubt, that they would be able to crowd in to hear the constable bully the boys as he searched them. One or two, who pretended to have missed things, managed to get in. The bearded man told me to come in, as he said that I should be needed as a witness. The others were driven out into the street, where, I suppose, their monkey–minds soon found other game, a horse fallen down, or a drunken woman in the gutter, to divert their idleness. Such sights seem to attract a London crowd at once.

The boys were strictly searched by the constable. The booty from their pockets was turned out upon the table.

"Now, sir," said the constable to the bearded man, after he had made a note of my story. "What is it they 'ad of you, sir?"

"A shagreen leather pocket–book," said the man. "There it is."

"This one?" said the constable.

"Yes."

"Oh," said the constable, opening the clasps, so that he could examine the writing on the leaves. "What's inside?"

"A lot of figures," said the man. "Sums. Problems in arithmetic."

"Right," said the constable, handing over the book.

"Here you are, sir. What name, sir?"

"Edward Jermyn."

"Edward German," the constable repeated.

"Where d' you live, sir?"

Martin Hyde, The Duke's Messenger

"At Mr. Scott's in Fish Lane."

"Right, sir," said the constable, writing down the address, "You must appear tomorrow at ten before Mr. Garry, the magistrate. You, too, young master, to give your evidence."

At this the boys burst out crying, begging us not to appear, using all those deceptive arts which the London thieves practise from childhood. I, who was new to the world's deceits, was touched to the marrow by their seeming misery. The constable roughly silenced them. "I know you, he said. "I had my eye on you two ever since Christmas. Now you'll go abroad to do a bit of honest work, instead of nickin' pockets. Stow your blubbering now, or I'll give you Mogador Jack." He produced "Mogador Jack," a supple shark's backbone, from behind the door. The tears stopped on the instant.

After this, the bearded man showed me the way back to Fish Lane, where Ephraim, who was at the door, looking out for me) gave me a shrewd scolding, for venturing out without a guide.

Mr. Jermyn silenced him by giving him a shilling. The next day, Mr. Jermyn took me to the magistrate's house, where the two thieves were formally committed for trial. Mr. Jermyn told me that they would probably be transported for seven years, on conviction at the Assizes; but that, as they were young, the honest work abroad, in the plantations, might be the saving of them. "So do not be so sad, Mr. Martin," he said. "You do not know how good a thing you did when you looked out of the window yesterday. Do you know, by the way, how much my book is worth?"

"No, sir," I said.

"Well. It's worth more than the King's crown," he said.

"But I thought it was only sums, sir."

"Yes," he said, with a strange smile. "But some sums have to do with a great deal of money. Now I want you to think tonight of something to the value of twenty pounds or so. I want to give you something as a reward for your smartness. Don't decide at once. Think it over. Here we are at our homes, you see. We live just opposite to each other."

Martin Hyde, The Duke's Messenger

We were standing at this moment in the narrow lane at my uncle's door. As he spoke, he raised his hand in a farewell salute with that dignity of gesture which was in all his movements. On the instant, to my surprise, the door of the house opposite opened slowly, till it was about half open. No one opened it, as I could see; it swung back of itself. After my friend had stepped across the threshold it swung to with a click in the same mysterious way. It was as though it had a knowledge of Mr. Jermyn's mind, as though the raised hand had had a magical power over it. When I went indoors to my uncle's house I was excited. I felt that I was in the presence of something romantic, something mysterious. I liked Mr. Jermyn. He had been very kind. But I kept wondering why he wore a false beard, why his door opened so mysteriously, why he valued a book of sums above the worth of a King's crown. As for his offer of a present, I did not like it, though he had not given me time to say as much. I remembered how indignant the Oulton wherrymen had been when a gentleman offered them money for saving his daughter's life. I had seen the man robbed, what else could I have done? I could have done no less than tell him. I resolved that I would refuse the gift when next I saw him.

At dinner that day, I was full of Mr. Jermyn, much to my uncle's annoyance.

"Who is this Mr. Jermyn, Martin?" he asked. "I don't know him. Is he a gentleman?"

"Yes, uncle."

"Do you know him, Ephraim?"

"No, sir. I know him by sight, sir. Gentleman who lives over the way, Mr. Hyde."

"That's Mr. Scott's, though."

"No, sir. Mr. Jermyn's been there ever since February."

"But the house is empty."

"The lower floor is furnished, sir."

"Do you know anything of him? Do you know his man?"

"They say he's in the fruit way, sir. In the Spanish trade. His men are Spaniards. They do say he's not quite to be trusted."

"Who says this?" my uncle asked.

"I don't like to mention names, sir," Ephraim said.

"Quite right. Quite right. But what do they say?"

"Very queer things goes on in that 'ouse," said Ephraim. "I don't 'ardly like to say. But they think 'e raises the devil, sir. Awful noises goes on there. I seen some things myself there, as I don't like to talk of. Well. I saw a black bird as big as a man stand flapping in the window. Then I seen eyes glaring out at the door. They give the 'ouse a bad name, sir; everyone."

"H'm," said my uncle. "What's he like, Martin, this Mr. Jermyn?"

"A tall man, with a beard," I answered. I thought it wrong to mention that I knew the beard to be false. "He's always stroking the bridge of his nose with his hand."

"Ha," my uncle said, as though recognizing the trait. "But with a beard, you tell me?"

"Yes, sir. With a beard."

"H'm," he answered, musing, "I must have a look at this Mr. Jermyn. Remember, Martin, you're to have nothing more to do with him, till I know a little more of what he is. You understand?"

"Yes, uncle."

"One cannot be too careful in this town. I won't allow you in the streets, Martin. No matter who has his pockets picked. I told you that before."

"Please, uncle, may I go on the river, then, if I'm not to go into the street? I'm used to boats."

"Yes. You may do that. But you're not to go on board the ships, mind."

"Beg pardon, sir," Ephraim put in. "The fall at the Bridge is very risky, sir."

"It is?" said my uncle, testily. "Then of course you can't go in a boat, Martin. You must play in the garden, or read."

CHAPTER II. I LEAVE HOME AGAIN

I thought Ephraim a pig for putting in that word about the fall. Though I had only known Ephraim for a few days I disliked him perhaps as much as he disliked me. He was angry (I could feel it) at having a boy in the house, after many years of quiet alone with my uncle. I know that when he had occasion to speak to me, he always went away muttering about my being a charity brat who ought to be in the poor-house. Still, like most servants, he vented most of his malice indirectly, as in this hint of his about the river. I rose up from the dinner-table full of rebellion. I would go on the river, I said to myself, fall or no fall. I would see more of Mr. Jermyn, too. I would find out what went on in that house. I would find out everything. In all this, of course, I was very wrong, but having made sure that I was being treated unjustly I felt that I was only doing right in rebelling. So after waiting till Ephraim was in the pantry, washing up the dinner-things with the housemaid, I slipped down the garden to the boat-house. The door was padlocked, as I had feared; but with an old hammer-head I managed to pry off the staple. I felt like a burglar when the lock came off in my hand. I felt that I was acting deceitfully. Then the thought of Ephraim came over me, making me rebellious to my finger-tips. I would go on the river, I said to myself, I would go aboard all the ships in the Pool. I would show them all that I could handle a boat anywhere. So in a moment my good angel was beaten. I was in the boat-house, prying at the staple of the outer door, like the young rogue that I was. Well, I paid a heavy price for that day of disobedience. It was the most dearly bought day's row I ever heard of.

It took me a few moments to open the outer door. Then, with a thrill of pleasure, such as only those who love the water can fed, I thrust out into the river, on to the last of the ebb, then fast ebbing. The fall under the bridge at that state of the tide was truly terrifying. It roared so loudly that I could hear nothing else. It boiled about the bridge piers so fiercely that I was scared to see it. I had seen the sea in storm; but then one does not put to sea in a storm. This waterfall tumbled daily, even in a calm. I shuddered to think of small boats, caught in the current above it, being drawn down, slowly at first, then with a whirl, till all was whelmed in the tumble below the arches. I saw how hatefully the back wash seemed to saunter back to the fall along the banks. I thought that if I was not careful I might be caught in the back wash, drawn slowly along it by the undertow, till the cataract sank me. As I watched the fall, fascinated, yet scared by it, there came a shooting rush, with shouts of triumph. A four–oared wherry with two passengers shot through the arch over the worst of the water into the quiet of the midstream. They waved to me, evidently very pleased with their exploit. That set me wondering whether the water were really as bad as it looked. My first feat was to back up cautiously almost to the fall, till my boat was dancing so vigorously that I was spattered all over. Standing up in the boat there, I could see the oily water, like a great arched snake's back, swirl past the arch towards me, bubbleless, almost without a ripple, till it showed all its teeth at once in breaking down. The piers of the arches jutted far out below the fall, like pointed islands. I was about to try to climb on the top of one from the boat, a piece of madness which would probably have ended in my death, but some boys in one of the houses on the bridge began to pelt me with pebbles, so that I had to sheer off. I pulled down among the shipping, examining every vessel in the Pool. Then I pulled down the stream, with the ebb, as far as Wapping, where I was much shocked by the sight of the pirates' gallows, with seven dead men hung in chains together there, for taking the ship Delight, so a waterman told me, on the Guinea Coast, the year before. I left my boat at Wapping Stairs, while I went into a pastry–cook's shop to buy cake; for I was now hungry. The pastry–cook was also a vintner. His tables were pretty well crowded with men, mostly seafaring men, who were drinking wine together, talking of politics. I knew nothing whatever about politics, but hearing the Duke of Monmouth named I pricked up my ears to listen. My father had told me, in his last illness, when the news of the death of Charles the Second reached us, that trouble would come to England through this Duke, because, he said, "he will never agree with King James." Many people (the Duke himself being one of them) believed that this James Scott, Duke of Monmouth, was the son of a very beautiful woman by Charles the Second, who (so the tale went) had married her in his wanderings abroad, while Cromwell ruled in England here. I myself shall ever believe this story. I am quite sure, now, in my own mind, that Monmouth was our rightful King. I have heard accounts of this marriage of Charles the Second from people who were with him in his wanderings. When Charles the Second died (being poisoned, some said, by his brother James, who wished to seize the throne while Monmouth was abroad, unable to claim his rights) James succeeded to the crown. At the time of which I write he had been King for about two months. I did not know anything about his merits as a King; but hearing the name of Monmouth I felt sure, from the first, that I should hear more of what my father had told me.

One of the seamen, a sour–looking, pale–faced man, was saying that Holland was full of talk that the Duke was coming over, to try for the Kingdom. Another said that it wasn't the Duke of Monmouth but the Duke of Argyle that was coming, to try, not for England, but for Scotland. A third said that all this was talk, for how could a single man, without twenty friends in the world, get through a cruising fleet? "How could he do anything, even if he did land?"

"Ah," said another man. "They say that the West is ready to rally around him. That's what they say."

"Well," said the first, raising his cup. "Here's to King James, I say. England's had enough of civil troubles." The other men drank the toast with applause. It is curious to remember how cautious people were in those troublous days. One could never be sure of your friend's true opinion. It was a time when there were so many spies abroad that everybody was suspicious of his neighbour. I am sure that a good half of that company was disloyal; yet they drank that toast, stamping their feet, as though they would have shed their blood for King James with all the pleasure in life. "Are you for King James, young waterman?" said one of the men to me. "Yes," I said, "I am for the rightful King." At this they all laughed. One of the men said that if there were many like me the Duke of Monmouth might spare himself the trouble of coming over.

I finished my cake quietly, after that. Then, as the tide was not yet making, to help me back up the river, I wandered into Wapping fields, where a gang of beggars camped. They were a dirtier, more troublesome company than the worst of the Oulton gipsies. They crowded round me, whining about their miseries, with the fawning smiles of professional beggars. There were children among them who lied about their wants as glibly as their parents lied. The Oulton beggars had taught me to refuse such people, as being, nearly always, knaves; so I said that I had nothing for them. I felt the hands of these thieves lightly feeling the outsides of my pockets for something worth taking. One of them with a sudden thrust upon me snatched my handkerchief. He tossed it to a friend. As he started to run from me, a young man with an evil, weak face pushed me backwards with a violent shove. I staggered back, from the push, to fall over a boy who had crouched behind me there, ready to upset me. When I got up, rather shaken from my fall, the dirty gang was scattering to its burrow; for they lived, like beasts, in holes scratched in the ground, thatched over with sacks or old clothes. I hurried back toward Wapping in the hope of finding a constable to recover my handkerchief for me. The constable (when I found him) refused to stir until I made it worth his while. Sixpence was his fee, he said, but he was sure that a handsome young gentleman like myself would not grudge a sixpence to recover a handkerchief. On searching for my purse (in which I had about two shillings) I found that that had gone, too, "nicked" by these thieves. I told the Constable that my purse had been stolen.

"Oh," he said. "How much was in it?" I told him.

"Could you describe the man who took it?"

"No." I said. "I did not see the man take it."

"Then how do you know that anybody took it?"

Of course I did not know that anybody had taken it but thought it highly probable. "That won't do here," he said, settling down in his chair to his tobacco. "I'll look into it. If I hear of it, why, next time you come here, you shall have it."

"But my handkerchief," I said.

"Sixpence is my fee," the brute answered. "Do you want to rob a poor man of his earnings? Why, what a rogue you must be, young master." I tried to move him to recover my handkerchief, but without success. At last, growing weary of the sound of my pipe, as he said, he rounded on me.

"If you don't run away 'ome," he said, "I'll commit you for a nuisance. Think I'm goin' to be bothered by yer. Be off, now."

At that, I set off down to the river. There I found two dirty little boys in my uncle's boat, busy with the dipper, trying to fill her with water. I boxed the ears of one of them, when the other, coming behind me, hit me over the head with the stretcher. I turned sharply, giving him a punch which made his nose bleed. The other, seeing his chance (my back being turned) promptly soused me with the dipper. I saw that I would have to settle one of them at a time, so, paying no attention to the dipper, I followed up my blow on the nose with one or two more, which drove the stretcher–boy out of the boat. The other was a harder lad; who would, perhaps, have beaten me, had not a waterman on the stairs taken my part. He took my enemy by the ear. "Get out of that," he said, giving him a kick. "If I catch you messing boats again, I'll give you Mogador Jack." I pushed off from the stairs then, glad to get away with both oars. My enemies, running along the banks, flung stones at me as long as I was in range. If I had had my sling with me, would have warmed their legs for them. When was out of range of their shot, I laid in my oars, so that I could bail. The boys had poured about six inches of water into the boat. If the plug had been less tightly hammered in, they would no doubt have sunk her at her painter by pulling it out. Then should have been indeed in difficulty. It took me about twenty minutes to bail the boat clear. As I bailed her, I thought that Londoners must be the most unpleasant people in the world, since, already, in two days, I had met so many knaves. It did not occur to me at the time that I was a young knave, too, to be out in a stolen boat, against orders. I never once thought how well I had been served for my disobedience.

I had an uncomfortable journey upstream, for I was very wet from my sousing. I loitered at the Tower to watch the garrison drilling with the big guns. Then I loitered about among the ships, reading their names, or even climbing their gangways to look at their decks. I lingered a long time at the schooner La Reina, partly because she was much the prettiest ship in the Pool, but partly because I was beginning to dread Ephraim. I wondered whether Mr. Jermyn was on board of her. I was half tempted to climb aboard to find out. I clambered partly up her gangway, so that I could peer over the rail. To my surprise, I found that her hatches were battened down as in ships ready for the sea. Her cargo of oranges, that had smelt so sweetly, must have been a blind, for no ship, discharging cargo the day before, could be loaded, ready for sea, within twenty–four hours. Indeed, she was in excellent trim. She was not too light to put to sea. No doubt, I said to myself, she has taken in ballast to equal the weight of oranges sent ashore. But I knew just enough of ships to know that there was some mystery in the business. The schooner could not be the plain fruit–trader for which men took her. As I looked over her rail, noting this, I said to myself that "here is another mystery with which Mr. Jermyn has to do." I felt a thrill of excitement go through me. I was touching mysterious adventure at half a dozen different points. I felt inclined to creep to the hatchway of the little cabin, to listen there if any plots were being hatched. It was getting duskish by this time, it must have been nearly seven o'clock. Two men came up the cabin hatch together. One of them was Mr. Jermyn, the other a shorter fellow, to whom Mr. Jermyn seemed extremely respectful. I wished not to be seen, so I ducked down nimbly into my boat, drawing her forward by a guess–warp, till I could row without being heard by them. I heard Mr. Jermyn calling to a waterman; so very swiftly I paddled behind other ships in the tier, without being observed. Then I paddled back to my uncle's boat–house, the door of which, to my horror, was firmly fastened against me.

CHAPTER III. I LEAVE HOME A THIRD TIME

I must have made some little noise at the door, trying to get in. At any rate, Ephraim, who was waiting for such a signal, came forward with a churlish glee to rate me.

"So you're come back, Mr. Martin," he said. "These are nice carryings–on for a young gentleman." I thought that I might as well be hanged for a sheep as for a lamb. Ephraim's tone jarred me, so I told him to shut up, as I didn't want any of his jaw. This rather staggered him, so I told him further to open the boat–house, instead of standing like a stock, as ,I wanted to moor the boat. He opened the door for me, glowering at me moodily. "Mr. Hyde shall know of this," he said when all was secured. He caught me by the arm to drag me out of the boat–house; so I, expecting this, rapped him shrewdly with the stretcher on the elbow. I thought for a moment that he would beat me. I could see his face very fierce in the dusk. I heard his teeth gritting. Then fear of my uncle restrained him. All that he said was, "If I 'ad my way I'd 'ave it out of you for this. A good sound whippin's what you want."

"Is it?" I asked contemptuously. "Lock the door."

Ephraim left me in the sitting–room while he made his report to my uncle. It was not a long report. He returned in a few minutes to say that I was to be locked into my room without supper. "Mr. 'Ide is in a fine taking," he said. "Per'aps 'e'll knock some of your pride out of you." I made no answer, but let him march me to my room, to the execution of the sentence. "There," he said, through the door, as he turned the key on me. "Per'aps that'll bring you to your senses."

"Ephraim the stiff–neck!" I answered loudly.; "Old Ephraim Stiff–neck! Stiff–neck!"

"Ah," he answered, clumping down the corridor. He was thinking how small I should sing when, in the morning, he gave me the option of apologizing to him, or going without breakfast.

It was pretty dark by this time. Fish Lane was as quiet as a country road. No one was stirring there. I thought that, as my uncle would shortly go to supper, I might soon venture out by the window, high up as it was, to buy myself some food in the town. I liked the notion; but when I came to look down from the window it seemed a giddy height from the pavement. Going down would be easy; but getting back would be quite another matter. Thinking it over, I remembered that I had seen a short gardener's ladder hooked to the garden wall. If I could make a rope, by which to let myself down, I could, I thought, make use of this ladder to get back by, for it would cover nearly half the height to my window sill, a full thirty feet from the ground. If, by standing on the upper rungs, could reach within five yards of the window, I knew that I should be able to scramble up so far by a rope. There was no difficulty about a rope. I had a good eighteen yards of choice stout rope there in the room with me, the lashings of my two trunks. I was about to pay this out into the lane, when I thought that would be far more effective if I fashioned a ladder for myself, using the two trunk lashings as the uprights. This was a glorious thought. I tied the lashings together behind the wooden bed–post which was to be my support in midair. Then I rummaged out a hank of sailor's spunyarn, a kind of very strong tarred string, with which to make my steps, or rungs. did not do this very well, for I was working in the dark, but you may be sure that I made those steps with all my strength, since my bones were to depend upon them. I ran short of spunyarn before I had finished, so my last three steps were made of the fire–irons. They made a good finish to the whole; for, being heavy, they kept the ladder steady. At least thought that they would keep the ladder steady, in the innocence of my heart.

I was so excited, when I finished the tying of the tongs, that I almost forgot to take some money from the little store which I kept locked up in my trunk. A shilling would be ample, I thought; but I took rather more than that, so as to he on the safe side. I took the precaution, before leaving, of bolting my door from the inside, lest Ephraim should visit me in my absence.

Then, having tested all my knots, I paid out my ladder from the window. No one was within sight along the lane. Downstairs they were at supper, for I heard the dining–room bell ring. Very cautiously I swung myself over the window ledge on my adventure. Now a rope ladder is an unsteady thing at the best of times; but when I swung myself on to this one it jumped about like a wild colt, banging the fire–irons against the wall, making noise enough to raise the town. I had to climb down it on the inner side, or I should have had Ephraim out to see what the matter was. Even so, my heart was in my mouth, with fright, as I stepped on to the pavement. After making sure that no one saw, I hooked up the lower ends of my ladder as far as I could reach, so that a passer–by might run less chance of seeing them. Then I scuttled off to the delights of Eastcheap, thinking what glorious sport I could have with this ladder in time to come. I thought of the moonlight adventures on the river, skulking along in my boat, like a pirate on a night attack. I thought how, perhaps, I should overhear gangs of highwaymen making their plans, or robbers in their dens, carousing after a victory. It seemed to me that London might be a wonderful place, to one with such a means of getting out at night.

I ate a good supper at a cook–shop, sauntered about the streets for awhile, then sauntered slowly home, after buying a tinder box, with which to light my candles. I found my ladder dangling unnoticed, so I nimbly climbed to my room, pulling it up after me, like the savages in Polynesia. I lit my candles, intending to read; but I found that I was far too well inclined to mischief to pay much heed to my book. Casting about for something to do, I thought that I would open a little locked door which led to some (apparently disused) room beyond my own. I had some difficulty in breaking the lock of this door; but a naughty boy is generally very patient. I opened it at last, with some misgivings as to what my uncle might say on the morrow, though with the feeling that I was a sort of conspirator, or, shall we say, a man haunting a house, playing ghost, coming at night to his secret chamber. I was disappointed with the room. Like my own room, it was nothing more than a long, bare attic. It had a false floor, like many houses of the time, but there was no thought of concealment here. Half a dozen of the long flooring planks were stored in a stack against the wall, so that anyone could see what lay in the hollow below. There was nothing romantic there. A long array of docketed, ticketed bundles of receipts filled more than half the space. I suppose that nearly every bill which my uncle had ever paid lay there, gathering dust. The rest of the space was filled with Ephraim's dirty old account books, jumbled higgledy–piggledy with collections of printed, unbound sermons, such as used to be sold forty years before, in the great Puritan time. I examined a few of the sermons, hoping to find some lighter fare among them. I examined also a few of the old account books, in the same hope. Other rubbish lay scattered in the corners of the room; old mouse–eaten saddle–bags mostly. There were one or two empty baskets, which had once been lined with silk. In one of them, I can't think why, there was an old empty, dusty powder–horn, the only thing in that room at all to my taste. I stuck it into my belt with a scrap of spunyarn, feeling that it made me a wonderful piratical figure. If I had had a lantern I should have been a very king there.

As I sat among the rubbish there, with my pistol (a sailmaker's fid) in my belt, it occurred to me that I would sit up till everyone had gone to bed. Then, at eleven or twelve o'clock, I would, I thought, creep downstairs, to explore all over the house, down even to the cellars. It shocked me when I remembered that I was locked in. I dared not pick the lock of that door. My scheme (after all) would have to wait for another night, when the difficulties would be less. That scheme of mine has waited until the present time. Though I never thought it, that was the last hour I was to spend in my uncle's house. I walked past it, only the other day, thinking how strange my life has been, feeling sad, too, that I should never know to what room a door at the end of the upper passage led. Well, I never shall know, now. I was a wild, disobedient young rogue. Read on.

When I decided not to pick the lock of my door I thought of the mysterious Mr. Jermyn as an alternative excitement. I crept to my window to look out at the house, watching it with a sort of terrified pleasure, half expecting to see a ghost flapping his wings, outside the window.

I was surprised to see that the window of the upper floor (which I knew to be uninhabited) was open. I watched it, (it was just opposite) hoping that something would happen. Presently two men came quickly up the lane from the river. As they neared the house they seemed to me to shuffle in their walk rather more than vas necessary. It must have been a signal, for, as they came opposite the door, I saw it swing back upon its hinges, as it had swung that morning, with Mr. Jermyn. Both men entered the house swiftly, just as the city churches, one after the other, chimed half–past nine o'clock. Almost directly afterwards I got the start of my life. I was looking into the dark upper room across the lane, expecting nothing, when suddenly, out of the darkness, so terribly that I was scared beyond screaming, two large red eyes glowed, over a mouth that trembled in fire. I started back in my seat, sick with fright, but I could not take my eyes away. I watched that horrid thing, with my hair stiffening on my head. Then in the room below it, the luminous figure of an owl gleamed out. That was not the worst, either. I heard that savage, "chacking" noise which brown owls make when they are perched. This great gleaming owl, five times greater than any earthly owl, was making that chacking noise, as though it would soon spread its wings, to swoop on some such wretched mouse as myself. I could see its eyes roll. I thought I saw the feathers stiffen on its breast. Then, as the sweat rolled down my face, both the horrible things vanished as suddenly as they had appeared. They were gone for more than a minute, then they appeared again, only to disappear a second time. They were exactly alike at each appearance. Soon my horror left me, for I saw that the things disappeared at regular intervals. I found that I could time each reappearance by counting ninety slowly from the instant the things vanished. That calmed me. "I believe they're only clock–work," I said to myself. A moment later I saw Mr. Jermyn's head in sharp outline against the brightness of the owl. He seemed to be fixing something with his hand. It made me burst into a cackle of laughter, to find how easily I had been scared. "Why, it's only clock–work," I said aloud. "They're carved turnips with candles inside them, fixed to a revolving pole, like those we used to play with at Oulton, on the 5th of November." My fear was gone in an instant. I thought to myself how fine it would be if I could get into that house, to stop the works, in revenge for the scare they had given me. I wondered how I could do that.

CHAPTER IV. I LEAVE HOME FOR THE LAST TIME

I was thoroughly ripe for mischief of any kind; my scare had driven away all desire for sleep. I looked at the window, wondering if it would be best to go down my ladder again, to get the ladder in the garden. I was about to do thus, when I remembered the planks in the box–room. How splendid it would be, I thought, if I could get a couple of those long planks across the lane as a sort of bridge. They were strong, thick planks not likely to sag in the middle if I could only get them across. Getting them across was the difficulty; for though I was strong for my age, I found the first plank very contrary. After blowing out my candles I fixed one end of the board under my heavy four–post bed, pointing the other end out through the window, slanting upwards. Straddling across it, I very gingerly edged it out, a hand's breadth at a time, till I had some ten feet wagging about in the air over the lane. It was as much as I could do unaided, to aim the thing. It seemed to have a wild, contrary kind of life in it. Once or twice I came near to dropping it into the lane, which would have been the end of everything. When I got it across, the end caught on the window ledge for about ten perilous minutes.

I was quite tired out before I got it properly across with two feet of the end in the other house. I did not at all look forward to the job of getting it back again after my trip. One plank was hardly safe, I thought; so I slid a second over it, without much trouble. It seemed firm enough then for anybody, no matter how heavy. So carefully I straddled across it, hopping forward a little at a time, as though I were playing leap–frog. When once I had started, I was much too nervous to go back. My head was strong enough. I was well used to being high up in trees. But the danger of this adventure made me dizzy. At every hop the two planks clacked together. I could feel the upper plank shaking out behind me a little to one side of the other. Then a tired waterman shambled slowly up from the river, carrying his oars. He passed underneath me, while I was in mid–air. It was lucky for me, I thought, that few people when walking look above their own heads. He passed on without seeing me. I waited up aloft till he had gone, feeling my head grow dizzier at each second. I was, I trust, truly thankful when I was able to dive down over the window–sill into the strange house. When I had rested for a moment, I felt that it was not so difficult after all. "Going back," I said to myself, "will be much less ticklish." Turning my head, I saw the eyes of the devil–face glaring at me. They smelt very strongly of kitchen tallow.

I was not in the least frightened. I crept cautiously along the floor, on tip–toe, to examine the contrivance. A hollow shaft of light wood, a sort of big wooden pipe, led down through the floor, probably to the ground–floor or basement, much as a mast goes down through a ship's decks into the hold. It was slowly revolving, being worked by some simple, not very strong mill–contrivance downstairs. A shelf had been fixed up inside the pipe. On the shelf (as I could see by looking in) was a tallow candle in a sconce. Two oval bits of red glass, let into the wood, made the eyes of this lantern–devil. The mouth was a smear of some gleaming stuff, evidently some chemical. This was all the monster which had frightened me. The clacking noise was made by the machine which moved it round. As for the owl, that was probably painted with the same chemical. People were more superstitious then than now. I have no doubt that an ignorant person like Ephraim, who had lived all his life in London, had been scared out of his wits by this machine. Like most ignorant people, he probably reckoned the thing as devilish, merely because he did not understand it. One or two neighbours, a housemaid or so, perhaps, had seen it, too. On the strength of their reports the house had gotten a bad name. The two unoccupied floors had failed to get tenants, while Mr. Jermyn, the contriver of the whole, had been left alone, as no doubt he had planned. I thought that Londoners must be a very foolish people to be so easily misled. Now that I am older, I see that Londoners often live in very narrow grooves. They are apt to be frightened at anything to which they have not been accustomed; unless, of course, it is a war, when they can scream about themselves so loudly that they forget that they are screaming.

I examined the machine critically, by its own candle, which I removed for the purpose. I meant to fix up one very like it in Ephraim's bed–room as soon as I found an opportunity. Then I looked about the room for some other toy, feeling in a fine state of excitement with the success of my adventure. The room was quite bare. But for this ghost–machine, there was nothing which could interest me, except a curious drawing, done with a burnt stick on the plaster of the wall, of a man–of–war under sail. After examining this drawing, I listened carefully at the door lest my faint footsteps should have roused someone below. I could hear no one stirring; the house was silent. "I must be careful," I said to myself. "They all may have gone to bed." Understand, I did not know then what I was doing. I was merely a wrong–headed boy, up to a prank, begun in a moment of rebellion. When I paused in the landing, outside the ghost–room, shading the candle with my hand, I was not aware that I was doing wrong. I was only thinking how fine it would be to find out about Mr. Jermyn, before crawling back, over the plank, to my bed. I wanted to steal about these deserted floors, like a conspirator; then, having, perhaps, found out about the mystery, to go back home. It did not enter my head that I might be shot as a burglar. My original intention, you must remember, had only been to stop the works of the ghost. It was later on that my intention became criminal, instead of merely boyish, or, in other words, crack–brained. As to stopping the ghost, I could not stop the revolving pipe. I could do no more than take away the light from the ghost–face. As for the owl on the lower floor, when I came to it, could not do so much, for it was a great big picture on board, done in some shining paint. I had nothing with which I could smear it over, nor could I reach the head. As for stopping the machine, that I dared not attempt to do, lest I should bring someone up to me, from the works, wherever they were. Standing by the ghost of the owl, hearing the chack–chack of the machine at intervals below me, I became aware of voices in the room downstairs. When the chack–chack stopped, I could hear men talking. I could hear what they said, for they were talking in the ordinary tone of conversation. There was an open space as it happened, all around the great pipe, where it passed through the floor. I could peep through this into the room below, getting a good sight of what was going on. It was very wicked of me, for there is nothing quite so contemptible as an eavesdropper, but I could not resist the temptation to look down. When once I had looked down I am ashamed to say that I listened to what the men were saying. But first of all, I put out my candle, lest anyone looking up should se the light through the open space.

At the head of the table, there was a very handsome man, dressed all in black, as though in mourning. His beauty was so great that afterwards it passed into a proverb. Later in the year, when I saw this gentleman nearly every day, I noticed that people (even those who did not know who he was) would look after him when he passed them. I will say only this about his handsomeness. It was a bodily kind of beauty, of colour rather than of form; there was not much character in it. Had he lived, I daresay he would have become ugly like the rest of his family, none of whom, except his great–great–grandmother, was accounted much for looks.

Next to this handsome man, on the right, sat Mr. Jermyn, looking fifteen years younger without his false beard. Then came a very black–looking man, with a face all eyebrows. Then a soldier in uniform. Then a little, wiry man, who jumped about as though excited—I could only see him when he jumped: he had an unpleasant, saturnine face, which frightened me. That, as far as I could see, was the whole company. When I first began to listen, the man in uniform was speaking to the handsome man at the head of the table. I knew at once, when he said Your Majesty, that he was talking to James, the Duke of Monmouth, of whom I had heard that afternoon.

"No, your Majesty," he said. "No, your Majesty," he repeated, "I can't answer for the army. If things had been different in February" (he meant, "if you had been in England when Charles II died") "there would have been another King in England. As it is, I'm against a rising."

"Don't you think his Majesty could succeed by raising an army in the West?" said Mr. Jermyn. "The present usurper (he meant James II) is a great coward. The West is ripe to rebel. Any strong demonstration there would paralyse him. Besides, the army wouldn't fire on their own countrymen. We'd enough of that in the Civil War. What do you think of a Western rising?"

The soldier smiled. "Ah no," he said. "No, your Majesty. Whatever you do, Sire, don't do it with untrained men. A rising in the West would only put you at the head of a mob. A regiment of steady trained men in good discipline can destroy any mob in twenty minutes. No, your Majesty. No. Don't try. it, Sire."

"Then what do you advise, Lane?" said the Duke.

"I would say wait, your Majesty. Wait till the usurper, the poisoner, commits himself with the Papists. When he's made himself thoroughly unpopular throughout the country, then sound a few regiments. It's only a matter of a year or two. If you'll wait for a year or two you'll see yourself invited over. Besides, a sudden rising in the West must fail, sir. Your Majesty would be in between two great garrisons, Bristol and Portsmouth. We can't be sure that either would be true to us."

"Yes," the Duke answered. "Yes, Lane. But as I plan it, the army will be tempted north. Argyle will make a strong feint in Scotland, with the great clans, just when the Western gentry declare for us."

"I take it," Lane answered, "that Argyle has sounded the clans. He knows, I suppose, what force of drilled men will rally to him. You know nothing, sir, about the West. You know that many men are for you; but you know not how many nor how good. You will need mounted men, sir, if you are to dash down upon London with any speed. You cannot raise cavalry in a week. All that you will get in the West will be squireens, or dashing young farmers, both kinds unaccustomed to being ordered; both kinds totally unfitted for war."

"Yes," said the saturnine little man. "But a rising in the West would have this natural effect. Argyle will draw troops to the north, as his Majesty has explained. Very well, then. Let Devon declare for the King, the business will be done. The usurper will not dare to send the few troops left to him out of the capital, lest the town should rise on him."

"Very true. True. A good point," said the man with the eyebrows.

"I think that disposes of your argument, Lane," said the Duke, with a smile.

"It's a supposition, sir, against a certainty. I've told you of a military danger. Falk, there, only tells you of a bare, military possibility."

"But it's as certain as anything can be," said the man with the eyebrows. "You can see. That's just what must happen."

"It is what may happen if you wait for a year or two, your Majesty," Lane replied. "But a newly crowned King is always popular. I doubt if you will find public opinion so much on your side, your Majesty. No for a year or two, till he's made himself disliked. They've settled down now to this usurper. They'll resent an interruption. The trades−men will resent an interruption."

"I think you over–rate the difficulties, Lane," said Mr. Jermyn.

"Yes," said the Duke, "I'm a great believer in putting a matter to the test. Much must necessarily be left to chance. If we wait, we may not find public opinion turning against our enemies. We may even lose the good opinion of the West by waiting. Besides, by waiting, Lane, we should lose the extraordinary: help of Argyle's diversion in the north."

"Yes," the others said in chorus. "We mustn't lose that. A rising this early summer, when the roads are good. A rising as soon as Argyle is ready."

"Well, your Majesty," said Lane, shaking his head. "I see you're resolved. You shall not find me backward when the time comes, for all my doubts at this meeting. To your Majesty's happy success." They all drank the toast; but I noticed that Mr. Lane looked melancholy, as though he foresaw something of what actually happened in that terrible June.

"Very good," said the Duke, "I thank you, gentlemen. Now, Jermyn. We two shall have to be off to the Low Countries in another half hour. How about messengers to the West? You, Lane, are tied here to your regiment. Falk, how about you, Falk?"

"No, your Majesty," said Falk. "There's danger in sending me. I'm suspected. I'm known to be in your interests."

"You, then, Candlish," said the Duke to the man with the eyebrows.

"Not me, Sire," said Candlish. "I can't disguise myself. I'm stamped by nature for the paths of virtue."

"It would be a good thing," said Falk, "if we could get some Western carrier."

"The Western carriers are all watched," Lane replied. "They are followed, wherever they go, as on as they arrive at their inns here."

"Haven't you found some more gipsies, Falk?" Candlish asked. "The last gipsy we had was very good."

"He was caught by a press—gang," said Falk, "Gipsies aren't to be trusted, though. They would sell us at once if they had the chance. Ramon was an exception."

Mr. Jermyn had risen at the Duke's last speech as though to put on his coat, ready to leave the house.. The Duke was listening to the conversation, making 'idle sketches, as he listened, on the paper before him, I think I hardly realised, as I craned over the open space, that I had been listening to a conversation which would have condemned all present to death for treason. I repeated to myself, in a dazed sort of way, that the West was ready to rise. "King James is an usurper," I said softly. "These men are going to rebel against him. There's going to be a civil war in England about it." I had hardly repeated this to myself, when it came over me with a shock that I was in terrible personal danger. The men were just leaving the house. They would probably look up, on leaving, to see what sort of a night it was. They would see my wonderful bridge. It would be all over with me then. I was so I could hardly stand up. I took a few cautious steps towards the door, saying to myself that I would never again be disobedient if I might escape this once. I was at the door, just about to open it, when I heard a step upon the landing just outside, coming towards me. I gave up hope then; but I had just sense enough to step to my left, so that, when the door should open (if the stranger entered) it might, possibly, screen me from him. Then I heard the Duke's voice from down below calling to Mr. Jermyn.

"Jermyn," he called. "Bring down my books, will you. They're on my bed. What are you doing up there?"

"Just seeing to the ghosts, your Majesty. I won't keep you waiting."

"I'll come, too," he answered. "I'd like to see your ghosts again." Then I heard Mr. Jermyn loitering at the stair—head while the Duke left the council—room. My hair was rising on my scalp; there was cold sweat on my forehead; it was as much as I could do to keep my teeth from chattering. I heard the Duke's feet upon the stairs; there were eleven stairs, I counted them. Presently I heard him say, "Now, Jermyn." Then came Jermyn's answer of "This way, your Majesty." He flung the door wide open, so that the Duke might enter. The two men passed into the room to examine the horrible owl. The Duke chuckled as the machine moved round to him. "How bright he keeps," he said. "Yes,"

Jermyn answered. "He won't need painting for a long while yet." "No," the Duke answered, "I hear, Jermyn, he's given you a most uncanny reputation." "Yes," said Jermyn, "the house has a bad name. What in the world is this?" In walking round the owl his foot had struck upon the unlucky tin candle-sconce which I had brought from the room above. "Sounds like a tin candle-stick," said the Duke. "Yes," said Mr. Jermyn, groping. "That's what it is. Now how in the world did it get here? It's the candle-stick from the dragon's head in the room above." "Are you sure, Jermyn?" the Duke asked, in a voice which showed that he was agitated. "Yes, sir. Quite sure. But no one's been up there." "There must be a spy," said the Duke. The two voices spoke together for a moment in whispers. I could not hear what they said; but a moment later I heard the rasping, clinking noise of two swords being drawn. "Come out of that," said Mr. Jermyn's voice. I felt that I was discovered; but I dared not stir from my covert. I heard the two men walking swiftly to the door. A hand plucked it from in front of me. I shrank back into the wall, covering my eyes with my hands, so that I should not see the two long sword-blades pointing at my throat. "Make no sound. Make no sound, now," said the Duke, pressing his sword-point on my chest, so that I could feel it thrust hard upon me, as though it needed very little force to send it through. I made no sound.

"Who are you?" said Mr. Jermyn, backing to the opening in the floor. "Kill him if he moves, sir. Candlish, Candlish. Bring a light. Bring a light. We've caught a moth."

I tried to swallow, but my throat seemed choked with dust. I heard the people downstairs bustling out of the room with candles. I tried to speak; but I could not. I was too much scared. I stood pressed hard against the wall, with the Duke's sword-point still in place.

"Bring it in here, Candlish," said Mr. Jermyn. There came a clattering noise from the window. Mr. Jermyn had released some heavy rolled up curtain-blinds, which covered the whole window. There was no chance, now, of being seen from the street, or from my uncle's house. Candlish entered carrying a candle.

The others followed at his heels.

"A boy. Eh?" he said.

"What do you do here?" the Duke asked, staring hard at me.

"He's frightened out of his wits, sir," said Lane. "We aren't going to hurt you, boy, if you'll only tell the truth."

"Why," said Mr. Jermyn. "It's Martin Hyde, nephew to old Hyde across the way."

"But he's overheard us," put in Falk. "He's overheard us."

"Come on downstairs. Bring him with you," said the Duke. Lane took me by one arm. Mr. Jermyn took me by the other. They marched me downstairs to the council–room.

"Here, boy," said Candlish, not unkindly. "Drink this wine." He made me swallow a glass of Burgundy, which certainly did me a great deal of good. I was able to speak after drinking it.

"Now, Mr. Hyde," said Mr. Jermyn. "How do you come to be in this house?"

"Take your time, boy," said Lane.

"He's not a London boy?" said the Duke to Mr. Jermyn.

"No, sir," he answered in a whisper. "Just come here from the country."

"Please, your Majesty," I began.

"So you're a young rebel," said the Duke. "That shows he overheard us," said Falk.

"Let him alone, Falk," the Duke said.

"He'll tell the truth. No use in frightening him."

"Please, your Majesty," I said again, "I was locked up in my room for taking my uncle's boat this afternoon." One of two of them smiled when I said this: it gave me confidence.

"But how did you get into this house?" Mr. Jermyn asked.

"Please, sir," I answered, "1 saw your upper window open. So I laid a couple of planks across the lane from my window. Then I just straddled across, sir."

"Are you used to burglary, may I ask?" said the Duke.

"No, your Majesty. But I saw the ghosts. I wanted to see how they were made."

"Well. That's one for you, Jermyn," said Lane. "Your ghosts haven't frightened this one."

"Sir," I answered. "They frightened me horribly. I wanted to be revenged for that. But after a bit I was sure they were only clockwork. I wanted to stop them. I did stop the devil upstairs, sir."

"So you stopped the devil upstairs," the Duke said. "What did you do then?"

"I came down to this room, sir. I looked at the owl. But I couldn't see how to stop the owl, sir. I saw you all sitting round the room. I'm afraid I listened, sir."

"That was not a gentlemanly thing to do," said Lane. "Was it now?"

"No, sir."

"You understood all that was said. Eh, boy?" said Candlish.

"Yes, sir. I understood it all."

"Well, young man," said Falk. "You'll be sorry you did."

"Be quiet, Falk," said the Duke. "No one shall bully the boy. What's your name, boy?"

"Martin Hyde, sir."

"A very smart lad too, sir," said Jermyn. "He saved my book of cipher correspondence yesterday. We should have been in trouble if that had got into the wrong hands."

"You understand," said the Duke, "that what you have heard might get us all, perhaps many more besides ourselves, into very terrible danger if repeated?"

"Yes, your Majesty, I understand," I answered. "Lock him into the pantry, Jermyn," said the Duke, "while we decide what to do with him. Go with Mr. Jermyn, boy. We sha'n't hurt you. Don't be frightened. Give him some oranges, Jermyn."

CHAPTER V. I GO TO SEA

Mr. Jermyn led me to the pantry (a little room on the ground floor), where he placed a plate of oranges before me.

"See how many you can eat," he said. "But don't try to burgle yourself free. This is a strong room." He locked the heavy door, leaving me alone with a well–filled pantry, which seemed to be without a window. A little iron grating near the ceiling served as a ventilator. There was no chance of getting out through that. The door was plated with iron. The floor was of concrete. I was a prisoner now in good earnest. I was no longer frightened; but I had had such scares that night that I had little stomach for the fruit. I was only anxious to be allowed to go back to my bed. I heard a dull noise in the upper part of the house, followed by the falling of a plank. "There goes my bridge," I thought. "Are they going to be so mean as to call my uncle out of bed, to show him what I've been doing?" I thought that perhaps they would do this, as my uncle (for all that I knew) might be in their plot. "Well," I said to myself, "I shall get a good thrashing. Perhaps that brute Ephraim will be told to thrash me. But thrashing or no, I've had enough of going out at night. I'll ask my uncle not to thrash me, but to put me into the Navy. I should love that. I know that I shall never get on in London." This sudden plan of the Navy, about which I had never before thought, seemed to me to be a good way of getting out of my deserts. I felt sure that my uncle would be charmed to be rid of me; while I knew very well that boys of that generation often entered the Navy, in the care of the captains, as naval cadets (or, as they were then called, "captain's servants") at the ages of eight or nine. I wondered why the debate lasted so long. Naturally, in that gloomy little prison, lit by a single tallow candle, with all my anxieties heavy on my mind, the time passed slowly. But they were so long in making up their minds that it seemed as though they had forgotten me. I began to remember horrible tales of people shut up in secret rooms until they starved to death, or till the rats ate them. I remembered the tale of the nun being walled up in a vault of her convent, brick by brick, till the last brick shut off the last glimmer of the bricklayer's lantern, till the last layer of mortar made for her the last sound she would hear, the patting clink of the trowel on the brick, before it was all horrible dark silence for ever. I wondered how many people had been silenced in that way. I wondered how long I should live, if that was what these men decided.

My fears were ended by the opening of the door. "Come on," said Mr. Lane. "This way," He led me back to the council-room, where all the conspirators sat at their places by the table. I noticed that Mr. Jermyn (cloaked now, as for travel) was wearing his false beard again.

"Mr. Hyde," the Duke said. "I understand that you are well disposed to my cause."

"Yes, your Majesty," I answered; though indeed I only followed what my father had told me. I had no real knowledge about it, one way or the other. I knew only what others had told me. Still, in this instance, as far as I have been able to judge by what I learned long afterwards, I was right. The Duke had truly a claim to the throne; he was also a better man than that disgraceful king who took his place.

"Very well, Mr. Hyde," the Duke answered. "Have you any objections to entering my service?"

I was not very sure of what he meant; it came rather suddenly upon me, so I stammered, without replying.

"His Majesty means, would you like to join our party?" said Mr. Lane. "To be one of us. To serve him abroad."

I was flushed with pleasure at the thought of going abroad, among a company of conspirators. I had no knowledge of what the consequences might be, except that I should escape a sound whipping from my uncle or from Ephraim. I did not like the thought of living on in London, with the prospect of entering a merchant's office at the end of my boyhood. I thought that in the Duke's service I should soon become a general, so that I might return to my uncle, very splendidly dressed, to show him how well I had managed my own life for myself. I thought that life was always like that to the adventurous man. Besides I hoped that I should escape school, the very thought of which I hated. Looking at the matter in that secret council–room, it seemed so very attractive. It seemed to give me a pathway of escape, whichever way I looked at it, from all that I most disliked.

"Yes, your Majesty," I said, "I should very much like to enter your service."

"You understand, Hyde," said Mr. Jermyn, "that we are engaged in a very dangerous work. It is so dangerous that we should not be justified in allowing you to go free after what you have heard tonight. But its very danger makes it necessary that we should tell you something of what your work under his Majesty will be, before you decide finally to throw in your lot with us. It is one thing to be a prisoner among us, Hyde; but quite another to be what is called a rebel, engaged in treasonable practices against a ruling King."

"Still," said Lane, "don't think that your imprisonment with us would be unpleasant. If you would rather not join us, you have only to say so. We shall then send you over to Holland, where you will, no doubt, find plenty of boats with which to amuse yourself. You will be kept in Holland till a certain much–wished event takes place, about the middle of June. After that you will be brought back here to your uncle who, by that time, will have forgiven you."

"That's a very pretty ladder you made," said the Duke. "You've evidently lived among sailors."

"Among fishermen mostly, your Majesty," I said "My father was rector in the Broads country." I knew from his remark that someone had been across to my uncle's house to remove all traces of my bridge. My ladder, I knew, would now be dangling from my window, to show by which way I had escaped.

"We want you, Hyde," Mr. Jermyn said. "That is—we shall want you in the event of your joining us, to be our messenger to the West. You will travel continually from Holland to the West of England, generally to the country near Taunton, but sometimes to Exeter, sometimes still further to the West. You will carry letters sewn into the flap of your leather travelling satchel. You will travel alone by your own name, giving out, in case any one should ask you, that you are going to one of certain people, whose names will be given to you. There will be no danger to yourself; for the persons to whom you will be sent are not suspected; indeed one of them is a clergyman. We think that a boy will have less difficulty in getting about the country in its present state than any man, provided, of course, that you travel by different routes on each journey. If, however, by some extraordinary .chance, you should be caught with these letters in your wallet, we shall take steps to bring you off; for we have a good deal of power, in one way or another, by which we get things done. Still, it may well fall out, Hyde, in spite of all our care, that you will come into the hands of men with whom we have no influence. If you should, (remember, it is quite possible) you will be transported to serve in one of the Virginian or West Indian plantations. That will be the end of you as far as we are concerned. We shan't be able to help you then. If you think the cause is right, join us, provided that you do not think the risks too great."

"If all goes well," said the Duke, "if the summer should prove prosperous, I may be able to reward a faithful servant, even if he is only a boy."

"I will serve your Majesty gladly," I answered. "I should like to join your service."

"Very well then, Jermyn," he said, rising swiftly on his way to the door; "bring him on board at once."

"We're off to Holland tonight, in the schooner there," said Mr. Jermyn. "So put these biscuits in your pocket. Give him another glass of wine, Falk. Now, then. Good–bye, Lane. Good–bye everybody."

"Good–bye," they said. "Good–bye, boy." In another minute we were in the narrow road, within earshot of the tumbling water, going down to the stairs at the lane end, to take boat. The last that I saw of my uncle's house was the white of my ladder ropes, swinging about against the darkness of the bricks.

"Remember, Hyde," said Mr. Jermyn in a low voice, "that his Majesty is always plain Mr. Scott. Remember that. Remember, too, that you are never to speak to him unless he speaks to you. But you won't have much to do with him. Were you ever at sea, before?"

"No, sir. Only about the Broads in a coracle."

"You'll find it very interesting, then. If you're not seasick. Here we are at the boat. Now, jump in. Get into the bows."

"Mr. Scott" was already snug under a boat–cloak in the sternsheets. As soon as we had stepped in, the boatman shoved off. The boat rippled the water into a gleaming track as she gathered way. We were off. I was on my way to Holland. I was a conspirator, travelling with a King. There ahead of me was the fine hull of the schooner La Reina, waiting to carry us to all sorts of adventure, none of them (as I planned them then) so strange, or so terrible, as those which happened to me. As we drew up alongside her, I heard the clack–clack of the sailors heaving at the windlass. They were getting up the anchor, so that we might sail from this horrible city to all the wonderful romance which awaited me, as I thought, beyond, in the great world. Five minutes after I had stepped upon her deck we were gliding down on the ebb, bound for Holland.

"Hyde," said Mr. Jermyn, as we drew past the battery on the Tower platform, "do you see the high ground, beyond the towers there?"

"Yes, sir," I said.

"Do you know what that is?"

"No, sir."

"That's Tower Hill," he answered, "where traitors, I mean conspirators like you or me, are beheaded. Do you know what that means?"

"Yes, sir," I replied. "To have your head cut off."

"Yes," he said. "With all that hill black with people. The scaffold hung with black making a sort of platform in the middle. Then soldiers, with drums, all round. You put your head over a block, so that your neck rests on the wood. Then the executioner comes at you with an axe. Then your head is shown to the people. 'This is the head of a traitor.' We may all end in that way, on that little hill there. You must be very careful how you carry the letters, Hyde."

After this hint, he showed me a hammock in the schooner's 'tweendecks, telling me that I should soon be accustomed to that kind of bed. "It is a little awkward at first," he said, "especially the getting in part; but, when once snugly in, it is the most comfortable kind of bed in the world." After undressing by the light of a huge ship's lantern, which Mr.

Martin Hyde, The Duke's Messenger

Jermyn called a battle–lantern, I turned into my hammock, rather glad to be alone. Now that I was pledged to this conspiracy business, with some knowledge of what it might lead to, I half wished myself well out of it. The 'tweendecks was much less comfortable than the bedroom which I had left so gaily such a very little time before. I had exchanged a good prison for a bad one. The smell of oranges, so near to the hold in which they were stored, was overpowering, mixed, as it was, with the horrible ship–smell of decaying water (known as bilge–water) which flopped about at each roll a few feet below me. My hammock was slung in a draught from the main hatchway. People came down the hatchway during the night to fetch coils of rope or tackles. Tired as I was, I slept very badly that first night on board ship. The schooner seemed to be full of queer, unrelated movements. The noise (f the water slipping past was like somebody talking. The striking of the bells kept me from sleeping. I did not get to sleep till well into the middle watch (about two in the morning) after which I slept brokenly until a rough voice bawled in my ear to get up out of that, as it was time to wash down.

I put my clothes on hurriedly, wondering where I should find a basin in which to wash myself. I could see none in the 'tweendecks; but I supposed that there would be some in the cabins, which opened off the 'tweendecks on each side. Now a 'tweendecks (I may as well tell you here) is nothing more than a deck of a ship below the upper deck. If some of my readers have never been in a ship, let them try to imagine themselves descending from the upper deck—where all the masts stand—by a ladder fixed in a square opening known as a hatchway. About six feet down this ladder is the 'tweendecks, a long narrow room, with a ceiling so low that unless you bend, you bump your head against the beams.

If you will imagine a long narrow room, only six feet high, you will know what a 'tweendecks is like. Only in a real 'tween–decks it is always rather dark, for the windows (if you care to call them so) are thick glass bull's–eyes which let in very little light. A glare of light comes down the hatchways. Away from the hatchways a few battle–lanterns are hung, to keep up some pretence of light in the darkest corners. At one end of this long narrow room in La Reina a wooden partition, running right across from side to side, made a biggish chamber called "the cabin," where the officers took their meals. A little further along the room, one on each side of it, were two tiny partitioned cabins, about seven feet square, in which the officers slept, two in each cabin one above the other, in shelf–beds, or bunks. My hammock had been slung between these cabins, a little forward of them. When I turned out, I saw that the rest of the 'tweendecks was piled with stores of all kinds, lashed down firmly to ringbolts. Right forward, in the darkness of the ship's bows, I saw other hammocks where the sailors slept.

I was wondering what I was to do about washing, when the rough man who had called me a few minutes before came down to ask me why I was not up on deck. I said that I was wondering where I could wash myself.

"Wash yourself," he said. "You haven't made yourself dirty yet. You don't wash at sea till your work's done for the day. Why, haven't you lashed your hammock yet?"

"Please, sir," I said, "I don't know how."

"Well, for once," he said, "I'll show you how. Tomorrow you'll do it for yourself."

"There," he said, when he had lashed up the hammock, by what seemed to me to be art–magic, "don't you say you don't know how to lash a 'ammick. I've showed you once. Now shove it in the rack there. Up on deck with you."

I ran up the ladder to the deck, thinking that this was not at all the kind of service which I had expected. When I got to the deck I felt happier; for it was a lovely bright morning. The schooner was under all sail, tearing along at what seemed to me to be great speed. We were out at sea now. England lay behind us, some miles away. I could see the windows gleaming in a little town on the shore. Ships were in sight, with rollers of foam whitening under them. Gulls dipped after fish. The clouds drove past. A fishing boat piled with fish was labouring up to London, her sails dark with spray. On the deck of the schooner some barefooted sailors were filling the wash–deck tubs at a hand–pump. One man was at work high aloft on the topsail yard, sitting across the yard with his legs dangling down, keeping his seat (as I thought) by balance. I found the scene so delightful that I gazed at it like a boy in a trance. was still staring, when the surly boor who had called me (he was the schooner's mate it seemed) came up behind me.

"Well," he said, in the rough, bullying speech of a sailor, "do ye see it?"

"See what, sir?"

"What you're looking at."

Martin Hyde, The Duke's Messenger

"Yes, sir," I answered.

"Then you got no butter in your eyes, then. Why ain't you at work?"

"What am I to do, sir?"

"Do," he said. "Ain't you Mr. Scott's servant?"

"Yes, sir."

"Then get a bucket of fresh water out of the cask there. Take this scrubber. You'll find some soap in the locker there. Now scrub out the cabin as quick as you know how."

He showed me down to the cabin. It was a dingy, dirty little room about twelve feet square over all, but made, in reality, much smaller by the lockers which ran along each side.

It was lighted by two large wooden ports, known as "chase ports," through which the chase guns or "stern-chasers pointed. Only one gun (a long three pounder on a swivel) was mounted; for guns take up a lot of room. With two guns in that little cabin there would not have been room enough to swing a cat. You need six feet for the proper swinging of a cat, so a man-of-war boatswain told me. The cat meant is the cat of nine tails with which they used to flog seamen. To flog properly one needs a good swing, so my friend said.

"There you are," said the mate of the schooner. "Now down on your knees. Scrub the floor here. See you get it mucho blanco."

He left me feeling much ashamed at having to work like a common ship's boy, instead of like a prince's page, which is what I had thought myself. Like many middle-class English boys I had been brought up to look on manual work as degrading. I was filled with shame at having to scrub this dirty deck. I, who, only yesterday, had lorded it over Ephraim, as though I were a superior being. You boys who go to good schools try to learn a little humbleness. You may think your parents very fine gentlefolk; but in the world, outside a narrow class, the having gentle parents will not help one much. It may be that you, for all your birth, have neither the instincts nor the intellect to preserve the gentility your parents made for you. You are no gentleman till you have proved it. Your right level may be the level of the betting publican, or of the sneak–thief, or of things even lower than these. It is nothing to be proud of that your parents are rich enough to keep your hands clean of joyless, killing toil, at an age when many better men are old in slavery. Try to be thankful for it; not proud. Leisure is the most sacred thing life has. A wise man would give his left hand for leisure. You that have it given to you by the mercy of gentle birth, regard it as a trust; make noble use of it. Many great men waste half their energies in the struggle for that which you regard, poor fools, as your right, as something to brag of.

I had never scrubbed a floor in my life; but I had seen it done, without taking much account of the art in it. I set to work, feeling more degraded each moment, as the hardness of the deck began to make my knees sore. When I had done about half of the cabin (in a lazy, neglectful way, leaving patches unscrubbed, only just wetted over, so as to seem clean to a chance observer) I thought that I would do no more; but wait till Mr. Jermyn came to me. I would tell him that I wished to go home, that I was not going to be a common sailor, but a trusted messenger, with a lot more to the same tune, meaning, really, that I hated this job of washing decks like poison. I dare say, if the truth were known, the sudden change in my fortunes had made me a little homesick. But even so, I was skulking work which had been given to me. What was worse, I was being dishonest. For I was pretending to do the work, even when I took least trouble with it. At last I took it into my head to wet the whole floor with water, meaning to do no more to it. While I was doing this the mate came into the cabin.

"Look here," he said. "I've been watching you. You ain't working. You're skulking. You ain't trying to wash that deck. You're making believe, thinking I won't know any different. Don't answer me. I know what you're doing. Now then. You go over every bit of that deck which you've just slopped at. Do it over. I'm going to stand here till it's done."

It was in my mind to be rebellious; but this man did not look like a good man to rebel from. He was a big grim sailor with a length of rope in his hand. lie called it his "manrope." "You see my manrope," he said. "His name's Mogador Jack. He likes little skulks like you." Afterwards I learned that a manrope is the rope rail at a ship's gangway, or (sometimes) a length of rope in the gangway–side for boatmen to catch as they came alongside the ship. I did not like the look of Mogador Jack, so I went at my scrubbing with all my strength, keeping my thoughts to myself. My knees felt very sore. My back ached with the continual bending down. I had had no food that morning, either, that was another thing. "Spell, oh," said the man at last. "Straighten your back a bit. Empty your bucket over the side. No. Not through the sternport. Carry in on deck. Empty it there. Then fill it again. Lively, too. It'll be breakfast time before you've done. You've got to have this cabin ready by eight bells."

I will not tell you how I finished the deck. I will say only this, that at the end I began to take a sort of pride or pleasure in making the planks white. Afterwards, I always found that there is this pleasure in manual work. There is always pleasure of a sort in doing anything that is not very easy. "There," the mate said. "Now lay the table for breakfast. You'll find the things in them lockers. Lay for three places. Don't break the ship's crockery while you're doing it."

CHAPTER VI. THE SEA! THE SEA!

He left me, then, as he had to watch the men on deck. I felt, when he went on deck, that the morning had been a nightmare; but now I was to be flunkey well as slave, a new humiliation. I did not think how many times I had humiliated others by letting them do such things for me. I had done so all my life without a thought. Now, forsooth, I was at the point of tears at having to do it for others, even though one of the others was my rightful King. Grubbing about among the lockers, I found a canvas table–cloth, which had once been part of a sail. I spread this cloth with the breakfast gear, imitating the arrangements made at home at Oulton. The mate came down some minutes after I had finished. He caught me sitting down on the top of the lockers, looking out at the ships through the open port.

"Here," he said roughly. "You've got to learn manners, or I'll have to teach you. Remember this once for all, my son. No one sits in the cabin except a captain or a passenger. You'll take your cap off to the cabin door before I've done with you. Nor you don't sit down till your work's done. That's another thing. Why ain't you at work?"

"Please, sir," I said, "I've laid the table. What else am I to do?"

"Do," he said. "Give the windows a rub. Then clean your hands, ready to wait at table. No. Hold on. Have you called Mr. Scott yet?"

"No, sir. I didn't know I had to."

"My," he answered. "Have you any sense at all? Go call them. No. Get their hot water first at the galley."

I suppose I stared at him; for I did not know that this would be a duty of mine. "Here. Don't look at me like that," he said. "You make me forget myself." He went to the locker, in which he rummaged till he produced a big copper kettle. "Here's the hot water can," he said. "Nip with it to the galley, before the cook puts his fire out. On deck, boy. Don't you know where the galley is?"

I did not know where the galley was in this particular ship. I thought that it would probably be below decks, round a space of brick floor to prevent fire. But as the mate said "on deck" I ran on deck at once. I ran on deck, up the hatch, so vigorously, that I charged into a seaman who was carrying a can of slush, or melted salt fat used in the greasing of ropes. I butted into him, spattering the slush all over him, besides making a filthy mess of grease on the deck, then newly cleansed. The seaman, who was the boatswain or second mate, boxed my ears with a couple of cuffs which made my head sing. "You young hound," he said, "Cubbadar when your chief passes." I went forward to the galley, crying as if my heart would break, not only at the pain of the blows, which stung me horribly, but at the misery of my life in this new service, that had seemed so grand only seven or eight hours before. At the galley door was the cook, a morose little Londoner with earrings in his ears. "Miaow, Miaow," he said, pretending to mimic my sobs. "Why haven't you come for this 'ot water before? 'Ere 'ave I been keepin' my fire lit while you been enjoyin' a stuffin' loaf down in that there cabin." I was too miserable to answer him. I just held out my kettle, thinking that he would fill it for me. "Wot are you 'oldin' out the kettle for?" he asked. "Think I'm goin' to do yer dirty work? Fill it at the 'ob yourself." I filled it as he bade me, choking down my tears. When I had filled it, I hurried back to the 'tweendecks, hoping to hide my misery down in the semi–darkness there. I did not pass the second mate on my way back; but I passed some of the seamen, to whom a boy in tears was fair game. One asked me what I meant by coming aft all salt, like a head sea, making the deck wet after he'd squeegeed it down. Another told me to wait till the second mate caught me. "I'd be sorry then," he said, "that ever I spilt the slush;" with other sea–jests, all of them pretty brutal. It is said that if a strange rook comes to a rookery the other rooks peck it to death, or at any rate drive it away. I know not if this be true of rooks (I know that sparrows will attack owls or canaries, whenever they have a chance), but it is true enough of human beings. We all hate the new-comer, we are all suspicious of him, as of a possible enemy. The seamen did to me what school-boys do to the new boy. I did not know then that there is no mercy for one sensitive enough to take such "jests" to heart. At sea, the rough, ready tom-fool boy is the boy to thrive. Such an one might have spilt all the slush in the ship, without getting so much as a cuff. I was a merry boy enough, but I was sad when I made my first appearance. The sailors saw me crying. If I had only had the wit to dodge the bosun's blows, the matter of the slush would have been turned off with a laugh, since he only struck me in the irritation of the moment. He would have enjoyed chasing me round the deck. If I had only come up merrily that is what would have happened. As it was I came up sad, with the result that I got my ears boxed, which, of course, made me too wretched to put the cook in a good temper; a cause of much woe to me later. The seamen who saw me crying at once put me down as a cry-baby, which I really was not; so that, for the rest of my time in the ship I was cruelly misjudged. I hope that my readers will remember how little a thing may make a great difference in a person's life. I hope that they will also remember how easy it is to misjudge a person. It will be well for them if, as I trust, they may never experience how terrible it feels to be misjudged.

After I had called the two gentlemen, I gave the glass bull's-eyes in the swing ports a rub with a cloth. I was at work in this way when the two gentlemen entered. Mr. Jermyn smiled to see me with my coat off, rubbing at the glass. He also wished me good morning, which Mr. Scott failed to do. Mr. Scott took no notice of me one way or the other; but sat down at the locker, asking when breakfast would be ready. "Get breakfast, boy," Mr. Jermyn said. At that I put my glass-rag into the locker. I hurried off to the galley to bring the breakfast, not knowing rightly whether it would be there or in another place. The cook, surly brute, made a lot of offensive remarks to me, to which I made no answer. He was glad to have someone to bully, for he had the common man's love of power, with all his hatred of anything more polished than himself. I took the breakfast aft to the cabin, where, by this time, the ship's captain was seated. I placed the dish before Mr. Jermyn.

"Why haven't you washed your hands, boy?" he asked, looking at my hands.

"Please, sir, I haven't had time."

"Wash them now, then. Don't come to wait at table with hands like that again. I didn't think you were a dirty boy."

I was not a dirty boy; but, having been at work since before six that morning, I had had no chance of washing myself. I could not answer; but the injustice of Mr. Jermyn's words gave me some of the most bitter misery which I have known. For brutal, thoughtless injustice, it is difficult to beat the merchant ship. I stole away to wash myself, very glad of the chance to get away from the cabin. When I was ready, it was time to clear the breakfast things to the galley, to wash them with the cook. Luckily, I had overheard Mr. Jermyn say "how well this cook can devil kidneys." I repeated this to the cook, who was pleased to hear it. It made him rather more kind in his manner to me. He did not know who Mr. Scott really was. He asked me a lot of questions about what I knew of Mr. Scott. I replied that I'd heard that he was a Spanish merchant, a friend of Mr. Jermyn's. As for Mr. Jermyn, he knew' an uncle of mine. I had helped him to recover his pocket-book; that was all that I knew of him; that was why he had given me my present post as servant. More I dared not say; for I remembered the Duke's sharp sword on my chest. We talked thus, as we washed the dishes; the cook in a sweeter mood (having had his morning dram of brandy); I, myself, trying hard to win him to a good opinion of me. I asked him if I might clean his copper for him; it was in a sad state of dirt. "You'll have work enough 'ere, boy," he said, tartly, "without you running round for more. You mind your own business." After this little snap at my head (no thought of thanks occurred to him) he prepared breakfast for us, out of the remains of the cabin breakfast. I was much cheered by the prospect of food, for nearly three hours of hard work had given me an appetite. At a word from the cook, I brought out two little stools from under the bunk. Then I placed the "bread-barge," or wooden bowl of ship's biscuits, ready for our meal, beside our two plates.

Breakfast was just about to begin, when my enemy, the boatswain, appeared at the galley door. "Here, cook," he said, "where's that limb of a boy? Oh, you're there, are you? Feeding your face. Get a three-cornered scraper right now. You'll scrape up that slush you spilled, before you eat so much as a reefer's nut." I had to go on deck again for another hour, while I scraped up the slush, which was, surely, spilled as much by himself as by me, since he was not looking where he was going any more than I was. I got no breakfast. For after the grease was cleaned I was sent to black the gentlemen's boots; then to make up their beds; then to scrub their cabin clean. After all this, being faint with hunger, I took a ship's biscuit from the locker in the cabin to eat as I worked. I did not know it; but this biscuit was what is known as "captain's bread," a whiter (but less pleasant) kind of ship's biscuit, baked for officers. As I was eating it (I was polishing the cabin door–knobs at the time) the captain came down for a dram of brandy. He saw what I was eating. At once he read me a lecture, calling me a greedy young thief. Let me not eat another cabin biscuit, he said, or he'd do to me what they always did to thieves:—drag them under the ship from one side to another, so that the barnacles would cut them (as he said) into Spanish sennet–work. When I answered him, he lost his temper, in sailor fashion, saying that if I said another word he'd make me sick that ever I learned to speak.

I will not go into the details of the rest of that first day's misery. I was kept hard at work for the whole time of daylight, often at work beyond my strength, always at work quite strange to me. Nobody in the ship, except perhaps the mate, troubled to show me how to do these strange tasks; but all swore at me for not doing them rightly. What I felt most keenly was the injustice of their verdicts upon me. I was being condemned by them as a dirty, snivelling, lying, thieving young hound. They took a savage pleasure in telling me how I should come to dance on air at Cuckold's Haven, or, in other words, to the gallows, if I went on as I had begun. Whereas (but for my dishonest moment in the morning) I had worked like a slave since dawn under every possible disadvantage which hasty men could place in my way. After serving the cabin supper that night I was free to go to my hammock. There was not much to be glad for, except the rest after so much work. I went with a glad heart, for I was tired out. The wind had drawn to the east, freshening as it came ahead, so that there was no chance of our reaching our destination for some days. I had the prospect of similar daily slavery in the schooner at least till our arrival. My nights would be my only pleasant hours till then. The noise of the waves breaking on board the schooner kept me awake during the night, tired as I was. It is a dreadful noise, when heard for the first time. I did not then know what a mass of water can come aboard a ship without doing much harm. So, when the head of a wave, rushing across the deck, came with a swish down the hatch to wash the 'tweendecks I started up in my hammock, pretty well startled. I soon learned that all was well, for I heard the sailors laughing in their rough, swearing fashion as they piled a tarpaulin over the open hatch–mouth. A moment later, eight bells were struck. Some of the sailors having finished their watch, came down into the 'tweendecks to rest. Two of them stepped very quietly to the chest below my hammock, where they sat down to play cards, by the light of the nearest battle–lantern. If they had made a noise I should probably have fallen asleep again in a few minutes; for what would one rough noise have been among all the noise on deck? But they kept very quiet, talking in low voices as they called the cards, rapping gently on the chest–lid, opening the lantern gently to get lights for their pipes. Their quietness was like the stealthy approach of an enemy, it kept a restless man awake, just as the snapping of twigs in a forest will keep an Indian awake, while he will sleep soundly when trees are falling. I kept awake, too, in spite of myself (or half awake), wishing that the men would go, but fearing to speak to them. At last, fearing that I should never get to sleep at all, I looked over the edge of the hammock intending to ask them to go. I saw then that one of them was my enemy the boatswain, while the other was the ship's carpenter, who had eaten supper in the galley with me, at the cook's invitation. As these were, in a sense, officers, I dared not open my mouth to them, so I lay down again, hoping that either they would go soon, or that they would let me get to sleep before the morning. As I lay there, I overheard their talk. I could not help it. I could hear every word spoken by them. I did not want their talk, goodness knows, but as I could not help it, I listened.

"Heigho," said the boatswain, yawning. "I sha'n't have much to spend on Hollands when I get there. Them rubbers at bowls in London have pretty near cleaned my purse out."

"Ah, come off," said the carpenter. "You can always get rid of a coil of rope to someone, on the sly, you boatswains can. A coil of rope comes to a few guilders. Eh, mynheer?"

"I sold too many coils off this hooker," said the boatswain. "I run the ship short."

"Who sleeps in the hammock there?" the carpenter asked.

"The loblolly boy for the cabin," the boatswain answered. "Young clumsy hound. I clumped his fat chops for him this morning."

"Mr. Jermyn's boy?" said the carpenter, sinking his voice. "There's something queer about that Mr. Jermyn. 'E wears a false beard. That Mr. Scott isn't all what he pretends neither."

"I don't see how that can be," the boatswain said, "I wish I'd a drink of something. I'm as dry as foul block."

"There'd be more'n a dram to us two, if Mr. Scott was what I think," said the carpenter. "I'm going to keep my eye on that gang."

"Keep your eye on the moon," said the boatswain.

"I tell you what'd raise drinks pretty quick."

"What would?"

"That loblolly boy would."

"Eh?" said the carpenter. "Go easy, Joe. He may be awake."

"Not he," said the boatswain, carelessly glancing into my hammock, where I lay like all the Seven Sleepers condensed. "Not he. Snoring young hound. Do him good to raise drinks for the crowd."

"Eh," said the carpenter, a quieter, more cautious scoundrel than the other (therefore much more dangerous). "How would a boy like that?" He left his sentence unfinished.

"Sell him to one of these Dutch East India merchants," said the boatswain. "There's always one or two of them in the Canal, bound for Java. A likely young lad like that would fetch twenty pounds from a Dutch skipper. A white boy would sell for forty in the East. Even if we only got ten, there'd be pretty drinking while it lasted."

This evidently made an impression on the carpenter, for he did not answer at once. "Yes," he said presently. "But a lad like that's got good friends. He don't talk like you or I, Joe."

"Friends in your eye," said the other. "What's a lad with good friends doing as loblolly boy?"

"Run away," the carpenter said. "Besides, Mr. Jermyn isn't likely to let the lad loose in Haarlem."

"He might. We could keep a watch," the boatswain answered. "If he goes ashore, we could tip off Longshore Jack to keep an eye on him. Jack gets good chances, working the town."

"Yes," said the other. "I mean to put Longshore Jack on to this Mr. Jermyn. If I aren't foul of the buoy there's money in Mr. Jermyn. More than in East Indian slaves."

"Oh," the boatswain answered, carelessly, "I don't bother about my betters, myself. What d'ye think to get from Mr. Jermyn?"

The carpenter made no answer; but lighted his pipe at the lantern, evidently turning over some scheme in his mind. After that, the talk ran on other topics, some of which I could not understand. It was mostly about the Gold Coast, about a place called Whydah, where there was good trading for negroes, so the boatswain said. He had been there in a Bristol brig, under Captain Travers, collecting trade, i.e. negro slaves. At Whydah they had made King Jellybags so drunk with "Samboe" (whatever Samboe was) that they had carried him off to sea, with his whole court. "The blacks was mad after," he said, "the next ship's crew that put in there was all set on the beach. I seed their bones after. All picked clean. But old King Jellybags fetched thirty pound in Port Royal, duty free." He seemed to think that this story was something laugh at.

I strained my ears to hear more of what they said. I could catch nothing more relating to myself. Nothing more was said about me. They told each other stories about the African shore, where the schooners anchored in the creeks, among the swamp—smells, in search of slaves or gold dust. They told tales of Tortuga, where the pirates lived together in a town, whenever they were at home after a cruise. "Rum is cheaper than water there," the bo'sun said. "A sloop comes off once a month with stores from Port Royal. Its happy days, being in Tortuga." Presently the two men crept aft to the empty cabin to steal the captain's brandy. Soon afterwards they passed forward to their hammocks.

When they had gone, I lay awake, wondering I was to avoid this terrible danger of being sold to the Dutch East India merchants. I wondered who Longshore Jack might be. I feared that the carpenter suspected our party. I kept repeating his words, "There's money in Mr. Jermyn," till at last, through sheer weariness, I fell asleep. In the morning, as cleared away breakfast, from the cabin—table, I told Mr. Jermyn all that I had heard. The Duke seemed agitated. He kept referring to an astronomical book which told him how his ruling planets stood. "Yes," he kept saying, "I've no very favourable stars till July. I don't like this, Jermyn." Mr. Jermyn smoked a pipe of tobacco (a practise rare among gentlemen at that time) while he thought of what could be done. At last he spoke.

"I know what we'll do, sir. We'll sell this man as carpenter to the Dutch East India man. We'll give the two of them a sleeping draught in their drink. We'll get rid of them both together."

"It sounds very cruel," said the Duke.

"Yes," said Mr. Jermyn, "it is cruel. But who knows what the sly man may not pick up? We're playing akes, we two. We've got many enemies. One word of what this man suspects may bring a whole pack of spies upon us. Besides, if the spies get hold of this boy we shall have some trouble."

"The boy's done very well," said the Duke.

"He's got a talent for overhearing," Mr. Jermyn answered. "Well, Martin Hyde. How do you like your work?"

"Sir," I answered, "I don't like it at all."

"Well," he said, "we shall be in the Canal to–night, now the wind has changed. Hold out till then. think, sir," he said, turning to the Duke, "the boy has done really very creditably. The work is not at all the work for one of his condition."

The Duke rewarded me with his languid beautiful smile.

"Who lives will see," he said. "A King never forgets a faithful servant."

The phrase seemed queer on the lips of that man's father's son; but I bowed very low, for I felt that I was already a captain of a man–of–war, with a big blazing decoration on my heart. Well, who lives, sees. I lived to see a lot of strange things in that King's service.

CHAPTER VII. LAND RATS AND WATER RATS

I will say no more about our passage except that we were three days at sea. Then, when I woke one morning, I found that we were fast moored to a gay little wharf, paved with clean white cobbles, on the north side of the canal. Strange, outlandish figures, in immense blue baggy trousers, clattered past in wooden shoes. A few Dutch galliots lay moored ahead of us, with long scarlet pennons on their mastheads. On the other side of the canal was a huge East Indiaman, with her lower yards cockbilled, loading all three hatches at once. It was a beautiful morning. The sun was so bright that all the scene had thrice its natural beauty. The clean neat trimness of the town, the water slapping past in the canal, the ships with their flags, the Sunday trim of the schooner, all filled me with delight, lit up, as they were, by the April sun. I looked about me at my ease, for the deck was deserted. Even the never–sleeping mate was resting, now that we were in port. While I looked, a man sidled along the wharf from a warehouse towards me. He looked at the schooner in a way which convinced me that he was not a sailor. Then, sheltering behind a bollard, he lighted his pipe.

He was a short, active, wiry man, with a sharp, thin face, disfigured by a green patch over his right eye. He looked to me to have a horsey look, as though were a groom or coachman. After lighting his pipe, he advanced to a point abreast of the schooner's gang–way, from which he could look down upon her, as she lay with her deck a foot or two below the level of the wharf.

"Chips aboard?" he asked, meaning, "Is the carpenter on board?"

"Yes," I said. "Will you come aboard?"

He did not answer, but looked about the ship, as though making notes of everything. Presently he turned to me.

"You're new," he said. "Are you Mr. Jermyn's boy?" I told him that I was.

"How is Mr. Jermyn keeping?" he asked. "Is that cough of his better?" This made me feel that probably the man knew Mr. Jermyn. "Yes," I said. "He's got no cough, now." "He'd a bad one last time he was here," the man answered. For a while he kept silent. He seemed to me to be puzzling out the relative heights of our masts. Suddenly he turned to me, with a very natural air. "How's Mr. Scott's business going?" he asked. "You know, eh? You know what I mean?" I was taken off my guard. I'm afraid I hesitated, though I knew that the man's sharp eyes noted every little change on my face. Then, in the most natural way, the man reassured me. "You know," he said. "What demand for oranges in London?" I was thankful that he had not meant the other business. I said with a good deal too much of eagerness that there was, I believed, a big demand for oranges. "Yes," he said, "I suppose so many young boys makes a brisk demand." I was uneasy at the man's manner. He seemed to be pumping me, but he had such a natural easy way, under the pale mask of his face, that I could not be sure if he were in the secret or not. I was on my guard now, ready for any question, as I thought, but eager for an excuse to get away from this man before I betrayed any trust. "Nice ship," he said easily. "Did you join her in Spain?" "No," I answered. "In London." In London?" he said. "I thought you'd something of a Spanish look." "No," I said. "I'm English. Did you want the carpenter, sir?"

"Yes," he answered. "I do. But no hurry. No hurry, lad." Here he pulled out a watch, which he wound up, staring vacantly about the decks as he did so. "Tell me, boy," he said gently. "Is Lane come over with you?" To tell the truth, it flashed across my mind, when he pulled out his watch, that he was making me unready for a difficult question. I was not a very bright boy; but I had this sudden prompting or instinct, which set me on my guard. No one is more difficult to pump than a boy who is ready for his questioner, so I stared at him. "Lane?" I said, "Lane? Do you mean the bo'sun?"

"No," he said. "The Colonel. You know? Eh?"

"No." I said. "I don't know."

"Oh well," he answered. "It's all one. I suppose he's not come over." At this moment the mate came on deck with the carpenter, carrying a model ship which they had been making together in their spare time. They nodded to the stranger, who gave them a curt "How do?" as though they had parted from him only the night before. The mate growled at me for wasting time on deck when I should be at work. He sent me down to my usual job of getting the cabin ready for the breakfast of the gentlemen. As I passed down the hatchway, I heard the carpenter say to the stranger, "Well. So what's the news with Jack?" It flashed into my mind that this man might be his friend, the "Longshore Jack" who was to keep an eye upon me as well as upon Mr. Jermyn. It gave me a most horrid qualm to think this. The man was so sly, so calm, so guarded, that the thought of him being on the look−out for me, to sell me to the Dutch captains, almost scared me out of my wits. The mate brought him to the cabin as I was laying the table. "This is the cabin," he was saying, "where the gentlemen messes. That's our stern−chaser, the gun there."

"Oh," said the stranger, looking about him like one who has never seen a ship before. "But where do they sleep? Do they sleep on the sofa (he meant the lockers), there?"

"Why, no," said the mate. "They sleep in the little cabins yonder. But we musn't stay down here now. I'm not supposed to use this cabin. I mustn't let the captain see me." So they went on deck again, leaving me alone. When the gentlemen came in to breakfast, I had to go on deck for the dishes. As I passed to the galley, I noticed the stranger talking to the carpenter by the main–rigging. They gave me a meaning look, which I did not at all relish. Then, as I stood in the galley, while the cook dished up, I noticed that the stranger raised his hand to a tall, lanky, ill–favoured man who was loafing about on the wharf, carrying a large black package. This man came right up to the edge of the wharf, directly he saw the stranger's signal. It made me uneasy somehow. I was in a thoroughly anxious mood, longing to confide in some one, even in the crusty cook, yet fearing to open my mouth to any one, even to Mr. Jermyn, to whom I dared not speak with the captain present in the room. Well, I had my work to do, so I kept my thoughts to myself. I took the dishes down below to the cabin, where, after removing the covers, I waited on the gentlemen.

"Martin," said Mr. Jermyn. "This skylight over our heads makes rather a draught. We can't have it open in the morning for breakfast.

"Did you open it?" the captain asked. "What made you open it?"

"Please, sir, I didn't open it."

"Then shut it," said the captain. "Go on deck. The catch is fast outside.

I ran very nimbly on deck to shut the skylight, but the catch was very stiff; it took me some few moments to undo. I noticed, as I worked at it, that the deck was empty, except for the lanky man with the package, who was now forward, apparently undoing his package on the forehatch. I thought that he was a sort of pedlar or bumboatman, come to sell onions, soft bread, or cheap jewellery to the sailors. The carpenter's head showed for an instant at the galley–door, He was looking forward at the pedlar. The hands were all down below in the forecastle, eating their breakfast. The other stranger seemed to have gone. I could not see him about the deck. At last the skylight came down with a clatter, leaving me free to go below again. As I went down the hatchway, into the 'tweendecks gloom, I saw a figure apparently at work among the ship's stores lashed to the deck there. I could not see who it was; it was too dark for that but the thing seemed strange to me. I guessed that it might be my enemy the boatswain, so I passed aft to the cabin on the other side.

Soon after that, it might be ten minutes after, while the gentlemen were talking lazily about going ashore, we heard loud shouts on deck.

"What's that?" said the captain, starting up from his chair.

"Sounds like fire," said Mr. Jermyn.

"Fire forward," said the captain, turning very white. "There's five tons of powder forward."

"What?" cried the Duke.

At that instant we heard the boatswain roaring to the men to come on deck. "Aft for the hose there, Bill," we heard. Feet rushed aft along the deck, helter–skelter. Some one shoved the skylight open with a violent heave. Looking up, we saw the carpenter's head. He looked as scared as a man can be.

"On deck," he cried. "We're all in a blaze forward. The lamp in the bo'sun's locker. Quick."

"Just over the powder," the captain said, rushing out.

"Quick, sir," said Jermyn to the Duke. "We may blow up at any moment."

"No," said the Duke, rising leisurely. "Not with these stars. Impossible."

All the same, the two men followed the captain in pretty quick time. Mr. Jermyn rushed the Duke out by the arm. I was rushing out, too, when I saw the Duke's hat lying on the lockers. I darted at it, for I knew that he would want it, with the result that my heel slipped on a copper nail–head, which had been worn down even with the deck till it was smooth as glass. Down I came, bang, with a jolt which shook me almost sick. I rose up, stupid with the shock, so wretched with the present pain that the fire seemed a little matter to me. Indeed, I did not understand the risk. I did not know how a fire so far forward could affect the cabin.

Martin Hyde, The Duke's Messenger

A couple of minutes must have passed before I picked up the hat from where it lay. As I hurried through the 'tweendecks some slight noise or movement made me turn my head. Looking to my right. I saw the horsey man, the stranger, rummaging quickly in the lockers of the Duke's cabin, As I looked, I saw him snatch up something like a pocketbook or pocket case, with a hasty "Ah" of approval. At the same moment, he saw me watching him.

"Where's Mr. Scott?" he cried, darting out on me. "We may all blow up in another moment."

"He's on deck," I said. "Hasn't he gone on deck?"

"On deck?" said the man. "Then on deck with you, too." He pushed me up the hatch before him. "Quick," he cried. "Quick. There's Mr. Scott forward. Get him on to the wharf.

He gave me a hasty shove forward, to where the whole company was working in a cloud of smoke, passing buckets from hand to hand. A crowd of Dutchmen had gathered on the wharf. Everybody was shouting. The scene was confused like a bad dream. I caught sight of the pedlar man at the gangway as the stranger thrust me forward. In the twinkling of an eye the stranger passed something to him with the quick thrust known as the thieves' pass. I saw it, for all my confusion. I knew in an instant that he had stolen something. The pedlar person was an accomplice. As likely as not the fire was a diversion. I rushed at the gangway. The pedlar was moving quickly away with his hands in his pockets. It all happened in a moment. As I rushed at the gangway, with some wild notion of stopping the pedlar, the horsey man caught me by the collar.

"What," he said, in a loud voice. "Trying to desert, are you? You come forward where the danger is." He ran me forward. He was as strong as a bull.

"Mr. Jermyn," I cried. "Mr. Jermyn. This man's a thief."

The man twisted my collar on to my throat till I choked. "Quiet, you," he hissed.

Then Mr. Jermyn dropped his bucket to attend to me.

"A thief," I gasped. "A thief." Mr. Jermyn sprang aft, with his eyes on the man's eyes. The stranger flung me into Mr. Jermyn's way, with all the sweep of his arm. As I went staggering into the fore–bitts (for Mr. Jermyn dodged me) the man took a quick side step up the rail to the wharf. I steadied myself. Mr. Jermyn, failing to catch the man before he was off the ship, rushed below to see what was lost. The crowd of workers seemed to dissolve suddenly. The men surged all about me, swearing. The fire was out. Remember, all this happened in thirty seconds, from the passing of the stolen goods to the stranger's letting go my throat. The very instant that I found my feet against the bitts, I jumped off the ship on to the wharf. There was the stranger running down the wharf to the right, full tilt. There was the lanky pedlar slouching quickly away as though he were going on an errand, with his black box full of groceries.

"That's the man, Mr. Scott," I cried. "He's got it."

The captain (who, I believe, was a naval officer in the Duke's secret) was up on the wharf in an instant. I followed him, though the carpenter clutched at me as I scrambled up. I kicked out behind like a donkey. I didn't kick him, but some one thrust the carpenter aside in the hurry so that I was free. In another seconds I was past the captain, running after the pedlar, who started to run at a good speed, dropping his box with a clatter. Half a dozen joined in the pursuit. The captain had his sword out. They raised such a noise behind me that I thought the whole crew was at my heels. The pedlar kept glancing behind; he knew very little about running. He doubled from street to street, like a man at his wits' ends. I could see that he was blown. When he entered into that conspiracy, he had counted on the horsey man diverting suspicion from him. Suddenly, after twisting round a corner, he darted through a swing door into a stone–paved court, surrounded by brick walls. I was at his heels at the moment or I should have lost him there. I darted through the swing door after him. I went full sprawl over his body on the other side. He had, quite used up, collapsed there.

CHAPTER VIII. I MEET MY FRIEND

"Give it me," I said. "Give it me, Longshore Jack. Before they catch us." To my horror, I saw that the creature was a woman in a man's clothes. She took me for one of her gang. She was too much frightened to think things out. "I thought you were one of the other lot," she gasped, as she handed me a pocketbook.

"Didn't he get the letters, too?" I asked at a venture. "No," she said, sitting up, now, panting, to take a good look at me. I stared at her for a moment. I, myself, was out of breath.

"They're going," I said, hearing the noise of the pursuit passing away in the check. "I'll just spy out the land." I opened the door till it was an inch or two ajar, so that I could see what was going on outside. "They're gone," I said again, still keeping up the pretence of being on her side. As I said it, I glanced back to fix her features on my memory. She had a pale, resolute face with fierce eyes, which seemed fierce from pain, not from any cruelty of nature. It was a pleasant face, as far as one could judge of a face made up to resemble a dirty pedlar's face.

Seeing my look, she seemed to watch me curiously, raising herself up, till she stood unsteadily by the wall. "When did you come in?" she said, meaning, I suppose, when did I join the gang.

"Last week," I answered, swinging the door a little further open. Footsteps were coming rapidly along the road. I heard excited voices, I made sure that it was the search party going back to the schooner.

"Digame, muchacho," she said in Spanish. It must have been some sort of pass–word among them. Seeing by my face that I did not understand she repeated the words softly. Then at that very instant she was on me like a tigress with a knife. I slipped to one side instinctively. I suppose I half saw her as the knife went home. She grabbed at the pocket–book, which I swung away from her hand. The knife went deep into the door, with a drive which must have jarred her to the shoulder. "Give it me," she gasped, snatching at me like a fury. I dodged to one side, up the court, horribly scared. She followed, raving like a mad thing, quite ghastly white under her paint, wholly forgetful that she was acting a man's part. When once we were dodging I grew calmer. I led her to the end of the court, then ducked. She charged in, blindly, against the wall, while I raced to the door, very pleased with my success. I did not hear her follow me, so, when I got to the door, I looked back. Just at that instant, there came a smart report. The creature had fired at me with a pistol; the bullet sent a dozen chips of brick into my face. I went through the door just as the shot from the second barrel thudded into the lintel. Going through hurriedly I ran into Mr. Jermyn, as he came round the corner with the captain. "I've got it," I said. "Look out. She's in there."

"Who?" they said. "The thief? A woman?" They did not stay, but thrust through the door.

Mr. Jermyn dragged me through with them. "You say you've got it, Martin?"

"Yes," I answered, handing him the book. "Here it is."

"That's a mercy," he said. "Now then, where's the thief?"

I had been out of the court, I suppose thirty seconds; it cannot have been more. Yet, when I went back with those two men, the woman had gone, as though she had never been there. "She's over the wall," cried the captain, running up the court. But when we looked over the wall there was no trace of her, except some slight scratches upon the brick, where her toes had rested. On the other side of the wall was a tulip bed full of rows of late flowering tulips, not yet out. There was no footmark on the earth. Plainly she had not jumped down on the other side. "Check," said captain. "Is she in one of the houses?"

But the houses on the left side of the court (on the other side the court had no houses, only brick walls seven feet high) were all old, barred in, deserted mansions, with padlocks on the doors. She could not possibly have entered one of those.

"They're old plague–houses," said Mr. Jermyn.

"They've been deserted twenty years now, since the great sickness."

"Yes?" said the captain, carelessly. "But where can she have got to?"

"Well. It beats me," Mr. Jermyn replied. "But perhaps she ran along the wall to the end, then jumped down into the lane. That's the only thing she could have done. By the way, boy, you were shot at. Were you hit?"

"No," I answered. "But I got jolly near it. The bullet went just by me."

"Ah," he said. "Take this. You'll have to be armed in future."

He handed me a beautiful little double–barrelled pocket pistol. "Be careful," he said. "It's loaded. Put it in your pocket. You musn't be seen carrying arms here. That would never do."

"Boy," said the captain. "D'ye think you could shin up that water-spout, so as to look over the parapet there, on to the leads of the houses?"

"Yes," I said. "I think I could, from the top of the wall."

"Why," Mr. Jermyn said. "She couldn't have got up there."

"An active woman might," the captain said. "You see, the water-spout is only six feet long from the wall to the eaves. There's good footing on the brackets. It's three quick steps. Then one vigorous heave over the parapet. There you are, snug as a purser's billet, out of sight."

"No woman could have done it," Mr. Jermyn said. "Besides, look here. We can't go further in the matter. We've recovered the book. We must get back to the ship."

So the scheme of climbing up the water pipe came to nothing. We walked off together wondering where the woman had got to. Long afterwards I learned that she heard all that we said by the wall there. While we talked, she was busy reloading her pistol, waiting. At the door of the court we paused to pull out her knife from where it stuck. It was a not very large dagger-knife, with a small woman's grip, inlaid with silver, but bound at the guard with gold clasps. The end of the handle was also bound with gold. The edge of the broad, cutting blade curved to a long sharp point. The back was straight. On the blade was an inscription in Spanish, "Veneer o Morir" ("To conquer or die"), with the maker's name, Luis Socartes, Toledo, surrounded by a little twirligig. I have it in my hand as I write. I value it more than anything in my possession. It serves to remind me of a very remarkable woman.

"There, Martin," said Mr. Jermyn. "There's a curiosity for you. Get one of the seamen to make a sheath for it. Then you can wear it at your back on your belt like a sailor."

As we walked back to the ship, I told Mr. Jermyn all that I had seen of the morning's adventure. He said that the whole, as far as he could make it out, had been a carefully laid plot of some of James the Second's spies. He treated me as an equal now. He seemed to think that I had saved the Duke from a very dreadful danger. The horsey man, he said, was evidently a trusted secret agent, who must have made friends with the carpenter on some earlier visit of the schooner. He had planned his raid on the Duke's papers very cleverly. He had arrived on board when no one was about. He had bribed the carpenter (so we conjectured, piecing the evidence together) to shout fire, when we were busy at breakfast. Then, when all was ready, this woman, whoever she was, had gone forward to the bo'sun's locker, where she had set fire to half a dozen of those fumigating chemical candles which she had brought in her box. The candles at once sputtered out immense volumes of evil smelling smoke. The carpenter, watching his time, raised the alarm of fire, while the horsey man, hidden below, waited till all were on deck to force the spring–locks on the Duke's cabin–door. When once he had got inside the cabin, he had worked with feverish speed, emptying all the drawers, ripping up the mattress, even upsetting the books from the bookshelf, all in about two minutes. Luckily the Duke kept nearly all his secret papers about his person. The pocket–book was the only important exception. This, a very secret list of all the Western gentry ready to rise, was locked in a casket in a locked drawer.

"It shows you," said Mr. Jermyn, "how well worked, that he did all this in so little time. If you hadn't fallen on the nail, Martin, our friends in the West would have fared badly. It was very clever of you to bring us out of the danger." When we got back aboard the schooner, we found, as we had expected, that the men in league with the horsey man had deserted. Neither carpenter nor boatswain was to be found. Both had bolted off in pursuit of the horsey man at the moment of alarm, leaving their chests behind them. I suppose they thought that the plot had succeeded. I dare say, too, that the horsey man, who was evidently well known to them both, had given them orders to desert in the confusion, so that he might suck their brains at leisure elsewhere. Altogether, the morning's work from breakfast time till ten was as full of moving incident as a quiet person's life. I have never had a more exciting two hours. When I sat down to my own breakfast (which I ate in the cabin among the gentlemen) I seemed to have grown five years older. All three men made much of me. They brought out all sorts of sweetmeats for me, saying I had saved them from disaster. The Duke was especially kind. "Why, Jermyn," he said, "we thought we'd found a clever messenger; but we've found a guardian angel." He gave me a belt made of green Spanish leather, with a wonderfully wrought steel clasp. "Here," he said. "Wear this, Martin. Here's a holster on it for your pistol. These pouches hold cartridges. Then this sheath at the back will hold your dagger, the spoils of war."

"There," said the captain. "Now I'll give you something else to fit you out. I'll give you a pocket flask. What's more, I'll teach you how to make cartridges. We'll make a stock this morning."

While he was speaking, the mate came down to tell us how sorry he was that it was through him that the horsey man was shown over the ship. "He told me he'd important letters for Mr. Scott," he said, "so I thought it was only right to show him about, while you was dressing. The carpenter came to me. 'This gentleman's got letters for Mr. Scott,' he said. So I was just taken in. He was such a smooth spoken chap. After I got to know, I could 'a' bit my head off." They spoke kindly to the man, who was evidently distressed at his mistake. They told him to give orders for a watchman to walk the gangway all day long in future, which to me sounded like locking the stable door too late. After that, I learned how to make pistol cartridges until the company prepared to go ashore. The chests of the deserters were locked up in the lazaret, or store cupboard, so that if the men came aboard again they might not take away their things.

"Before we start," the Duke said, "I must just say this. We know, from this morning's work, that the spies of the English court know much more than we supposed. We may count it as certain that this ship is being watched at this moment. Now, we must put them off the scent, because I must see Argyle without their knowledge. It is not much good putting to sea again, as a blind, for they can't help knowing that we are here to see Argyle. They have only to watch Argyle's house to see us enter, sooner or later. I suggest this as a blind. We ought to ride far out into the country to Zaandam, say, by way of Amsterdam. That's about twenty miles. Meanwhile Argyle shall come aboard here. The schooner shall take him up to Egmont; he'll get there this afternoon. He must come aboard disguised though. At Zaandam, we three will separate, Jermyn will personate me, remaining in Zaandam. The boy shall carry letters in a hurry to Hoorn; dummy letters, of course. While I shall creep off to meet Argyle—somewhere else. If we start in a hurry they won't have time to organize a pursuit. There are probably only a few secret agents waiting for us here. What do you say?"

"Yes," said Mr. Jermyn. "I myself should say this. Send the boy on at once to Egmont with a note to Stendhal the merchant there. They won't suspect the boy. They won't bother to follow him, probably. Tell Stendhal to send Out a galliot to take Argyle off the schooner while at sea. The galliot can land Argyle somewhere on the coast. That would puzzle them rarely. She can then ply to England, or elsewhere, so that her men won't have a chance of talking. As for the schooner, she can proceed north to anchor at the Texel till further orders. At the same time, we could ride south to Noordwyk; find a barge there going north. Hide in her cabin till she arrives, say, at Alkmaar. Meet Argyle somewhere near there. Then remain hidden till it is time to move. We can set all the balls moving, by sticking up a few bills in the towns." I did not know what he meant by this. Afterwards I learned that the conspirators took their instructions from advertisements for servants, or of things lost, which were stuck up in public places. To the initiated, these bills, seemingly innocent, gave warning of the Duke's plan. Very few people in Holland (not more than thirty I believe) were in the secret of his expedition. Most of these thirty knew other loyalists, to whom, when the time came, they gave the word. When the time came we were only about eighty men all told. That is not a large force, is it, for the invasion of a populous kingdom?

They talked it out for a little while, making improvements on Mr. Jermyn's plan. They had a map by them during some of the time. Before they made their decision, they turned me out of the cabin, so that I know not to this day what the Duke did during the next few days. I know only this, that he disappeared from his enemies, so completely that the spies were baffled. Not only James's spies, that is nothing: but the spies of William of Orange were baffled. They knew no more of his whereabouts than I knew. They had to write home that he had gone, they could not guess where; but possibly to Scotland to sound the clans. All that I know of his doings during the next week is this. After about half an hour of debate, the captain went ashore to one of the famous inns in the town. From this inn, :he despatched, one by one, at brief intervals, three horses, each to a different inn along the Egmont highway. He gave instructions to the ostlers who rode them to wait outside the inns named till the gentlemen called for them. He got the third horse off, in this quiet way, at the end of about an hour. I believe that he then sent a printed book (with certain words in it underlined, so as to form a message) by the hand of a little girl, to the Duke of Argyle's lodging. I have heard that it was a book on the training of horses to do tricks. There was probably some cipher message in it, as well as the underlined message. Whatever it was, it gave the Duke his instructions.

CHAPTER IX. I SEE MORE OF MY FRIEND

After waiting for about an hour in the schooner, I was sent ashore with a bottle–basket, with very precise instructions in what I was to do. I was to follow the road towards

Martin Hyde, The Duke's Messenger

Haarlem, till I came to the inn near the turning of the Egmont highway. There I was to leave my bottle–basket, asking (or, rather, handing over a written request) for it to be filled with bottles of the very best gin. After paying for this, I was to direct it to be sent aboard the schooner by the ostler (who was waiting at the door with a horse) the last of those ordered by the captain. I was then to walk the horse along the Egmont road, till I saw or heard an open carriage coming behind. Then I was to trot, keeping ahead of the carriage, but not far from it, till I was past the third tavern. After that, if I was not recalled by those in the carriage, I was free to quicken up my pace. I was then to ride straight ahead, till I got to Egmont, a twenty mile ride to the north. There I was to deliver up my horse at the Zwolle–Haus inn, before enquiring for M. Stendhal, the East India merchant. To him I was to give a letter, which for safety was rolled into a blank cartridge in my little pistol cartridge box. After that, I was to stay at M. Stendhal's house, keeping out of harm's way, till I received further orders from my masters.

You may be sure that I thought myself a fine figure of gallantry as I stepped out with my bottle–basket. I was a King's secret agent. I had a King's letter hidden about my person. I was armed with fine weapons, which I longed to be using. I had been under fire for my King's sake. I was also still tingling with my King's praise. It was a warm, sunny April day; that was another thing to fill me with gladness. Soon I should be mounted on a nag, riding out in a strange land, on a secret mission, with a pocket full of special service money. Whatever I had felt in the few days of the sea–passage was all forgotten now. I did not even worry about not knowing the language. It would keep me from loitering to chatter. My schoolboy French would probably be enough for all purposes if I vent astray. I was "to avoid chance acquaintances, particularly if they spoke English." That was my last order. Repeating it to myself I walked on briskly.

I had not gone more than three hundred yards upon my way, when a lady, very richly dressed, cantered slowly past me on a fine bay mare. She was followed by a gentleman in scarlet, riding on a little black Arab. They had not gone a hundred yards past me when the Arab picked up a stone. The man dismounted to pick it out, while the lady rode back to hold the horse, which was a ticklish job, since he was as fresh as a colt. He went squirming about like an eel. The man had no hook to pick the stone with; nor could he get it out by his fingers. I could hear him growling under his breath in some strange language, while the horse sidled about as wicked as he could be.

Martin Hyde, The Duke's Messenger

As I approached, the horse grew so troublesome that the man decided to take him back to the town, to have the stone pulled there. He was just starting to lead him back when I came up with them. He asked me some question in a tongue which I did not know. He probably asked me if I had a hook. I shook my head. The lady said something to him in French, which made him laugh. Then he began to lead back the horse towards the town. The lady, after waving her hand to him, started to ride slowly forward in front of me. Like most ladies at that time she wore a little black velvet domino mask over her eyes. All people could ride in those days; but I remember it occurred to me that this lady rode beautifully. So many women look like meal–sacks in the saddle. This one rode as though she were a part of the horse.

She kept about twenty yards ahead of me till I sighted the inn, where an ostler was walking the little nag which I was to ride. She halted at the inn–door, looking back towards the town for her companion. Then, without calling to anybody, she dismounted, flinging her mare's reins over a hook in the wall. She went into the inn boldly, drawing her whip through her left hand. When I entered the inn–door a moment later, she was talking in Dutch to the landlord, who was bowing to her as though she were a great lady.

I handed over my bottle–basket, with the letter, to a woman who served the customers at the drinking bar. Then, as I was going out to take my horse, the lady spoke to me in broken English.

"Walk my horse, so he not take cold," she said. It was in the twilight of the passage from the door, so that I could not see her very clearly, but the voice was certainly like the voice of the woman who had fired at me in the courtyard. Or was I right? That voice was on my nerves. It seemed to be the voice of all the strangers in the town. I looked up at her quickly. She was masked; yet the grey eyes seemed to gleam beyond the velvet, much as that woman's eyes had gleamed. Her mouth; her chin; the general poise of her body, all convinced me. She was the woman who had carried away the book from Longshore Jack. I was quite sure of it. I pretended not to understand her. I dropped my eyes, without stopping; she flicked me lightly with her whip to draw my attention.

"Walk my horse," she said again, with a little petulance in her voice. I saw no way out of it. If I refused, she would guess (if she did not know already) that I was not there only for bottles of gin. "Oui, mademoiselle," I said. "Oui. Merci." So out I went to where the mare stood. She followed me to the door to see me take the mare. There was no escape; she was going to delay me at the door till the man returned. I patted the lovely creature's neck. I was very well used to horses, for in the Broad Country a man must ride almost as much as he must row. But I was not so taken up with this mare that I did not take good stock of the lady, who, for her part, watched me pretty narrowly, as though she meant never to forget me. I began to walk the beast in the road in front of the inn, wondering how in the world I was to get out of the difficulty before the Duke's carriage arrived. There was the woman watching me, with a satirical smile. She was evidently enjoying the sight of my crestfallen face.

Now in my misery a wild thought occurred to me. I began to time my walking of the mare so that I was walking towards Sandfoort, while the other horse–boy was walking with my nag towards Egmont on the other side of the inn. I had read that in desperate cases the desperate remedy is the only measure to be tried. While I was walking away from the inn I drew the dagger, the spoils of war. I drew it very gently as though I were merely buttoning my waistcoat. Then with one swift cut I drew it nine–tenths through the girth. I did nothing more for that turn, though I only bided my time. After a turn or two more, the other horse–boy was called up to the inn by the lady to receive a drink of beer. No doubt she was going to question him (as he drank) about the reason for his being there. He walked up leisurely, full of smiles at the beer, leaving his nag fast to a hook in the wall some dozen yards from the door. This was a better chance than I had hoped for; so drawing my dagger, I resolved to put things to the test. I ripped the reins off the mare close to the bit. Then with a loud shout followed by a whack in the flank, I frightened that lovely mare right into them, almost into the inn–door. Before they knew what had happened I was at my own horse's head swiftly casting off the reins from the hook. Before they had turned to pursue me, I was in the saddle, going at a quick trot towards Egmont, while the mare was charging down the road behind me, with her saddle under her belly, giving her the fright of her life.

An awful thought came to me. "Supposing the lady is not the English spy, what an awful thing I have done. Even if she be, what right have I to cut her horse's harness? They may put me in prison for it. Besides, what an ass I have been. If she is what I think, she will know now that I am her enemy, engaged on very special service." Looking back at the inn–door, I saw a party of people gesticulating in the road. A man was shouting to me. Others seemed to be laughing. Then, to my great joy, round the turn of the road came an open carriage with two horses, going at a good pace. There came my masters. All was well. I chuckled to myself as I thought of the lady's face, when these two passed her, leaving her without means of following them. When we were well out of sight of the inn, I rode back to the carriage to report, wondering how they would receive my news. They received it with displeasure, saying that I had disobeyed my orders, not only in acting as I had done; but in coming back to tell them. They bade me ride on at once to Egmont, before I was arrested for cutting the lady's harness. As for their own plans, whatever they were, my action altered them. I do not know what they did. I know that I turned away with a flea in my ear from the Duke's reproof. I remember not very much of my ride to Egmont, except that I seemed to ride most of the time among sand–dunes. I glanced back anxiously to see if I was being pursued; but no one followed. I rode on at the steady lope, losing sight of the carriage, passing by dune after dune, rising windmill after windmill, to drop them behind me as I rode. In that low country, I had the gleam of the sea to my left hand, with the sails of ships passing by me. The wind freshened as I rode, till at last my left cheek felt the continual stinging of the sand grains, whirled up by the wind from the bents. Where the sea–beach broadened, I rode on the sands. The miles dropped past quickly enough, though I rode only at the lope, not daring to hurry my horse. I kept this my pace even when going through villages, where the people in their strange Dutch clothes hurried out to stare at me as I bucketed by. I passed by acre after acre of bulb–fields, mostly tulip–fields, now beginning to be full of colour. Once, for ten minutes, I rode by a broad canal, where a barge with a scarlet transom drove along under sail, spreading the ripples, keeping alongside me. The helmsman, who was smoking a pipe as he eyed the luff of his sail, waved his hand to me, as I loped along beside him. You would not believe it; but he was one of the Oulton fishermen, a man whom I had known for years. I had seen that tan–sailed barge many, many times, rushing up the Waveney from Somer Leyton, with that same quiet figure at her helm. I would have loved to have called out "Oh, Hendry. How are you? Fancy seeing you here." But I dared not betray myself; nor did Hendry recognize me. After the road swung away from the canal, I watched that barge as long as she remained in sight, thinking that while she was there I had a little bit of Oulton by me.

At last, far away I saw the church of Egmont, rising out of a flat land (not unlike the Broad land) on which sails were passing in a misty distance. I rose in my stirrups with a holloa; for now, I thought, I was near my journey's end. I clapped my horse's neck, promising him an apple for his supper. Then, glancing back, I looked out over the land. The Oulton barge was far away now, a patch of dark sail drawing itself slowly across the sky. Out to sea a great ship seemed to stand still upon the skyline. But directly behind me, perhaps a mile away, perhaps two miles, clearly visible on the white straight ribbon of road, a clump of gallopers advanced, quartering across the road towards me. There may have been twenty of them all told; some of them seemed to ride in ranks like soldiers. I made no doubt when I caught sight of them that they were coming after me, about that matter of the lady's harness. My first impulse was to pull up, so that Old Blunderbore, as I had christened my horse, might get his breath. But I decided not to stop, as I knew how dangerous a thing it is to stop a horse in his pace after he has settled down to it. had still three miles to go to shelter. If I could manage the three miles all would be well. But could manage them? Old Blunderbore had taken the eighteen miles we had come together very easily. Now I was thankful that I had not pressed him in the early part of the ride. But Egmont seemed a long, long way from me. I dared not begin to gallop so far from shelter. I went loping on as before, with my heart in my mouth, feeling like one pursued in a nightmare.

As I looked around, to see these gallopers coming on, while I was still lollopping forward, I felt that I was tied by the legs, unable to move. Each instant made it more difficult for me to keep from shaking up my horse. Continual promptings flashed into my mind, urging me to bolt down somewhere among the dunes. These plans I set aside as worthless; for a boy would soon have been caught among those desolate sandhills. There was no real hiding among them. You could see any person among them from a mile away. I kept on ahead, longing for that wonderful minute when I could hurry my horse, in the wild rush to Egmont town, the final wild rush, on the nag's last strength, with my pursuers, now going their fastest, trailing away behind, as their beasts foundered. The air came singing past. I heard behind me the patter of the turf sent flying by Old Blunderbore's hoofs. The excitement of the ride took vigorous hold on me. I felt on glancing back that I should do it, that I should carry my message, that the Dutchman should see my mettle, before they stopped me. They were coming up fast on horses still pretty fresh. I would show them, I said to myself, what a boy can do on a spent horse.

Old Blunderbore lollopped on. I clapped him on the neck. "Come up, boy! Up!" I cried. "Egmont—Egmont! Come on, Old Blunderbore!" The good old fellow shook his head up with a whinny. He could see Egmont. He could smell the good corn perhaps. I banged him with my cap on the shoulder. "Up, boy!" I cried. I felt that even if I died, even if I was shot there, as I sailed along with my King's orders, I should have tasted life in that wild gallop.

Martin Hyde, The Duke's Messenger

A countryman carrying a sack put down his load to stare at me, for now, with only a mile to go, I was going a brave gait, as fast as Old Blunderbore could manage. I saw the man put up his hands in pretended terror. The next instant he was far behind, wondering no doubt why the charging squadron beyond were galloping after a boy. Now we were rushing at our full speed, with half a mile, a quarter of a mile, two hundred yards to the town gates. Carts drew to one side, hearing the clatter. I shouted to drive away the children. Poultry scattered as though the king of the foxes was abroad. After me came the thundering clatter of the pursuit. I could hear distant shouts. The nearest man there was a quarter of a mile away. A man started out to catch my rein, thinking that my horse had run away with me. I banged him in the face with my cap as I swung past him. In another second, as it seemed, I was pulled up inside the gates.

As far as I remember,– but it is all rather blurred now,—the place where I pulled up was a sort of public square. I swung myself off Old Blunderbore just outside a tavern. An ostler ran up to me at once to hold him. So I gave him a silver piece !what it was worth I did not know) saying firmly "Zwolle–Haus. Go on. Zwolle–Haus."

The ostler smiled as he repeated Zwolle–Haus, pointing to the tavern itself, which, by good luck, was the very house.

"M. Stendhal," I said. "Where is M. Stendhal? Mynheer Stendhal? Mynheer Stendhal Haus?"

The ostler repeated, "Stendhal? Stendhal? Ah, ja. Stendhal. Da." He pointed down a narrow street which led, as I could see, to a canal wharf.

I thanked him in English, giving him another silver piece. Then off I went, tottering on my toes with the strangeness of walking after so long a ride. I was not out of the wood yet, by a long way. At every second, as I hurried on, I expected to hear cries of my pursuers, as they charged down the narrow street after me. I tried to run, but my legs felt so funny, it was like running in a dream. I just felt that I was walking on pillows, instead of legs. Luckily that little narrow street was only fifty yards long. It was with a great gasp of relief that I got to the end of it. When I could turn to my right out of sight of the square I felt that I was saved. I had been but a minute ahead of the pursuers outside on the open. Directly after my entrance, some cart or waggon went out of the town, filling the narrow gateway full, so that my enemies were forced to pull up. This gave me a fair start, without

66

which I could hardly have won clear. If it had not been for that lucky waggon, who knows what would have happened?

As it was, I tottered along with drawn pistol to the door of a great house (luckily for me the only house), which fronted the canal. I must have seemed a queer object, coming in from my ride like that, in a peaceful Dutch town. If I had chanced upon a magistrate I suppose I should have been locked up; but luck was with me on that day. I chanced only on Mynheer Stendhal as he sat smoking among his tulips in the front of his mansion. He jumped up with a "God bless me!" when he saw me.

"Mynheer Stendhal?" I asked.

"Yes," he said in good English. "What is it, boy?"

"Take me in quick," I said. "They're after me."

CHAPTER X. SOUNDS IN THE NIGHT

In another minute, after Mr. Stendhal had read my note, I was skinning off my clothes in an upper bedroom. Within three minutes I was dressed like a Dutch boy, in huge baggy striped trousers belonging to Stendhal's son. In four minutes the swift Mr. Stendhal had walked me across the wharf in sabots to one of the galliots in the canal, which he ordered under way at once, to pick up Argyle at sea. So that when my pursuers rode up to Mr. Stendhal's door in search of me, I was a dirty little Dutch boy casting off a stern-hawser from a ring bolt. They seemed to storm at Mr. Stendhal; but I don't know what they said; he acted the part of surprised indignation to the life. When I looked my last on Mr. Stendhal he was at the door, begging a search party to enter to see for themselves that I was not hidden there. The galliot got under way, at that moment, with a good deal of crying out from her sailors. As she swung away into the canal, I saw the handsome lady idly looking on. She was waiting at the door with the other riders. She was the only woman there. To show her that I was a skilled seaman I cast off the stern-hawser nimbly, then dropped on to the deck like one bred to the trade. A moment later I was aloft, casting loose the gaff-topsail. From that fine height as the barge began to move I saw the horsemen turning away foiled. I saw the lady's leathered hat, making a little dash of green among the drab of the riding coats. Then an outhouse hid them all from sight. I was in a sea–going barge, bound out, under all sail, along a waterway lined with old reeds, all blowing down with a rattling shiver.

Now I am not going to tell you much more of my Holland experiences. I was in that barge for about one whole fortnight, during which I think I saw the greater part of the Dutch canals. We picked up Argyle at sea on the first day. After that we went to Amsterdam with a cargo of hides. Then we wandered about at the wind's will, thinking that it might puzzle people, if any one should have stumbled on the right scent. All that fortnight was a long delightful picnic to me. The barge was so like an Oulton wherry that I was at home in her. I knew what to do, it was not like being in the schooner. When we were lying up by a wharf, I used to spend my spare hours in fishing, or in flinging fiat pebbles from a cleft–stick at the water–rats. When we were under sail I used to sit aloft in the cross–trees, looking out at the distant sea. At night, after a supper of strong soup, we all turned in to our bunks in the tiny cabin, from the scuttle of which I could see a little patch of sky full of stars.

A boy lives very much in the present. I do not think that I thought much of the Duke's service, nor of our venture for the crown. If I thought at all of our adventures, I thought of the handsome woman with the grey, fierce eyes. In a way, I hoped that might have another tussle with her, not because I liked adventure, no sane creature does, but because I thought of her with liking. I felt that she would be such a brave, witty person to have for a friend. I felt sad somehow at the thought of not seeing her again. She was quite young, not more than twenty, if her looks did not belie her. I used to wonder how it was that she had come to be a secret agent. I believed that the sharp–faced horsey man had somehow driven her to it against her will. Thinking of her at night, before I fell asleep, I used to long to help her. It is curious, but I always thought tenderly of this woman, even though she had twice tried to kill me. A man's bad angel is only his good angel a little warped.

On the second of May, though I did not know it then, Argyle set sail for Scotland, to raise the clans for a foray across the Border. On the same day I was summoned from my quarters in the barge to take up my King's service. Late one evening, when it was almost dark night, Mr. Jermyn halted at the wharf–side to call me from my supper. "Mount behind me, Martin," he said softly, peering down the hatch. "It's time, now." I thought he must mean that it was time to invade England. You must remember that I knew little of the rights of the case, except that the Duke's cause was the one favoured by my father, dead such a little while before. Yet when I heard that sudden summons, it went through me with a shock that now this England was to be the scene of a bloody civil war, father fighting son, brother against brother. I would rather have been anywhere at that moment than where I was, hearing that order. Still, I had put my hand to the plough. There was no drawing back. I rose up with my eyes full of tears to say good–bye to the kind Dutch bargemen. I never saw them again. In a moment I was up the wharf, scrambling into the big double saddle behind Mr. Jermyn. Before my eyes were accustomed to the darkness we were trotting off into the night I knew not whither.

"Martin," said Mr. Jermyn, half turning in his saddle, "talk in a low voice. There may be spies anywhere."

"Yes, sir," I answered, meekly. For a while after that we were silent; I was waiting for him to tell me more.

"Martin," he said at length, "we're going to send you to England, with a message."

"Yes, sir?" I answered.

"You understand that there's danger, boy?"

"Yes, sir."

"Life is full of danger. But for his King a Christian man must be content to run risks. You aren't afraid, Martin?"

"No, sir," I answered bravely. I was afraid, all the same. I doubt if any boy my age would have felt very brave, riding in the night like that, with danger of spies all about.

"That's right, Martin," he said kindly. "That's the kind of boy I thought you." Again we were quiet, till at last he said:

"You're going in a barquentine to Dartmouth. Can you remember Blick of Kingswear?"

"Blick of Kingswear," I repeated. "Yes, sir."

"He's the man you're to go to."

"Yes, sir. What am I to tell him?"

"Tell him this, Martin. Listen carefully. This, now. King Golden Cap. After Six One."

"King Golden Cap. After Six One," I repeated. "Blick of Kingswear. King Golden Cap. After Six One."

"That's right," he said. "Repeat it over. Don't forget a word of it. But I know you're too careful a lad to do that." There was no fear of my forgetting it. I think that message is burned in into my brain under the skull–bones.

"There'll be cipher messages, too, Martin. They're also for Mr. Blick. You'll carry a little leather satchel, with letters sewn into the flap. You'll carry stockings in the satchel. Or school–books. You are Mr. Blick's sister's son, left an orphan in Holland. You'll be in mourning. Your mother died of low–fever, remember, coming over to collect a debt from her factor. Your mother was an Oulton fish–boat owner. Pay attention now. I'm going to cross–examine you in your past history."

As we rode on into the gloom, in the still, flat, misty land, which gleamed out at whiles with water dykes, he cross–examined me in detail, in several different ways, just as a magistrate would have done it. I was soon letter–perfect about my mother. I knew Mr. Blick's past history as well as I knew my own.

"Martin," said Mr. Jermyn suddenly. "Do you hear anything?"

"Yes, sir," I answered. "I think I do, sir."

"What is it you hear, Martin?"

"I think I hear a horse's hoofs, sir."

"Behind us?"

"Yes, sir. A long way behind."

"Hold on then, boy. I'm going to pull up."

Martin Hyde, The Duke's Messenger

We halted for an instant in the midst of a wide fiat desert, the loneliest place on God's earth. For an instant in the stillness we heard the trot trot of a horse's hoofs. Then the unseen rider behind us halted, too, as though uncertain how to ride, with our hoofs silent.

"There," said Mr. Jermyn. "You see. Now we'll make him go on again." He shook the horse into his trot again, talking to him in a little low voice that shook with excitement. Sure enough, after a moment the trot sounded out behind us. It was as though our wraiths were riding behind us, following us home. "I'll make sure," said Mr. Jermyn, pulling up again.

"You're a cunning dog," he said gently. "You heard that?" Indeed, it sounded uncanny. The unseen rider had feared to pull up, guessing that we had guessed his intentions. Instead of pulling up he did a much more ominous thing, he slowed his pace perceptibly. We could hear the change in the beat of the horse–hoofs. "Cunning lad," said Mr. Jermyn. "I've a good mind to shoot that man, Martin. He's following us. Pity it's so dark. One can never be sure in the dark like this. But I don't know. I'd like to see who it is."

We trotted on again at our usual pace. Presently,, something occurred to me. Mr. Jermyn, I said; "would you like me to see who it is? I could slip off as we go. I could lie down flat so that he would pass against the sky. Then you could come back for me."

He did not like the scheme at first. He said that it would be too dark for me to see anybody; but that when we were nearer to the town it might be done., So we rode on at our quick trot for a couple of more, hearing always behind us a faint beat of

upon the road, like the echo of our own hoofs. After a time they stopped suddenly, nor did we hear them again.

"D'you know what he's done, Martin?" said Mr. Jermyn.

"No, sir," I answered.

"He's muffled his horse's hoofs with duffle shoes. A sort of thick felt slippers. He was in too great a hurry to do that before. There are the lights of the town."

"Shall I get down, sir?"

"If you can without my pulling up. Don't speak. But lay your head on the road. You'll hear the horse, then, if I'm right."

"Then I'll lie still," I said, "to see if I can see who it is."

"Yes. But make no sign. He may shoot. He may take you for a footpad. I'll ride back to you in a minute."

He slowed down the horse so that I could slip off unheard on to the turf by the roadside. When he had gone a little distance, I laid my ear to the road. Sure enough, the noise of the other horse was faint but plain in the distance, coming along on the road, avoiding the turf. The turf vas trenched in many drains, so as to make dangerous riding at night. I lay down flat on the turf, with my pistol in my hand. I was excited; but I remember that I enjoyed it. I felt so like an ancient Briton lying in wait for his enemy. I tried to guess the distance of this strange horse from me. It is always difficult to judge either distance or location by sound, when the wind is blowing. The horse hoofs sounded about a quarter of a mile away. I know not how far they really were. Very soon I could see the black moving mass coming quietly along the road. The duffle hoof–wraps made a dull plodding noise near at hand. Nearer the unknown rider came, suspecting nothing. I could see him bent forward, peering out ahead. I could even take stock of him, dark though it was. He was a not very tall man, wearing a full Spanish riding cloak. It seemed to me that he checked his horse's speed somewhere in the thirty yards before he passed me. Then, just as he passed, just as I had a full view of him, blackly outlined against the stars, his horse shied violently at me, on to the other side of the road. The rider swung him about on the instant to make him face the danger. I could see him staring down at me, as he bent forward to pat his horse's neck. I bent my head down so that my face was hidden in the grass.

The stranger did not see me. I am quite sure that he did not see me. He turned his horse back along the road for a few snorting paces. Then with a sounding slap on his shoulder he drove him at a fast pace along the turf towards me. I heard the brute whinny. He was uneasy; he was trying to shy; he was twisting away, trying to avoid the strange thing which lay there. I hid my head no longer. I saw the horse above me. I saw the rider glaring down. He was going to ride over me. I saw his face, a grey blur under his hat. The horse seemed to be right on top of me. I started up to my feet with a cry. The horse shied into the road, with a violence which made the rider rock. Then, throwing up his head, he bolted towards the town, half mad with the scare. Fifty yards down the road he tore past Mr. Jermyn, who was trotting back to pick me up. We heard the frantic hoofs pass away into the night, growing louder as the duffle wraps were kicked off. Perhaps you have noticed how the very sound of the gallop of a scared horse conveys fear. That is what we felt, we two conspirators, as we talked together, hearing that clattering alarm–note die away.

"Martin," said Mr. Jermyn. "That was a woman. She chuckled as she galloped past me."

"Are you sure, sir?" I asked, half–hoping that he might be right. I felt my heart leap at the thought of being in another adventure with the lady.

"Yes," he said, "I'm quite sure. Now we must be quick, so as to give her no time in the town." When I had mounted, we forced the horse to a gallop till we were within a quarter of a mile of the walls, where we pulled up at a cross–roads.

"Get down, Martin," he said. "We must enter the town by different roads. Turn off here to the right. Then take the next two turns to the left, which will bring you into the square. I shall meet you there. Take your time. There's no hurry."

About ten minutes later, I was stopped in a dark quiet alley by a hand on the back of my neck. I saw no one. I heard no noise of breathing. In the pitch blackness of the night the hand arrested me. It was like my spine suddenly stiffening to a rod of ice. "Quiet," said a strange voice before I could scream. "Off with those Dutch clothes. Put on these. Off with those sabots." I was in a suit of English clothes in less than a minute. "Boots," the voice said in my ear. "Pull them on." They were long leather knee–boots, supple from careful greasing. In one of them I felt something hard. My heart leapt as I felt it.

It was a long Italian stiletto. I felt myself a seaman indeed, nay, more than a seaman, a secret agent, with a pair of such boots upon me, "heeled," as the sailors call it, with such a weapon. "Go straight on," said the voice.

As I started to go straight on, there was a sort of rustling behind me. Some black figure seemed to vanish from me. Whoever the man was that had brought me the clothes, he had vanished, just as an Indian will vanish into grass six inches high. Thinking over my strange adventures, I think that that changing of my clothes in the night was almost the most strange of all. It was so eerie, that he should be there at all, a part of Mr. Jermyn's plan, fitting into it exactly, though undreamed of by me. Would indeed that all Mr. Jermyn's plans had carried through so well. But it was not to be. One ought not to grumble.

A few steps farther on, I came to a public square, on one side of which (quite close to where I stood) was a wharf, crowded with shipping. I had hardly expected the sea to be so near, somehow, but seeing it like that I naturally stopped to look for the ship which was to carry me. The only barquentine among the ships lay apart from the others, pointing towards the harbour entrance. She seemed to be a fine big vessel, as far as I could judge in that light. I lingered there for some few minutes, looking at the ships, wondering why it was that Mr. Jermyn had not met me. I was nervous about it. My nerves were tense from all the excitement of the night. One cannot stand much excitement for long. I had had enough excitement that night to last me through the week. As I stood looking at the ships, I began to feel a horror of the wharf–side. I felt as though the very stones of the place were my enemies, lying in wait for me. I cannot explain the feeling more clearly than that. It was due probably to the loneliness of the great empty square, dark as a tomb. Then, expecting Mr. Jermyn, but failing to meet with him, was another cause for dread. I thought, in my nervousness, that I should be in a fine pickle if any enemies made away with Mr. Jermyn, leaving me alone, in a strange land, with only a few silver pieces in my pocket. Still, Mr. Jermyn was long in coming. My anxiety was almost more than I could bear.

At last, growing fearful that I had somehow missed him at the mouth of the dark alley, I walked slowly back in my tracks, wishing that I had a thicker jacket, since it was beginning to rain rather smartly. There was a great sort of inn on the side of the square to which I walked. It had lights on the second floor. The great windows of that story opened on to balconies, in what is, I believe, the Spanish way of building. I remember feeling bitterly how cheery the warm lights looked, inside there, where the people were. I stood underneath the balcony out of the rain, looking out sharply towards the alley, expecting at each instant to see Mr. Jermyn. Still he did not come. I dared not move from where I was lest I should miss him. I racked my brains to try to remember if I had obeyed orders exactly. I wondered whether I had come to the right square. I began to imagine all kinds of evil things which might have happened to him. Perhaps that secret fiend of a woman had been too many for him. Perhaps some other secret service people had waylaid him as he entered the town. Perhaps he was even then in bonds in some cellar, being examined for letters by some of the usurper's men.

CHAPTER XI. AURELIA

While I was fretting myself into a state of hysteria, the catch of one of the great window-doors above me was pushed back. Someone came out on the balcony just over my head. It was a woman, evidently in some great distress, for she was sobbing bitterly. I thought it mean to stand there hearing her cry, so I moved away. As I walked off, the window opened again. A big heavy-looted man came out.

"Stop crying, Aurelia," the voice said. "Here's the stuff. Put it in your pocket."

"I can't," the woman answered. "I can't."

I stopped moving away when I heard that voice. It was the voice of the Longshore Jack woman who had had those adventures with me. I should have known her voice anywhere, even choked as it then was with sobs. It was a good voice, of a pleasant quality, but with a quick, authoritative ring.

"I can't," she said. "I can't, Father."

"Put it in your pocket," her father said. "No rubbish of that sort. You must."

"It would kill me. I couldn't," she answered. "I should hate myself forever."

"No more of that to me," said the cold, hard voice with quiet passion. "Your silly scruples aren't going to outweigh a nation's need. There it is in your pocket. Be careful you don't use too much. If you fail again, remember, you'll earn your own living. Oh, you bungler! When I think of—"

"I'm no bungler. You know it," she answered passionately. "I planned everything. You silly men never backed me up. Who was it guessed right this time? I suppose you think you'd have come here without my help? That's like a man."

"Don't stand there rousing the town, Aurelia, the man said. "Come in out of the rain at once. Get yourself ready to start."

As the window banged to behind them, a figure loomed up out of the night—two figures, more. I sprang to one side; but they were too quick for me. Someone flung an old flour—sack over my head. Before I was ready to struggle I was lying flat on the pavement, with a man upon my chest.

"It's him," said a voice. "You young rip, where are the letters?"

"What letters?" I said, struggling, choking against the folds of the sack.

"Rip up his boots," said another. "Dig him with a knife if he won't answer."

"Bring him in to the Colonel," said the first.

"I've got no letters," I said.

"Lift him up quick," said the man who had suggested the knife. "In with him. Here's the watch."

"Quick, boys," the leader said. "We mustn't be caught at this game."

Steps sounded somewhere in the square. Hearing them, I squealed with all my strength, hoping that somebody would come.

"Choke him," said one of the men.

I gave one more loud squeal before they jammed the sack on my mouth. To my joy, the feet broke into a run. They were the feet of the watch, coming to my rescue.

"Up with him," said the leader among my captors. "Quick, in to the Colonel with him."

"No, no! Drop it. I'm off. Here's the watch," cried the other hurriedly.

They let me drop on to the pavement after half lifting me. In five seconds more they were scattering to shelter. As I rose to my feet, flinging off the flour—sack, I found myself in the midst of the city watch, about a dozen men, all armed, whose leader carried a lantern. The windows of the great inn were open; people were thronging on to the balcony to see what the matter was; citizens came to their house–doors. At that moment, Mr. Jermyn appeared. The captain of the guard was asking questions in Dutch. The guardsmen were peering at my face in the lantern light.

Mr. Jermyn questioned me quickly as to what had happened. He interpreted my tale to the guard. I was his servant, he told them. I had been attacked by unknown robbers, some of whom, at least, were English. One of them had tried to stifle me with a flour–sack, which, on examination under the lantern, proved to be the sack of Robert Harling, Corn–miller, Eastry. Goodness knows how it came to be there; for ship's flour travels in cask. Mr. Jermyn gave an address, where we could be found if any of the villains were caught; but he added that it was useless to expect me to identify any of them, since the attack had been made in the dark, with the victim securely blindfolded. He gave the leader of the men some money. The guard moved away to look for the culprits (long before in hiding, one would think), while Mr. Jermyn took me away with him.

As we went, I looked up at the inn balcony, from which several heads looked down upon us. Behind them, in the lighted room, in profile, in full view, was the lady of the fierce eyes. I knew her at once, in spite of the grey Spanish (man's) hat she wore, slouched over her face. She was all swathed in a Spanish riding cloak. One took her for a handsome young man. But I knew that she was my enemy. I knew her name now, too; Aurelia. She was looking down at me, or rather at us, for she could not have made out our faces. Her face was sad. She seemed uninterested; she had, perhaps, enough sorrow of her own at that moment, without the anxieties of others. A big, burly, hulking, handsome person of the swaggering sort which used to enter the army in those days, left the balcony hurriedly. I saw him at the window, speaking earnestly to her, pointing to the square, in which, already, the darkness hid us. I saw the listlessness fall from her. She seemed to waken up into intense life in an instant. She walked with a swift decision peculiar to her away from the window, leaving the hulking fellow, an elderly, dissolute–looking man, with the wild puffy eyes of the drinker, to pick his teeth in full view of the square.

When we left watching our enemies, Mr. Jermyn bade me walk on tiptoe. We scurried away across the square diagonally, pausing twice to listen for pursuers. No one seemed to be following. There was not much sense in following; for the guard was busy searching for suspicious persons. We heard them challenging passers–by, with a rattle of their halberds on the stones, to make their answers prompt. We were safe enough from persecution for the time. We went down a dark street into a dark alley. From the alley we entered a courtyard, the sides of which were vast houses. We entered one of these houses. The door seemed to open in the mysterious way which had puzzled me so much in Fish Lane. Mr. Jermyn smiled when I asked him how this was done. "Go on in, boy," he said. "There are many queer things in lives like ours." He gave me a shove across the threshold, while the door closed itself silently behind us.

He took me into a room which was not unlike a marine store of the better sort. There were many sailor things (all of the very best quality) lying in neat heaps on long oak shelves against the walls. In the middle of the room a table was laid for dinner.

Mr. Jermyn made me eat a hearty meal before starting, which I did. As I ate, he fidgeted about among some lockers at my back. Presently, as I began to sip some wine which he had poured out for me, he put something over my shoulders.

"Here," he said, "this is the satchel, Martin. Keep the straps drawn tight always. Don't take it off till you give it into Mr. Blick's hands. His own hands, remember. Don't take it off even at night. When you lie down, lash it around your neck with spun–yarn." All this I promised most faithfully to do. "But," I said, examining the satchel, which was like an ordinary small old weather–beaten satchel for carrying books, "where are the letters, sir?"

"Sewn into the double," he answered. "You wouldn't be able to sew so neatly as that. Would you, now?"

"Oh, yes, I should, sir," I replied. "I am a pretty good hand with a sail–needle. The Oulton fishermen used to teach me the stitches. I can do herring–bone stitch. I can even put a cringle into a sail."

"You're the eighth wonder of the world, I think," Mr. Jermyn said. "But choose, now. Choose a kit for yourself. You won't get a chance to change your clothes till you get to Mr. Blick's if you don't take some from here. So just look round the room here. Take whatever you want."

I felt myself to have been fairly well equipped by the stranger who had made me change my clothes in the alley. But I knew how cold the Channel may be even in June; so I chose out two changes of thick underwear. Weapons I had no need for, with the armory already in my belt; but a heavy tarred jacket with an ear–flap collar was likely to be useful, so I chose that instead. It was not more than ten sizes too large for me; that did not matter; at sea one tries to keep warm; appearances are not much regarded. Last of all, when I had packed my satchel, I noticed a sailor's canvas "housewife" very well stored with buttons, etc. I noticed that it held what is called a "palm," that is, the leather hand–guard used by sail–makers for pushing the needle through sail cloth. It occurred to me, vaguely, that such a "housewife" would be useful, in case my clothes got torn, so I stuffed it into my satchel with the other things. I saw that it contained a few small sail–needles (of the kind so excellent as egg–borers) as well as some of the strong fine sail–twine, each thread of which will support a weight of fifty pounds. I put the housewife into my store with a vague feeling of being rich in the world's goods, with such a little treasury of necessaries; I had really no thought of what that chance impulse was to do for me.

"Are you ready?" Mr. Jermyn asked.

"Yes, sir. Quite ready."

"Take this blank drawing–book," he said, handing me a small pocket–book, in which a pencil was stuck. "Make a practice of drawing what you see. Draw the ships. Make sketches of the coast. You will find that such drawings will give you great pleasure when you come to be old. They will help you, too, in impressing an object on your mind. Drawing thus will give you a sense of the extraordinary wonder of the universe. It will teach you a lot of things. Now let's be off. It's time we were on board."

When we went out of the house we were joined by three or four seamen who carried cases of bottles (probably gin bottles). We struck off towards the ship together at a brisk pace, singing one of those quick–time songs with choruses to which the sailors sometimes work. The song they sang was that very jolly one called "Leave her, Johnny." They made such a noise with the chorus of this ditty that Mr. Jermyn was able to refresh my memory in the message to be given to Mr. Blick.

The rain had ceased before we started. When we came into the square, we saw that cressets, or big flaming port–fires, had been placed along the wharf, to give light to some seamen who were rolling casks to the barquentine. A little crowd of idlers had gathered about the workers to watch them at their job; there may have been so many as twenty people there. They stood in a pretty strong, but very unsteady light, by which I could take stock of them. I looked carefully among them for the figure of a young man in a grey Spanish hat; but he was certainly not there. The barquentine had her sails loosed, but not hoisted. Some boats were in the canal ahead, ready to tow her. out. She had also laid out a hawser, by which to heave herself out with her capstan. I could see at a glance that she was at the point of sailing. As we came up the plank—gangway which led to her deck we were delayed for a moment by a seaman who was getting a cask aboard.

"Beg pardon, sir," he said to Mr. Jermyn. "I won't keep you waiting long. This cask's about as heavy as nitre."

"What 'a' you got in that cask, Dick?" said the boatswain, who kept a tally at the gangway.

"Nitre or bullets, I guess," said Dick, struggling to get the cask on to the gang plank. "It's as heavy as it knows how."

"Give Dick a hand there," the boatswain ordered. A seaman who was standing somewhere behind me came forward, jogging my elbow as he passed. In a minute or two they had the cask aboard.

"It's red lead," said the boatswain, examining the marks upon it. "Sling it down into the 'tweendecks."

After this little diversion, I was free to go down the gangway with Mr. Jermyn. The captain received us in the cabin. He seemed to know my "uncle Blick," as he called him, very well indeed. I somehow didn't like the looks of the man; he had a bluff air; but it seemed to sit ill upon him. He reminded me of the sort of farmer who stands well with his parson or squire, while he tyrannizes over his labourers with all the calculating cowardly cruelty of the mean mind. I did not take to Captain Barlow, for all his affected joviality.

However, the ship was sailing. They showed me the little trim cabin which was to be mine for the voyage. Mr. Jermyn ran ashore up the gangway, after shaking me by the hand. He called to me over his shoulder to remember him very kindly to my uncle. A moment later, as the hawsers were cast off, the little crowd on the wharf called out "Three cheers for the Gara barquentine," which the Gara's crew acknowledged with three cheers for Pierhead, in the sailor fashion. We were moving slowly under the influence of the oared boats ahead of us, when a seaman at the forward capstan began to sing the solo part of an old capstan chanty. The men broke in upon him with the chorus, which rang out, in its sweet clearness, making echoes in the city. I ran to the capstan to heave with them, so that I, too, might sing. I was at the capstan there, heaving round with the best of them, until we were standing out to sea, beyond the last of the fairway lights, with our sails trimmed to the strong northerly wind. After that, being tired with so many crowded excitements, which had given me a life's adventures since supper—time, I went below to my bunk, to turn in.

I took off my satchel, intending to tie it round my neck after I had undressed. Some inequality in the strap against my fingers made me hold it to the cabin lamp to examine it more closely. To my horror, I saw that the strap had been nearly cut through in five places. If it had not been of double leather with an inner lining of flexible wire, any one of those cuts would have cut the thong clean in two. Then a brisk twitch would have left the satchel at the cutter's mercy. It gave me a lively sense of the craft of our enemies, to see those cuts in the leather. I had felt nothing. I had suspected nothing. Only once, for that instant on the wharf, when we stopped to let Dick get his barrel aboard, had they had a chance to come about me. Yet in that instant of time they had suspected that that satchel contained letters. They had made their bold attempt to make away with it. They had slashed this leather in five places with a knife as sharp as a razor. But had it been on the wharf, that this was done? I began to wonder if it could have been on the wharf. Might it not have been done when I was at the capstan, heaving round on the bar? I thought not. I must have noticed a seaman doing such a thing. It would have been impossible for any one to have cut the strap there; for the capstan was always revolving. The man next to me on the bar never took his hands from the lever, of that I was certain. The men on the bar behind me could not have reached me. Even if they had reached me the mate must have noticed it. I knew that sailors were often clever thieves; but I did not believe that they could have been so clever under the mate's eye. If it had not been done at the capstan it could not have been done since I came aboard; for there had been no other opportunity. I was quite convinced, after a moment's thought, that it had been done on the wharf before I came aboard. Then I wondered if it had been done by common shore thieves, or "nickers," who are always present in our big seaport towns, ready to steal whenever they get a chance. But I was rather against this possibility; for my mind just then was much too full of Aurelia's party. I saw their hands in it. It would have needed very strong evidence to convince me that they were not at the bottom of this last attack, as they had doubtless been in the attack under the inn balcony.

Thinking of their cunning with some dismay, I went to my door to secure it. I was in my stockinged feet at the moment, as I had kicked my boots off on coming into the cabin. My step, therefore, must have been noiseless. Opening the door smartly, half–conscious of some slight noise on the far side, I almost ran into Captain Barlow, who was standing without. He showed a momentary confusion, I thought, at seeing me thus suddenly. It was a bad sign. To me, in my excited nervous state, it was a very bad sign. It convinced me that he had been standing there, trying to spy upon me through the keyhole, with what purpose I could guess only too well. His face changed to a jovial grin in an instant; but I felt that he was searching my face narrowly for some sign of suspicion.

"I was just coming in to see if you wanted anything," he said.

"No. Nothing, thanks," I answered. "But what time's breakfast, sir?"

"Oh, the boy'll call you," he answered. "Is that your school satchel? Hey? What you carry your books in? Let's see it?"

"Oh," I said, as lightly as I could, feeling that he was getting on ticklish ground. "I've not unpacked it yet. It's got all my things in it."

By this time he was well within my cabin. "Why," he said, "this strap's almost cut in two. Does your master let you bring your satchel to school in that state? How did it come to be cut like that? Hey?"

I made some confused remark about its having always been in that state; as it was an old satchel which my father used for a shooting–bag. I had never known boys to carry books in a satchel. That kind of school was unknown to me.

"Well," he said, fingering the strap affectionately, as though he was going to lift it off my head, "you let me take it away with me. I've got men in this ship, who can mend a cut leather strap as neat as you've no idea of. They'd sew up a cut like them so as you'd hardly know it had been cut."

I really feared that he would have the bag away from me by main force. But I rallied all my forces to save it. "I'm lagged now," I said. "I haven't undone my things. I'll give it to you in the morning."

It seemed to me that he looked at me rather hard when I said this; but he evidently thought "What can it matter? Tomorrow will serve just as well." So he just gave a little laugh. "Right," he said. "You turn in now. Give it to me in the morning. Good night, boy."

"Good night," I said, as he left the cabin, adding, under my breath, "Good riddance, too. You won't find quite so much when you come to examine this bag by daylight." After he had gone—but not at once, as I wished not to make him suspicious,—I locked my cabin–door. Then I hung my tarred sea–coat on the door–hook, so that the flap entirely covered the keyhole. There were bolts on the door, but the upper one alone could be pushed home. With this in its place felt secure from spies. Yet not too secure. I was not certain that the bulkheads were without crannies from which I could be watched. The crack by the door–hinge might, for all I knew, give a very good view of the inside of the cabin. Thinking that I might still be under observation I decided to put off what I had to do until the very early morning, so I undressed myself for bed. I took care to put out the light before turning in, so that I might not be seen lashing the satchel round my neck with a length of spunyarn. I slept with my head upon it.

CHAPTER XII. BRAVE CAPTAIN BARLOW

Very early the next morning, at about half–past four, a little before sunrise, I woke up with a start, wondering where I was. Looking through my little scuttle port, I could see the flashing of bright waves, which sometimes dowsed my window with a shower of drops. The ship was apparently making about three knots an hour, under all her sails. Directly I woke, I turned out of my bunk to do what I had to do. After dressing, I took my sail–making tools from my housewife. I had resolved to cut the letters from their hiding–place so that I might make them up into tiny rolls, small enough to hide in my pistol cartridges. Very carefully I cut the threads which bound the leather flaps of the satchel together. I worked standing up, with the satchel in my bunk. I could hardly have been seen from any point. In a few moments the letters were in my hands. They were small sheets of paper, each about four inches square. They were nine in number, all different. They were covered with a neat cipher very different from the not very neat, not quite formed hand of the Duke himself. What the cipher was, I did not know. It was one of the many figure ciphers then in use. I learned long afterwards that the figures which frequently occurred in them stood for King James II. Such as they were, those cipher letters made a good deal of difference to many thousands of people then living contentedly at home.

As soon as I had removed them, I rolled them up very carefully into pistol cartridges from which I drew the charges. I was just going to throw away the powder, when I thought, "No, I'll put the powder back. It'll make the fraud more difficult to detect." So I put the powder back with great care. Then I searched my mind for something with which to seal up the cartridge wads over the powder. I could think of nothing at all, till I remembered the tar–seams at my feet. I dug up a fragment of tar–seam from the dark corners of the cabin under my bunk. Then I lit my lamp with my little pocket tinder–box, so that I could heat the tar as I needed it. It took me a long time to finish the cartridges properly; but I flatter myself that I made neat jobs of them. I was trained to neat habits by my father. The Oulton seamen had given me a taste for doing clever neat work, such as plaits or pointing, so that I was not such a bungler at delicate handicraft as most boys of my age. I even took the trouble to hide the tar marks on my wads by smearing wetted gunpowder all over them. When I had hidden all the letters, I wrote out a few pencilled notes upon leaves neatly cut from my pocket–book. I wrote a varying arrangement of ciphers on each leaf, in the neatest hand I could command. I always made neat figures; but as I had not touched a pen for nearly a month, I was out of practice. Still, I did very creditably. I am quite sure that my neat ciphers gave the usurper James a very trying week of continual study. I daresay the whole privy council puzzled over those notes of mine. I felt very pleased with them when they were done.

I had not much more than a half–hour left to me when I finished writing them out. The ship's bells told me that it was seven o'clock. Cabin breakfast, as I knew very well, would be at eight. I could expect to be called at half past seven. I put the two flaps of the satchel evenly together, removing all traces of the thread used in the earlier sewing. Then I very trimly sewed the two flaps with my sail–needle, using all my strength to make secure stitches. I used some brown soap in the wash–stand as thread wax, to make the sewing more easy. "There," I thought, "no one will suspect that this was sewn by a boy." When I had finished, I thought of dirtying the twine to make the work look old; but I decided to let well alone. I might so easily betray my hand by trying to do too much. The slight trace of the soap made the work look old enough. But I took very great care to remove all traces of my work in the cabin. The little scraps of thread which I had cut out of the satchel I ate, as I could see no safer means of getting rid of them. I cannot say that they disagreed with me, though they were not very easy to get down. My palm, being a common sea–implement, not likely to seem strange in a ship's cabin, I hid in a locker below my bunk. My sail–needles I thrust at first into the linings of the pockets of my tarred sea–coat. On second thoughts, I drove them into the mattress of my bunk. My hank of twine I dropped on deck later, when I went out to breakfast. Having covered all traces of my morning's work, I washed with a light heart. When some one came to my cabin–door to call me, I cried out that I would be out in a minute.

When the breakfast bell rang, I walked aft to the great cabin, with my satchel over my shoulder. The captain asked me how I had slept; so I said that I had slept like a top, until a few minutes before I was called.

"That's the way with you young fellows," he said. "When you come to be my age you won't be able to do that." Presently, as we were sitting down to breakfast, he began his attack upon the satchel. "You still got your satchel, I see," he said. "Do you carry it about with you always? Or are you pretending to be a military man with a knapsack?"

I looked a little uncomfortable at this; but not from the reason which flashed through his mind. I said that I liked carrying it about, as it served instead of a side coat–pocket, which was perfectly true.

"By the way," he said; "you must let me take that beloved satchel after breakfast, so that I can get the strap sewn up for you."

It came into my mind to look blank at this. I stammered as I said that I didn't mind the straps being cut, because there was a wire heart to the leather which would hold till we got to England, when I could put on a new strap for myself.

"Oh, nonsense," he said, serving out some of the cold bacon from the dish in front of him. "Nonsense. What would your uncle say if you landed slovenly like that? Besides, now you're at sea you're a sailor. Sailors don't wear things like that at meals any more than they wear their hats."

After this, I saw that there was no further chance of retaining the satchel, so I took it from my neck, but grudgingly, as though I hated doing so. I heard no more about it till after breakfast, when he made a sudden playful pounce upon it, as it lay upon the chair beside me, at an instant when I was quite unprepared to save it.

"Aha," he cried, waving his booty. "Now then. Now."

I knew that he would expect a passionate outcry from me, nor did I spare it; because I meant him to think that I knew the satchel contained precious matters.

"No, no," I cried. "Let me have it. I don't want it mended."

"What?" he said. "Not want it mended? It must be mended."

At this I made a sort of playful rush to get it. He dodged away from me, laughing. I attacked again, playing my part admirably, as I thought, but taking care not to overdo it. At last, as though fearing to show too great an anxiety about the thing, I allowed him to keep it. I asked him if he would be able to sew the leather over the wire heart.

"Why, yes," he said. I could see that he smiled. He was thinking that I had stopped struggling in order to show him that I set no real value on the satchel. He was thinking that he saw through my cunning.

"Might I see you sew it up?" I said. "I should like to learn how to sew up leather."

He thought that this was another sign of there being letters in the satchel, this wish of mine to be present when the sewing was done.

"Why, yes," he said. "I'll do it here. You shall do it yourself if you like. I will teach you." So saying, he tossed me an orange from his pocket. "Eat that," he said, "while I go on deck to take the sights."

He left the cabin, swinging the satchel carelessly in his left hand. I thought to myself that I had better play anxiety; so, putting the orange on the table, I followed him into the 'tweendecks, halting at the door, as though in fear about the satchel's fate. Looking back, he saw me there. My presence confirmed him in his belief that he had got my treasure.

He waved to me. "Back in a minute," he said. "Stay in the cabin till I come back. There's a story–book in the locker."

I turned back into the cabin in a halting, irresolute way which no doubt deceived him as my other movements had deceived him. When I had shut the door, I went to the locker for the story–book.

Now the story–book, when I found it, was not a story–book, but a little thick book of Christian sermons by various good bishops. I read one of them through, to try, but I did not understand it. Then I put the book down with the sudden thought: "This Captain Barlow cannot read. He thinks that these sermons are stories. Now who is it in this ship to whom the letters will be shown? Or can there be no one here? Is he going to steal the letters to submit them to somebody ashore?"

I was pretty sure that there was somebody shut up in the ship who was concerned in the theft with Barlow. I cannot tell what made me so sure. I had deceived the captain so easily that I despised him. I did not give him credit for any intelligence whatsoever. Perhaps that was the reason. Then it came over me with a cold wave of dismay that perhaps the woman Aurelia was on board, hidden somewhere, but active for mischief. I remembered that scrap of conversation from the inn–balcony. I wondered if that secret mission mentioned then was to concern me in any way. What was it, I wondered, that was put into her pocket by her father as she stood crying there, just above me? If she were on board, then I must indeed look to myself, for she was probably too cunning a creature to be deceived by my forgeries. The very thought of having her in the ship with me was uncomfortable. I felt that I must find some more subtle hiding–place for my letters than I had found hitherto. I may have idealized the woman, in my alarm, into a miracle of shrewdness. At any rate I knew that she would be a much more dangerous opponent than Captain Barlow, the jocular donkey who allowed himself to be fooled by a schoolboy who was in his power. I knew, too, that she would probably search me other letters, whether my ciphered blinds deceived her or not. She was not one so easily satisfied as a merchant skipper; besides, she had now two scores against me, as well as excellent reason to think me a sharp young man.

Presently, after half an hour's absence, the captain came back with the satchel, evidently very pleased with himself. He seemed to find pleasure in the sight of my pretended distress. "Why," he said, with a grin; "you've not eaten your orange."

"No, sir," I said, "I'm not very hungry just after breakfast."

"Why, then," he answered, "you must keep it for your dinner. Look how nice I've mended your strap for you."

"Thank you very much, sir," I said. "But thought that you were going to do it here. You were going to teach me how to do it."

"Well, it's done now, isn't it?" he replied. "It's done pretty good, too. I'll teach you how to sew some other time. I suppose they don't learn you that, where you go to school?"

"No, sir," I said, "they don't."

"Ah," he said, picking up the book. "You're a great one for your book, I see. There's very good reading in a book like that."

"Yes," I said, looking at the mended strap. "There is. How very neatly you've mended the strap, sir. Thank you very much."

He looked at me with a look which said, very plainly, "You've got a fine nerve, my lad, to pretend in that way."

I could see from his manner during the next few minutes that he wished to keep me from examining the satchel flap. No doubt he thought that I was on tenter-hooks all the time, to look to see if the precious letters had been disturbed. At last, in a very easy way, after slinging the strap round my shoulder, I pulled out my handkerchief, intending to put it into the satchel as into an extra pocket.

"I'm going up on deck, sir," I said. "May I take the book with me?"

As he said that I might, I swiftly opened the satchel, to pop the book in. I could feel that he watched my face mighty narrowly all the time. No doubt I looked guilty enough to convince him of his cleverness. I had no more than a second's peep at the flap, but that was quite enough to show me that it had been tampered with. I had finished off my work that morning with an even neatness. The bold Captain Barlow had left two ends of thread sticking out from the place where he had ended his stitch. Besides, my thread had been soaped, to make it work more easily. The thread in the flap now was plainly not soaped; it was fibrous to the touch, not sleeked down, as mine had been.

When I went on deck, I found the ship driving fast down Channel, making an excellent passage. I took up my place by the mizzen–rigging, near which there were no seamen at work, so that I could puzzle out a new hiding–place for my letters. I noticed, as I stood there, that some men were getting a boat over the side.: It seemed a queer thing to be doing in the Channel, so far from the port to which we were bound; but I did not pay much attention to it at the time, as I was very anxious. I was wondering what in the world I could do with the pistol cartridges which I had made that morning. I feared Aurelia. For all that I could tell she was looking at me as I stood there, guessing, from my face, that I had other letters upon me. It did not occur to me that my anxiety might be taken for grief at having the satchel searched. At last it came into my head that Aurelia, if she were in the ship, would follow up that morning's work promptly, before I could devise a fresh hiding–place. At any rate I felt pretty sure that I should not be much out of that observation until the night. It came into my head that the next attack would be upon my boots; for in those days secret agents frequently hid their papers above a false boot–sole, or stitched them into the double leather where the beckets, or handles, joined the leg of the boot at the rim.

Sure enough, I had not been very long on deck when the ship's boy appeared before me. He was an abject looking lad, like most ship's boys. I suppose no one would become a ship's boy until he had proved himself unfit for life anywhere else. Personally, I had rather be a desert savage than a ship's boy. My experience on La Reina was enough to sicken me of such a life forever. This barquentine's boy came up to me, as I have said.

"Sir," he said, "can I take away your boots to black, please?"

"No," I answered, "my boots don't want blacking. I grease them myself."

"Please, sir," he said, "do let me take them away, sir."

"No," I said. "I grease them myself, thank you." I thought that this would end the business; but no such matter.

"Please, sir," he said, "I wish you would let me take them away. The captain'll wale me if I don't. He gave me orders, sir."

"Don't call me 'sir,'" I said. "I'll see the captain myself."

I walked quickly to the companion—way, below which (listening to us, like the creature he was) sat the captain, carving the end of a stick.

"Please, sir," I said, "I've already greased my boots this morning. I always grease them." (I had only had them about twelve hours.) "If I blacked them they'd get so dry that they would crack."

"All right. All right, boy," he answered. "I forgot you wore soft—leather boots. They're the kind they buy up to make salt beef of at the Navy Yard." He grinned in my face, as though he were pleased; but a few minutes later, when I had gone forward, I heard him thrashing the wretched boy, because he had failed to get the boots from me for him.

I soon found that I was pretty closely watched. If I went forward to the fo'c's'le, I found myself dogged by the ship's boy, who was blubbering from his whipping, poor lad, as though his heart would break. In between his sobs, he tried to tell me the use of everything forward, which was trying to me, as I knew more than he knew. If I went aft, the mate would come rolling up, to ask me if I could hear the dog—fish bark yet. If I went below the captain got on to my tracks at once. He was by far the worst of the three: the other two were only obeying his orders. I went into my cabin hoping to get rid of him there; but no, it was no use. In he came, too, with the excuse that he wished to see if I had enough clothes on my bunk. It was more worrying than words can tell. All the time I wondered whether he would end by knocking me senseless so that he might search my boots at his ease. I had the fear of that strongly on me. I was tempted, yet feared, to drive him from me by threatening him with my pistol. His constant dogging of me was intolerable. But had I threatened him, he would have had an excuse for maltreating me. My duty was to save the letters, not to worry about my own inconveniences. Often, since then, I have suffered agonies of remorse at not giving up the letters meekly. Had I done so, I might, who knows, have saved some two thousand lives. Well. We are all agents of a power greater than ourselves. Though I was, it may be, doing wrong then, I was doing wrong unwittingly. Had things happened only a little differently, my wrong would have turned out a glorious right. The name of Martin Hyde would have been in the history books. He watched me narrowly as I took off my waistcoat (pretending to be too hot), nor did he forget to eye the waistcoat. "See here," he said. "Do you know how a sailor folds a waistcoat? Give it to me now. I'll show you." He snatched it from my hands with that rudeness which, in a boorish nature, passes for fun; he only wished to feel it over so that if any letter were sewn within it he might hear the paper crackle. The sailor's way of folding a waistcoat, as shown by him then, was just the way which bent all the cloth in folds. He seemed to be much disgusted at hearing no crackling as he folded it. I could have laughed outright at his woeful face, had I been less anxious. Had he been worth his salt as a spy he would have lulled all my suspicions to sleep before beginning to search for letters. Instead of that he went to work as crudely as a common footpad..

CHAPTER XIII. IT BREEZES UP

After I had taken off my waistcoat, I went out into the 'tweendecks, then into the grand cabin, then into the space below the booms. He followed me everywhere, keeping me under observation, till I was tempted to tell him where the letters were, so as to have a little peace. At first he kept telling me stories, or making bad jokes; but very soon he grew weary of pretending; he became surly. At this point I asked him which was his cabin. He glowered at me for asking such a question, but he pointed it out to me. It was a cabin no larger than my own, on the opposite (that is the port) side of the 'tweendecks. I took the opportunity (it was a bold stroke, evidently displeasing to him) of looking in; for to tell the truth I had a suspicion that he slept in the grand cabin, on the top of the locker. I thought that the stateroom had another inmate. When I looked into it I expected to find myself in Aurelia's presence. I did not want to see her; but I wished very eagerly to know if she were in the ship or not. The stateroom was empty, but the bunk, which had been slept in, was not yet made up.

I do not know how much longer he would have dogged me about the ship. To my great joy he was called from me by the mate, who cried down the hatchway, bidding him come up at once, as there was "something in sight." Captain Barlow evidently wanted me to come on deck with him; but I was resolute. I said I would stop below to have another try at his stories. He went on deck surlily, saying something about "You wait," or "You whelp," I could not catch his exact words. He turned at the hatchway to see where I had gone. I had expected this move, so when he looked, he saw me entering the grand cabin, just as I had said. I watched him through the crack in the hinge; for I fully expected him to return suddenly. As he did not return on the instant, I darted into my own cabin just long enough to drop the letter cartridges into an old tin slush–pot which was stowed in the locker below the bunk. I had noted it in the early morning when I had done my sewing. I pressed the cartridges into the slush, till they were all hidden. In another instant of time the pot was back in the locker among the other oddments while I was back in the cabin hard at work at my sermons. I was conscious that the captain glanced through the skylight at me. No doubt what he saw reassured him. For the moment I felt perfectly safe.

About half an hour later, I heard a great noise of hauling on deck, followed by the threshing of our sails, as though they had suddenly come aback. I knew enough of the sea to know that if we were tacking there would be other orders, while, if the helmsman had let the ship come aback by accident I should have heard the officers rating him. I heard neither nor orders; something else was happening. A glance out of the stern windows showed me that the ship was no longer under way. She was not moving through the water. It struck me that I had better go on deck to see what was the matter. When I reached the deck I found that the barquentine was hove–to (that is, held motionless by a certain arrangement of the sails) about half a mile from a small full–rigged ship which had hove–to likewise. The barquentine's boat was rapidly pulling towards this full–rigged ship, with Captain Barlow sitting in the stern–sheets. The ship was a man–of–war; for she flew the St. George's banner, as well as a pennant. Her guns were pointing through her ports, eight bright brass guns to a broadside. She was waiting there, heaving in huge stately heaves, for Captain Barlow's message.

Now I had had alarms enough since I entered the Duke's service; but I confess this sight of the man–of–war daunted me worse than any of them. I knew that Captain Barlow had stopped her, so that he might hand over my letters to her captain; that was easily guessed The next question was, would the captain insist on taking the messenger to be examined in person. It was that which scared me worst. I had heard frightful tales about political prisoners. They were shut up in the Tower dungeons, away below the level of the Thames. They were examined there by masked magistrates who wrung the truth from them by the "bootikins," which squeezed the feet, or by the thumbscrews, which twisted the thumbs. My feet seemed to grow red–hot when I thought of that horror. I knew only too well that my youth would not save me. James the Second was never moved by pity towards a beaten enemy. I watched the arrival of the boat at the ship's side, with the perspiration running down my face. I began to understand, now, what was meant by the words high treason. I saw all the majesty of the English Navy, all the law, all the noble polity of England, arrayed to judge a boy to death, for a five minutes' prank. They would drag me on a hurdle to Tyburn, as soon as torture had made me tell my tale.

But enough of my state of mind. I saw Captain Barlow go up the ship's gangway, where an officer no doubt received him. Very soon afterwards he came down the gangway again, half followed by some one who seemed to be ordering him. His boat then shoved off for the barquentine. The man—of—war got under way again by swinging her great mainyard smartly about. The smother at her bows gleamed whiter at the very instant, as she gathered way. It was a blessed sight to me, after my suspense, I assure you; but I did not understand it till later. I learned later on that Captain Barlow was one of a kind of men very common in those troublous times. He was hedging, or trimming. He was quite willing to make money by selling the Duke's plans to the King; but he had the sense to see that the Duke's party might succeed, in which case the King's favour would not be worth much. So his treason to the Duke stopped short of the betrayal of men attached in any way to the Monmouth party. He would betray letters, when he could lay his hands on them unobserved; but he was not going to become an open enemy to the Duke until he knew that the Duke's was the losing side; then he would betray men fast enough. Until then, he would receive the trust of both factions, in order to betray a portion of the confidence received from them.

The day dragged by for me somehow, uncomfortably, under the captain's eye. It was one of the longest days I have ever known. It sickened me utterly of the life of adventure to which I now seemed pledged. I vowed that if I had the chance I would write to my uncle from Mr. Blick's house, begging to be received back. That seemed to be the only way of escape possible to me. It did not seem hopeful; but it gave me some solace to think of it. I longed to be free from these terrors. You don't know what an adventurous life is. I will tell you. It is a life of sordid unquiet, pursued without plan, like the life of an animal. Have you seen a dog trying to cross a busy street? There is the adventurer. Or the rabbit on the cliff, in his state of continual panic; he, too, lives the adventurous life. What does the world owe to the adventurer? But there. I become impatient. One patient hero in his garret is worth all these silly fireworks put together.

One thing more happened on that day. The breeze freshened all the afternoon till by bedtime it blew what is called a fresh gale. Captain Barlow drove his ship till she shook to her centre, not because he liked (like many sailors) to show his vessel's paces; but because he sat at his bottle too long after dinner. He was half drunk by supper time, too drunk to take the sail off her, so we drove on down Channel, trusting to the goodness of the gear. There would have been a pretty smash–up if we had had to alter our course hurriedly. As it was we were jumping like a young colt, in a welter of foam, with two men at the tiller, besides a gang on the tackles. I never knew any ship to bound about so wildly. I passed the evening after supper on deck, enjoying the splendour of that savage leaping rush down Channel, yet just a little nervous at the sight of our spars buckling under the strain. The captain was drunk before dark; we could hear him banging the table with his bottle. The mate, who was on the poop with me, kept glancing from the spars to the skylight; he was getting frightened at the gait we were going. "Young man," he said, "d'ye know the sailor's catechism?"

"No, sir," I answered. "Well," he said, "it's short but sweet, like a ration of rum. What is the complete duty of a sailorman? You don't know? It's this. OBEY ORDERS, IF YOU BREAK OWNERS. My orders are not to take off sail till Mr. drunken Barlow sees fit. You'll see a few happenings aloft just now if he don't see fit soon." Just at that instant she gave a lurch which sent one of the helmsmen flying. The mate leaped to his place with an angry exclamation. "Another man to the helm," he cried. "You, boy. Run below. Tell the captain she'll be dismasted in another five minutes." He was in the right of it. A blind man could have told that the ship was being over–driven. I ran down, as eager as the mate to put an end to the danger.

When I went below, I found the captain in my cabin, rummaging everywhere. He had flung out the contents of the lockers, my bedclothes, everything, in a jumble on the deck, which, in a drunken aimless way he was examining by the light of a couple of dip candles, stuck to the edge of the bunk. It was not a time to mind about that. "Sir," I said, "the ship is sinking. Come on deck, sir; take the sail off. The mate says the ship is sinking."

"Eh," said the captain furiously. "You young spy. I command this ship. What's the sail got to do with you?" He glared at me in drunken anger.

"You young whelp," he cried, grabbing me by the collar. "Where are your letters? Eh? Where've you hid your letters?"

At that instant, there came a more violent gust in the fierceness of wind which drove us. The ship gave a "yank;" there is no other word to express the frightful shock of her movement. She lay down on her lee beam ends with a crash of breaking crockery. Casks broke loose in the hold; gear fell from aloft; the captain was flung under me against the ship's side. The deck beneath us sloped up like a roof. In the roar of water rushing down the hatch I remember thinking that the Day of Judgment was come. Yells on deck mingled with all the uproar; I heard something thud like a sledge–hammer on the ship's side. The captain picked himself up holding his head, which was all one gore of blood from the crack against the ship's side. "Beam ends," he said stupidly. "Beam ends. Yes. Yes." He was dazed; he did not know what he said; but some sort of sailor's instinct told him that he was wanted on deck. At any rate he went out, pulling himself up the steep deck with a cleverness which I had not expected. He left me clutching the ledge of the bunk, staring up at the door away above me, while the wreck of my belongings banged about at my feet. I thought it was all over with the ship; but I was not scared at the prospect of death; only a little sickish from the shock of that sudden sweeping over. I found a fascination in the horrible open door, the black oblong hole in the air through which the captain had passed. I waited for the sea to pour down it. I expected to see a clear mass of water with fish in it; something quite calm, something beautiful, not the noisy horror of the sea outside. I suppose I waited like that for a full minute before the roar of the squall grew less. Then I told myself that I must go on deck; that the danger would be less, looking it in the face, than down there in the cabin. It was not pleasant to go on deck, any more than it is pleasant to go downstairs at two in the morning to look for burglars, but it was better to be moving than staying still. I clenched my fist upon the only dip which remained alight (the other was somewhere in the jumble under my feet). Then, catching hold of the door–hook I pulled myself up to the door, where I steadied myself for a moment. While I stood there I had a horrible feeling of the ship having died under my feet. She had been leaping so gallantly only five minutes before. Now she lay with her heart broken, while the seas beat her with great thumps.

Two battle–lanterns lit the after 'tweendecks. There was a great heap of staved in casks, slopping about in an inch or two of water, all along that side, thrown there by the smash. I could hear the men yelling on deck. Captain Barlow was swearing in loud shouts. I could hear all this in the lull of the squall. I heard more than that, as I stood listening. I heard the faint crying out of a woman's voice from the steward's pantry (next door to the captain's cabin) on the opposite side, across the steep, tipped up slippery decks. At first I thought it must be the poor cat; but as the wind passed, letting me hear more clearly, I recognized that it was a woman's voice, crying out there in the darkness with a note of pain. I did not think of Aurelia. She never entered my head. All that I thought was "Poor creature! What a place for a woman!" The ship was jerking, you might almost call it gasping, as the seas struck her; it was no easy job to climb along that roof–slope of the deck with nothing to hold on by. I got across somehow, partly by luck, partly by fingernails. I even managed to open the pantry door, which was another difficulty, as it opened inwards, into the cabin. As I opened it, a suck of wind blew out my light. There I was in the dark, with a hurt woman, in a ship which for all I knew, might sink with all hands in twenty seconds. It is queer; I didn't mind the ship sinking. What I disliked was being in the dark with an unknown somebody who whimpered.

"Are you much hurt?" I asked. "Hold on a minute. I'll strike a light." I shut myself into the cabin, so as to keep out the draught. My feet kicked among the steward's crockery. It was as dark in that cubby–hole as in a grave. The unknown person, probably fearing me, thinking me some rough drunken sailor, was crying out now more in terror than in pain. She was begging me not to hurt her. I probably frightened her a good deal by not replying. The tinder box took up all my attention for a good couple of minutes. A tinder box is not a thing to get light by hurriedly. You try some day, to see how quickly you can light a candle by one. When I got the candle lit, I thought of the battle–lanterns swinging outside all the time. I might have saved myself all that trouble by using a little common sense. Well. Wait till you stand as I stood, with your heart in your boots, down in a pit of death, you'll see how much common sense will remain in your fine brains.

When the flame took hold of the wick, so that I could look about me, I saw the lady Aurelia lying among the smashed up gear to leeward. She had been lying down, reading in a sort of bunk which had been rigged up for her on the locker–top. The shock had flung her clean out of the bunk on to the deck. At the same moment an avalanche of gear had fetched to leeward. A cask had rolled on to her left hand, pinning her down to the deck, while a box of bottles had cut the back of her head. A more complete picture of misery you could not hope to see. There was all the ill–smelling jumble of steward's gear, tumbled in a heap of smash, soaking in the oil from the fallen lamp. There was a good deal of blood about. Aurelia was lying in all the debris half covered with salted fish from one of the capsized casks. They looked like huge leaves. She seemed to have been buried under them, like a babe in the wood. She grew calm when she saw me. "There are candles under the bunk," she said. "Light two or three. Tell me what has happened."

I did not answer till I had lighted three or four more candles. "The ship's on her beam ends," I said. "It's the captain's fault. But never mind that. I must get you out. Are you badly hurt, do you think?"

"I'm all right," she said with a gasp. "But it's being pinned in here. I thought I was going to be pinned down while I was being drowned."

"Shut your eyes, please," I said. "Bite your lip. It'll hurt, I'm afraid, getting this cask off your hand. Are you ready. Now." I did it as gently as I could; but it made me turn all cold to think of the hand under all that weight.

"Can you withdraw your hand, now?" I asked, tilting the cask as far up as I could.

"No," she said. "Look out. I'll roll out." In another two seconds she was sitting up among the crockery with her face deathly white against the bulkhead; she had fainted. There was a water–carafe on a bracket up above my head. I splashed her face with water from it till she rallied. She came to herself with a little hysterical laugh, at the very instant when something giving way aloft let the ship right herself again. "Hold on a minute," I said. "Take this water. Now drink a little. I'll be back in a moment." The ship was rolling drunkenly in the trough of the sea; but I made a nimble rush to the cabin, where the captain's cruet of brandy bottles still swung from a hook in the beams. I ran back to her with a bottle of brandy. There were a few unbroken mugs in the pantry, so I gave her a drink of brandy, which brought the colour back to her cheeks. While she sat there, in the mess of gear which slid about as the ship rolled, I got a good big jug of water from the scuttle–butt in the 'tweendecks. I nipped on deck with it to ask the mate for some balsam, an excellent cure for cuts which most sailors carry to sea with them. There was mess enough on deck in all conscience. I found the foretopmast gone over the side, in a tangle of torn rope at which all hands were furiously hacking. The mate was on the fo'c'sle hacking at some gear with a tomahawk. I did not see the captain.

"Mr. mate," I cried. "I want some balsam, quick."

"Get out of this," he shouted. "Get out of this. I can't attend to your hurts. Don't come bothering here."

"It's for the lady," I said, "the lady down below."

"In my chest. Look in my chest till," he said. "Now stand dear. I've trouble enough without ladies in the case. Are you all clear, you, aft there?"

"All gone here, sir," the men shouted back. "Shall we sling a bowline over the foot?"

"No," he shouted. "Look out. She's going."

For just a second I saw the mass of spar all tangled up with sail rise up on a wave as it drifted past. I found myself wondering why we had all been in the shadow of death only a couple of minutes before. There was no thought of danger now. I ran below for the balsam, which I found without difficulty.

CHAPTER XIV. A DRINK OF SHERBET

I took what handkerchiefs I could find into the pantry with me. "There's no danger," I said. "The ship's all right. How are you now? Let me give you some more brandy." I gave her a little more brandy; then I helped her on to the top of the locker. Pouring out some water into the basin I bathed the cut on her head. It was a clean long cut which would probably have gone through the bone had not her hair been so thick. I dressed it as well as I could with balsam, then bound it tightly up with a white handkerchief. The hand was a good deal more, difficult to manage; it was nastily crushed; though no bones were broken. The wrist was so much swollen that I had to cut open the sleeve of her man's riding jacket. Then I bathed the hand with cold water mixed with vinegar (which I had heard was cooling) till I felt that the time had come to bandage it, so that the patient might lie down to rest. She had been much shaken by her fall. I don't think it ever once occurred to me to think of her as my enemy. I felt too much pity for her, being hurt, like that. "Look here," I said. "You'll have to wear that arm in a sling. I'll bandage it up for you nicely." She bore my surgery like the hero she was; it didn't look very wonderful when it was done; but she said that the pain was a good deal soothed. That was not the end though. I had to change cabins with her, since I could not let a hurt woman sleep in that bunk in the pantry; she might so easily be flung from it a second time. So I shifted her things into my cabin, where I made all tidy for her. As for the precious slush can, I stowed that carefully away, at the back of some lumber in one of the pantry lockers, where it would not be found. Altogether, it took me about twenty minutes to make everything ready, by which time the little accident on deck had been forgotten, except by those who had to do the work of sending up a new topmast; a job which kept all hands busy all night. The ship was making a steady three knots. under her reduced sail when I helped Aurelia across to her new room. There was no more thought of danger.

As I paused at the cabin door, to ask if there was anything more which I could do for her, the lady turned to me.

"What is your name?" she asked. I am ashamed to say that I hesitated, being half inclined to give her a false name; for my time of secret service had given me a thorough distrust of pretty nearly everybody. She noticed my hesitation. "As a friend to another friend," she added. "Life isn't all the King's service."

"My name is Martin Hyde," I said.

"Mine is Aurelia," she replied, "Aurelia Carew. Will you remember that?" I told her that I should certainly remember that. "We seem to have met before," she said, "more than once."

"Yes," I answered, smiling. She, too, smiled, but she quickly became grave again.

"Mr. Martin Hyde," she said, with a little catch in her voice, "we two are in opposite camps. But I don't know. After this, it's difficult. I warn you." Here she stopped, quite unable to go on. "I can't," she continued, more to herself than to me, "I can't. They oughtn't to have put this on me. They oughtn't. They oughtn't." She laid her unhurt hand on my shoulder for a moment. "Let me warn you," she said earnestly, "that you're in danger."

"In danger from you?" I asked.

"Don't ask me more," she said, "I hate myself for telling you even that. Oh, it's terrible to have to do it. Go now. Don't ask me more. But I had to warn you. But I can't do it myself." I did not know what to make of this; but I gathered that her task (whatever it was) from which she had shrunk so bitterly in the Dutch town only the night before, was now to be deputed to another, probably to the captain, perhaps to the Dartmouth justices. I did not like the thought; but I thanked her for warning me, it was generous of her to warn me. I took out the dagger with which she had tried to stab me. "You said we were in opposite camps, Miss Carew," I said. "But I wouldn't like to keep this. I mean I wouldn't like to think that we were enemies, really." I daresay I said other foolish things as well, at the same time.

"Yes, keep it," she said. "I couldn't bear to have it again. But be warned. Don't trust me. While we're in opposite camps you be warned. For I'm your enemy, then, when you least expect it."

Nothing much happened the next day until the evening, by which time we were off the Isle of Wight. With the aid of the mate, I doctored Aurelia's hand again; that was the only memorable event of the day. In the evening, the captain (who had been moody from his drunkenness of the night before) asked me to sing to him in the great cabin. I was surprised at the request; but I knew a few ballads, so I sang them to him. While I was singing, Aurelia entered the cabin; she sat down on one of the lockers below the great window. She looked very white, in the gloom there. She did not speak to me; but sat there restlessly, coughing in a dry hacking way, as though one of her ribs had been broken in the fall. I lowered my voice when I noticed this, as I was afraid that my singing might annoy her; I thought that she was suffering from her wound. The captain told me to pipe up; as he couldn't hear what my words were. I asked Aurelia if my singing worried her; but instead of answering she left the cabin for a few minutes. When she came back, she sat with her face in her hand, seemingly in great pain. I sang all the ballads known to me. When I had finished, the captain grunted a note of approval. "Well," he said, "so there's your ballads. That's your treat. Now you shall have mine." A little gong hung in the cabin. He banged upon it to summon his boy, who came in trembling, as he always did, expecting to be beaten before he went out. "Bring in a jug of cool water," he said. "Then fetch them limes I bought." As the boy went out, the captain turned to me with a grin. "Did you ever drink Turk's sherbet?" he said.

"No," I answered. "I've never even heard of it. What is it?"

"Why," he said, "it's a drink the heathen Turks make out of citron. A powder which fizzes. I got some of it last autumn when I made a voyage to Scanderoon. It's been too cold ever since to want to drink any, as it's a summer drink mostly. Now you shall have some." He took down some tumblers from the rack in which they stood. "Here's glasses," he said. "Now the sherbet is in this bottle here." He produced a pint glass bottle from one of the lockers. It was stopped with a wooden plug, carved in the likeness of a Turk's head.

Martin Hyde, The Duke's Messenger

It was about three parts full of a whitish powder. A label on the side of the bottle gave directions for its preparation.

When the boy returned with his tray, the captain squeezed the juice of half a lime into each of the three tumblers. "That's the first thing," he said. "Lime juice. Now the water." He poured water into each glass, till they were nearly full. "White of egg is said to make it better," he said to me. "But at sea I guess we must do without that. Now then. You're the singer, so you drink first. Be ready to drink it while it fizzes; for then it's at its best. Are you ready?" I was quite ready, so the captain filled his spoon with the soft white powder. Glancing round at Aurelia I saw that she had covered her eyes with her hand. "Won't Miss Carew drink first?" I asked.

"I don't want any," she said in a low voice. Before I could speak another word the captain had poured his heaped spoonful of powder into my glass. "Stir it up, boy," he cried. "Down with it while it fizzes." Aurelia rose to her feet, catching her breath sharply.

I remember a pleasant taste, as though all of the fruits of the world had been crushed together into a syrup; then a mist surged all about me, the cabin became darker, the captain seemed to grow vast, till his body filled the room. My legs melted from me. I was one little wavering flame blowing about on great waves. Something was hard upon my head. The captain's hand (I could feel) was lifting my eyelid. I heard him say "That's got him." Instantly a choir of voices began to chant "That's got him," in roaring, tumultuous bursts of music. Then the music became, as it were, present, but inaudible; there were waves of sound all round me, but my ears were deafened to them. I had been put out of action by some very powerful drug, I remember no more of that evening's entertainment. I was utterly unconscious.

I came to, very sick, some time in the night. I was in the bunk in the pantry; but far too helpless in my misery to rise, or to take an account of time. I lay half-conscious till the morning, when I fell into a deep sleep, which lasted, I may say, till the evening; for I did not feel sufficiently awake to get up until about half-past five. When I did get up, I felt so tottery that I could hardly keep my feet. Someone, I supposed that it was Aurelia, had placed a metal brandy flask, with a paper roll containing hard-boiled eggs, on my wash-hand-stand. I took a gulp of the brandy. In the midst of my sickness I remember the shame of it; the shame of being drugged by those two; for I knew that I had been drugged; the shame of having given up like that, at the moment when I had the cards in my hand; all the cards. I was locked into the pantry; all my clothes were gone. I found myself dressed in a sailor's serge–shirt. All my other property had vanished. I remember crying as I shook at the door to open it; it was too strong for me, in my weak state. As I wrestled with the door, I heard the dry rattling out of the cable. We had come to anchor; we were in Dartmouth; perhaps in a few minutes I should be going ashore. Looking through the port–hole, I saw a great steep hill rising up from the water, with houses clinging to its side, like barnacles on the side of a rock. I could see people walking on the wharf. I could see a banner blowing out from a flagstaff.

A few more gulps of brandy brought me to myself I was safe anyhow; my cartridges had not been found. I dropped them one by one into the metal–flask. Whatever happened, no one would look for them there. Then I banged at the door again, trying to make people hear. Nobody paid any attention to me; I might have spared myself the trouble. Long afterwards, I learned that I was detained while Captain Barlow spoke to a magistrate about me, asking if I might be "questioned," that is, put to the thumbscrews, till it could be learned whether I carried a verbal message to my uncle, Mr. Blick. The magistrate to whom he first applied was one of the Monmouth faction as it happened, so my thumbs escaped; but I had a narrow escape later, as you shall hear. About an hour after the ship came to anchor, the cabin–door was opened by a sailor, who flung in an armful of clothes to me, without speaking a word. They were mostly not my own clothes; the boots were not mine; my own boots, I guessed, had been cut to pieces in the letter–hunt. All the clothes which were mine had had the seams ripped up. All my cartridges had been taken. About half of my money was gone. The only things untouched were the weapons in the belt. I laughed to myself to think how little reward they had had for all their baseness. They had stooped to the methods of the lowest kind of thieves, yet they had failed. They had not found my letters. My joy was not very real; I was too wretched for that. Looking back at it all long after, I think that the hardest thing to bear was Aurelia's share in the work. I had not thought that Aurelia would join in tricking me in that way. But while I thought bitterly of her deceit, I thought of her tears on the balcony in the Dutch city. After all, she had been driven into it by that big bully of a man. I forgave her when I thought of him; he was the cause of it all. A brute he must have been to force her into such an action. Presently the mate came down with orders to me to leave the ship at once. I asked him for my own clothes; but he told me sharply to be thankful for what I had, since I'd done no work to earn them; by work he meant the brainless manual work done by people like himself. So going on deck I called a boatman, who for twopence put me ashore on the Kingswear side of the river. He gave me full directions for finding Mr.

Blick's house, telling me that in another five minutes I should come to it, if I followed my nose. As I started from the landing place I looked back at the barquentine, where I had had so many adventures. She was lying at anchor at a little distance from the Dartmouth landing place, making a fair show, under her flag, in spite of her jury foretopmast. As I looked, the boatman jogged my elbow, pointing across the river to the strip of road which edges the stream. "A young lady waving to you," he said. Sure enough a lady was waving to me. I supposed that it was Aurelia, asking pardon, trying to show me that we parted friends. I would not wave at first; I was surly; but after about a minute I waved my hat to her. Then I set off up the road to Mr. Blick's. Ten minutes later, I was in Mr. Blick's house, telling him all that I have now told you.

Mr. Blick kept me in his house for a day or two less than four weeks, when business took him to Exeter. I went with him; for he gave out that he was taking me to school there, as his dead sister had wished. His real reason was to pass the word through the country that King Monmouth was coming. He was one of the few men in full knowledge of the Duke's plans; but as we went about from town to town, spreading the word among the faithful, I saw that the Duke was expected by vast numbers of the country folk. Our clients were not much among the gentry; they hung by themselves, as, in this country, they always will, in times of popular stir. But among the poorer people, such as small farmers, or common labouring men, we were looked for as men sent from on high. At more than one little quiet village, when we went into the inn–parlour, we saw the men looking at us, half frightened, half expectant, as though we, being strangers, must needs have news of the King for whom they longed. Often some publican or maltster would tell us that Gyle (their name for the unfortunate Argyle, then a defeated man in Scotland, if not already put to death for his rebellion) was taken, looking at us carefully as he spoke, for fear lest we should be of the wrong side. Then, if we seemed sympathetic, he would tell us how perhaps another would have better luck elsewhere. After that, we would tell our news. It was dangerous work, though, carrying that message across the country. In many of the towns we found guards of the Devon red regiment of militia. I am quite sure that if Mr. Blick had not had me by his. side, as an excellent excuse for travelling to Exeter, he would have been lodged in gaol as a suspicious character. The soldiers had arrested many travellers already; the gaols were full. King James's great man in those parts, the Earl of Albemarle, knew very well that something was in the air; but as he was a great lord the hearts of the poor were hidden from him. He had no guess of what was planning. In a way, the Duke's affairs were very well planned. The eastern end of Devon, all Somerset, with the western end of Dorset, were all ripe to rise, directly he appeared.

They knew that he was coming; they were prepared to join him; they knew at about what time he would come, at about a fortnight from hay–harvest. Already, quite unknown to the authorities, we had men picked out to carry the news of the landing to different parts of the country. So far, I think, the Duke's affairs were well planned. But though we had all this enthusiasm in three counties, besides promises of similar risings in London, we were in no real case to take the field. Our adherents, however numerous, however brave, were only a mob, when all is said; they were not an army. The Duke thought that the regular army, or at least some regiments of it, would desert to him, as happened some years later, when the great Prince William did what my master attempted. But my master forgot that he had neither the arms nor the officers to make his faction a likely body for regular troops to join.

CHAPTER XV. THE ROAD TO LYME

We spread the tidings as far as Exeter, where Mr. Blick made some pretence of handing me over to a schoolmaster, one Hubble, a red–faced, cheery clergyman, one of the most ardent rebels on our side. Indeed, the clergymen everywhere supported us, as defenders of the Protestant faith, which that dastard James would have destroyed. Mr. Hubble made some excuse for not taking me in at the instant; but gave us letters of introduction to people in towns further on, so that we could pass the militia without difficulty, to give the news in western Dorset. So after waiting for a little while in Exeter, gathering all the news we could of the whereabouts of the troops of militia, we pushed on eastward, by way of Sidmouth, to the big town of Dorchester. As we came east, we found the militia very much more suspicious than they had been on the western side of Exeter. At every little town we found a strong guard so placed that no one could enter without passing under the captain's eye. We were brought before militia captains some two or three times a day. Sometimes we were searched; sometimes, if the captain happened to be drunk, we were bullied with threats of the gaol. Mr. Blick in these cases always insisted on being brought before the magistrate, to whom he would tell a fine indignant tale, saying what a shame it was that he could not take his orphan nephew peaceably to school, without being suspected of complicity in a rebellion. He would then show Mr. Hubble's letters, or some other papers signed by the Dartmouth magistrates. These always cleared our characters, so that we were allowed to proceed; but I did not like the way in which our descriptions were taken. Once on our journey, shortly after we had left Sidmouth, where the soldiers had been very suspicious, we turned out of the highway to leave word at a town called

Seaton. We spread the watchword at several villages near the sea, before we came to Seaton, so that we were rather late in arriving. Thinking no wrong, we put up at one of the inns in Seaton, intending to pass the night there. We were at supper in our inn, when some yeomanry rode up to the door, to ask the landlord if an elderly man had passed that way with a boy. The landlord, who was a good deal scared by the soldiers, showed the captain in to us at once. We were quite as much scared to see him as the landlord had been. The captain of the soldiers was the very man who had given us such a searching examination in Sidmouth that morning.

"Well," he said to Mr. Blick, "I thought you were going to Dorchester. What brings you here?" "Sir," said Mr. Blick, "we've been so much interrupted by soldiers that we hoped to travel away from the main–roads."

"Well, sir," said the captain, "I've had you watched. Since you left Sidmouth, you've been into every inn upon the road, listening to a lot of seditious talk about Argyle. That's not my point, though. You gave out to me that you were going to Dorchester. Instead of that you slink off the Dorchester road at the first opportunity. You will have to explain yourself to my superiors. You're under arrest."

"Sir," said Mr. Blick, "I am sorry that you should think ill of me. We will gladly come with you to answer for our conduct to the authorities. But while the horses are being saddled, perhaps you will join us at supper. Landlord, bring a couple of bottles more. The captain sups with us."

But though the captain drank his couple of bottles of port, he did not become any gentler with us. As soon as supper was over we had to ride on again, with the troopers all round us.

"Sir," said Mr. Blick, "may I ask you where we are going with you?"

"Axminster," said the captain.

"Well. That's on my way," said Mr. Blick.

"It'll probably end your way, for some time," said the captain.

Martin Hyde, The Duke's Messenger

"I'm perfectly willing to abide by the decision of the authorities," Mr. Blick answered calmly. "But what is the meaning of all these soldiers everywhere? I've asked the people; but nobody seems able to give a straight answer."

"I think you know what the soldiers mean well enough," answered the captain. "If you hadn't known you wouldn't have turned out of the highway."

At about midnight we reached Axminster. We were taken before a couple of officers who sat at work by candlelight over a mass of papers, in an upper chamber of an inn. They had a wild air of having been without sleep for some time. Their muddy riding boots were drying in front of the fire. They had a map of the countryside before them, all stuck about with little flags, some red, some yellow, to show where the different troops of militia were stationed. After saluting these officers, the captain made his report about us, saying that we were suspicious persons, who had started from Sialmouth, towards Dorchester. He had waited to receive word from the troops stationed along the highway of our arrival at various points upon the road; but, failing to hear about us, he had searched for us, with the result that he had found us at Seaton, some miles out of our way. The officers questioned us closely about our plans, making notes of what we said. They kept referring to a book of letters, as though to verify what we said. Mr. Blick's answers made them take a favourable view of us; but they told him in a friendly way that the officer had done right to arrest us. They complimented the captain on his zeal. Meanwhile, they said, since we were going to Dorchester, we could not object to going with a military escort. A troop of cavalry was to start in a couple of hours; we could go with that.

We were in Dorchester for a few days, always under the eye of the soldiers. It was a bustling, suspicious time full of false alarms. Mr. Blick told me that the message "King Golden Cap. After six one," meant that the Duke was to be expected off Golden Cap, a cliff a few miles from Lyme Regis, any day after the first of the sixth month. He was on tenter-hooks to be in Lyme to greet him on his arrival; but this he could not hope to do. We were watched too carefully to be able to get away to a place upon the sea-coast. We had to be very careful how we sent our secret message abroad into the country. I have never known a time so full of alarms. People would ride in to the town at night with word that Monmouth was landed, or that there was fighting all along the coast, or that King James was dead. The drums would beat; the cavalry would come out clattering. People would be crying out. The loyal would come to their doorsteps ready to fly further inland. Every night, if one lay awake, one could hear the noise of spades in back gardens where misers were burying their money. Then, every day, one would see the troopers coming in, generally two at a time, with a suspected man led by a cord knotted to his two thumbs. Dorchester gaol was full of suspected people, who were kept in prison indefinitely, without trial, in very great discomfort. King James was afraid, he did not really know of what, so he took measures not so much to prevent trouble as to avenge his own fear. Mr. Blick used to send me to the prison every morning with loaves of fresh bread for the prisoners.

At last, after midnight, in the night of the 11th of June, a memorable day for the West, riders came in with news which destroyed the night's rest of the town. Monmouth had landed at Lyme the evening before, after sailing about in sight of the town all day. That was news indeed. It made a strange uproar in the streets. The trumpets blew from every inn–door to summons the billeted soldiers. Officers ran about bawling for their sergeants; the sergeants hurried about with lanterns, rousing the men from where they slept. All the streets were full of cavalry men trying to form in the crowd. At last, when they were formed, a trumpet sounded, making everyone keep silence. Then in the stillness an officer shouted out an order, which no one, save a soldier, could understand. Instantly the kettle–drums began to pound; the swords jingled; the horses whinnied, tossing up their heads. The soldiers trotted off smartly towards Bridport, leaving the town strangely quiet, strangely scared, to discuss the great news from Lyme.

I was watching the crowd at my bed–room window when the horsemen trotted off. While I stood looking at them, Mr. Blick ran upstairs, bidding me to come down at once, as now there was a chance to get to Lyme. "Come quick," he said. "The troops are gone. We must follow on their tracks. It'll be too late later in the morning." In less than twenty minutes we were trotting after the soldiers at a good pace, passing some scores of men on foot who were hurrying, as they said, to see the battle. Mr. Blick wore a sword which clattered as he rode. The people hearing the noise thought that he was an officer, perhaps a colonel, riding with his servant. Many of the men asked him where the battle was to be, whether it would begin before daylight, whether Monmouth was come with the French, all sorts of questions, to which we answered at random. In the light summer night we had a fair view of things. When we dismounted to lead our horses up or down the steep hills of that road, the straggling sight–seers came all round us as we walked, to hear what we had to tell. We could see their faces all about us, strange in the dusk, like ghosts, not like real men. At the top of one hill, Mr. Blick warned them to look out for themselves. He told them that before morning the highway would be patrolled by troops who would take them in charge as suspicious characters trying to join Monmouth, which actually happened the next day when the militia officers realized that war had begun. His words scared off a number ,of them; but many kept on as they were going, to see the great battle, which, they said, would begin as soon as it was light.

When the sun began to peep, we turned off the highway in order to avoid Bridport, which we passed a little after dawn. A few miles further on we felt that we could turn into the road again as we were safe from the militia at that distance. Then, feeling happy at the thought of the coming contest, which, we felt sure, would be won by our side, we pressed our tired nags over the brook towards the steep hill which separates Charmouth from Lyme.

It was early morning, about five o'clock, when we came to Charmouth; but the little town was as busy as though it were noon on fair–day. The street was crowded. People were coming in from all the countryside. A man was haranguing the crowd from a horseless waggon drawn up at an inn. The horses had no doubt been pressed into Monmouth's service some hours before. I should think that there must have been three hundred people listening to the orator. Men, already half drunk, with green boughs in their hats, were marching about the town in uneven companies, armed with clubs torn from the hedges. Weeping women followed them, trying to persuade their sons or husbands to come home. Other men were bringing out horses from private stables. People were singing. One man, leaning out of a window, kept on firing his pistol as fast as he could load. Waving men cheered from the hill above. The men in the town cheered back. There was a great deal of noisy joking everywhere. They cheered us as we rode through them, telling us that Monmouth had arms for all. One poor woman begged Mr. Blick to tell her man to come home, as without him the children would all starve. The crowd groaned at her; but Mr. Blick stopped them, calling the husband, who was in a sad state of drunken vainglory, to leave the ranks in which he tried to march. "We don't want fathers of families," he cried. "We want these tight young bachelors. They're the boys." Indeed, the tight young bachelors felt that this was the case, so the woman got her man again; lucky she was to get him. As far as I could judge, the crowd imagined us to be great officers; at any rate our coming drew away the listeners from the waggon. They came flocking to our heels as though we were the Duke himself. A drummer beat up a quickstep; the crowd surged forward. We marched across the fields to Lyme, five hundred strong. One of the men, plucking a sprig of hawthorn from the hedge, asked me to wear it in my hat as the Duke's badge, which I did. He called me "Captain." "Captain," he said. "We had a brush with them already, this morning, along the road here. Two on 'em were killed. They didn't stay for no more." So fighting had begun then, the civil war had taken its first fruits of life. There could be no more shillyshallying; we had put our hands to a big business. In spite of the noise of the march, my spirits were rather dashed by the thought of those two men, lying dead somewhere on the road behind us, killed by their own countrymen.

We are said to be a sober people; but none of those who saw Lyme that morning would have had much opinion of our sobriety. Charmouth had been disorderly; Lyme was uproarious. Outside the town, in one of the fields above the church, we were stopped by a guard of men who all wore white scarves on their arms, as well as green sprays in their hats. They stopped us, apparently, because their captain wished to exercise them in military customs. They were evidently raw to the use of arms. They handled their muskets like spades. "Be you for Monmouth, masters?" they asked us, grinning. When we said that we were, this very unmilitary guard told us to pass on. "Her've got arms for all," they said. "The word be 'Fear nothing but God.'" Some of them joked with friends among our party. They waved their muskets to us.

CHAPTER XVI. THE LANDING

Inside the town, there was great confusion.Riotous men were foraging, that is, plundering from private houses, pretending that they did so at the Duke's orders. The streets were full of people, nearly all of them men, the green boughs in their hats. On the beach two long lines of men with green scarves on their arms were being drilled by an officer. Horses were picketed in a long line up the main street; they were mostly very poor cart–stock, ill–provided, as I learned afterwards, with harness. Men were bringing hay to them from whatever haystack was nearest. From time to time, there came a loud booming of guns, above the ringing of the church bells. Three ships in the bay, one of them La Reina, were firing salutes as they hoisted their colours. It was all like a very noisy fair or coronation day. It had little appearance of an armed invasion. We found the Duke busy with Mr. Jermyn enlisting men in a field above the town.

"That's not Mr. Jermyn. That's Lord Grey," Mr. Blick said, on hearing me exclaim. "Mr. Jermyn's only the name he goes by. He's my Lord now, you must remember."

Just then the Duke caught sight of us riding up. He took us for local gentry, coming in to volunteer. He came smiling to welcome us. It must have been a shrewd disappointment to him to find that we were not what he thought. All his hopes were in the gentry, poor man. By the time we were on our feet with our hats off he had turned his back upon us as though to speak to Lord Grey, but really, I believe, to hide his chagrin. When he turned to us again both of them welcomed us, saying that there was work enough for all, in enlisting men, making out billets, etc. So without more ado we gave our horses to the ostlers at an inn. Mr. Blick at once began to blarney the standers–by into joining, while I, sitting at a little table, in the open air, wrote out copies of a letter addressed to the local gentry. My copies were carried from Lyme by messengers that afternoon but, alas for my master, they did not bring many gentry to us.

Now while I was writing at the table, under the great flapping standard, with the Duke, in his purple coat, walking about in front of me, I had a pretty full view of the crowd which ringed us in. We were circled about by a crowd of gaping admirers; from whom, every minute, Mr. Blick, or the Duke, or Lord Grey, would select a sheepish grinning man to serve under our colours. Among the crowd I noticed a little old lame man with a long white beard. He was a puppet–man, who was making the people laugh by dancing his puppets almost under the Duke's nose. As he jerked the puppet–strings, he played continually on his pan–pipes the ribald tune of "Hey, boys, up go we," then very popular. The Duke spoke to him once; but he did not answer, only bowed very low, with his hat off, which made the people think him an idiot or a jester. They laughed heartily at him. After a bit, it occurred. to me that this old puppet–shaker always crept into the ring (with his hat off to receive alms) whenever the Duke spoke aside to Lord Grey, or to some other officer. I watched him narrowly to make sure, because something in his manner made me suspect that he was trying to catch what our leaders said to each other. I tried to recall where I had seen the old man; for I had seen him before. He had been at Exeter on the day we set out for Sidmouth, so much I remembered clearly; but looking at him carefully, with my head full of memories of faces, it seemed to me that he had been at Dorchester also. Surely an old man, lame in the left leg like this man, had gone down a narrow lane in front of me in Dorchester. I had not thought of it in Dorchester; but I thought of it now, with a feeling that it was strange to meet again thus in Lyme. I took good stock of the man, wondering if he were a spy. He was a dirty old man enough. His dirty fingers poked through ragged mittens. His cheeks were all swathed up in a woollen comforter. I made the mistake of looking at him so hard that I made him look at me. Seeing that I was staring at him, with a face full of suspicion, he walked boldly up to me, holding out his hat for my charity. We stared at each other, while he blew a blast on his pan—pipes, at which everybody laughed.

"Come, come, boy," said Lord Grey to me, "we want those letters done. Never mind about the puppets. Here, old man" (giving him a penny), "you take yourself off now. Or are you going to enlist?"

The people laughed again at this, while the old man, after a flourish of his hat to me, piped up lively quickstep, called "Jockeys to the Fair."

He disappeared after this. I did not see him again until our troubles began, later in the morning. I was finishing off the last of my letters, when some of our scouts rode in to make a grave report to the Duke. They had ridden in pretty hard, their horses were lathered all over. They themselves were in an internal lather; for they had just had their first sight of war. They had come into touch (so they declared) with the whole of Albemarle's militia, marching out to attack them. On being questioned, it turned out that they had heard this from an excited labourer who had run to them with the news, as they stood guard in a roadside field a few miles out of Lyme. They themselves had seen nothing, but the news seemed so probable that the Duke acted on it. He sent me off at once with a message to a clever, handsome gentleman who was in charge of the cavalry in the street. It was in giving the message that I saw the old man again. He was them limping up the street on the. Sidmouth road, going fast, in spite of his lameness. I gave my message to the captain, who commanded his trumpeter to call to arms. The trumpeter blew nobly; but the sight of the confusion afterwards showed me how little raw troops can be trusted. There was a hasty scramble for horses rather than a setting forth. Some men quarreled over weapons; others wrestled with harness; others ran about wildly, asking what was happening, was it to be a battle, what did blowing .on the trumpet mean? Some few, thinking the worst, got wisdom in those few moments. They took horses from the ranks, but instead of forming up with the regiments, they galloped off home, having had enough of soldiering at the first order. The foot behaved rather better, knowing, perhaps, that if they fought they would be behind hedges, in some sort of shelter. Even so, they seemed a raw lot of clumsy bumpkins as they marched up. Many of them were in ploughmen's smock—frocks; hardly any of them had any sense of handling their guns. They had drums with them, which beat up a quickstep, giving each man of them a high sense of his importance, especially if he had been drinking. People in the roadway cheered them, until they heard that there was to be a battle. Those who were coming in to join us found it a reason for hesitation.

Martin Hyde, The Duke's Messenger

After a lot of confusion, the army drew out of Lyme along the Sidmouth road, followed by a host of sightseers. Some of the best mounted rode on ahead at a trot, under the handsome man, Mr. Fletcher, who was their captain. I followed on with the foot-soldiers, who marched extremely slowly. They halted at their own discretion; nor did they seem to understand that orders given were to be obeyed. What they liked, poor fellows, was to see the women admiring them. The march up the hill out of Lyme was a long exhibition of vanity, the women waving their handkerchiefs, the men putting on all sorts of airs, jetting like gamecocks. When we got up to the top of the hill, I saw the old lame puppet-man, sitting on the edge of the wild, unenclosed, gorse-covered common-land which stretches away towards the town of Axminster. He was watching us with deep interest. Our men were spreading out into line upon this common. The horse was ranging on, bobbing about, far ahead. The foot were looking about eagerly as they got out of the ranks in which they had marched; but they could see no trace of any enemy. I caught sight of the Duke four hundred yards away, a little figure sitting alone on his horse, in front of half a dozen others. They were all scanning the country, all the way round. Presently I called out that I saw the enemy. Half a dozen cavalry were riding up a combe far off. But they were our own men, not the militia. They were some of our scouts riding off as "feelers" to spy out Albemarle's position. All the time that we were up there on the hill, the little old man portered about among the men, now listening to what they had to say, now asking the soldiers to look at his pretty puppets. When the returning scouts brought word that no troops were near us, so that we were free to march back again, he was still there, packing up his puppets in tarred canvas, as though about to march off to the next market-town. We marched past him, as he sat in the heather. I passed quite close to him, staring at him hard, for to tell the truth he was on my mind. I was suspicious of him. He took off his hat to me, with a smile; but he did not speak. Then my troops swung round, down the hill, leaving him alone there, watching the men pass.

Other things put him out of my mind during the afternoon. I was kept busy writing orders to scouts; for we were sending out scouts in every direction, partly to protect us from surprise, partly to direct new recruits to our headquarters. Mr. Blick, who knew the ground dictated the letters, helped by Mr. Fletcher, who studied a big map with great attention; I was writing all that afternoon. Lyme grew noisier during the day, as the recruits became more drunk. Many steady men turned away from us when they saw our disorder. I myself had been brought up to abhor drunkenness. I found the state of drunken uproar very terrible. I feared that such an army would never achieve any great deed. I thought that such sin would be punished. Our soldiers were not behaving like knights sworn to a good cause; but like boors at a fair. That day we lost our only good officer, Mr. Fletcher.

I have spoken of this gentleman. He was in command of the horse under Lord Grey. He was a much better soldier than my Lord; a better officer, too; a better man. Now in the day's confusion, with everything topsy turvy, the Duke's messenger, "Old Dare," rode into Lyme from Taunton, where he had galloped the day before to spread the news of our arrival. This Dare was a quick−tempered, not very clever, popular man with a great deal of influence in the countryside. On his way back to us from Taunton, someone lent, or gave, him a very fine horse. It may have been meant as a gift to the Duke; I do not know. Anyhow Old Dare rode in on this horse with letters from Taunton, which he handed to Mr. Fletcher to give to the Duke. Fletcher, our cavalry commander, had as yet no horse; so seeing the splendid charger on which Old Dare rode, he ordered Old Dare to give it up to him. He was the real commander of the army, with a military right, if no real right, to take what horse he liked from any subordinate officer. But Old Dare, like so many of our men, had no knowledge of what soldier's discipline meant. He saw, in Fletcher, a gentleman with whom he had lived as an equal for the last fortnight. He was not going to give up his horse like that; not he. Fletcher (speaking sharply) told him to obey without further words, at which Dare in a sudden flush of temper struck him with his riding switch. Fletcher was not a patient man. He could not let an act of gross mutiny pass unpunished, nor would he suffer an insult. He shot Dare dead upon the spot, in full view of some hundreds of us. It was all done in an instant. There was Dare lying dead, never to stir again. There was Fletcher, our only soldier, with a smoking pistol in his hand, thinking that he had taught the army a lesson in obedience. There was the army all about him, flocking round in a swarm, not looking at it as a military punishment but as a savage murder, for which he deserved to be hanged. Then the Duke hastened up to make things quiet, before the army avenged their friend. He drew Fletcher aside, though the people murmured at him for speaking to a murderer. He was unnerved by Fletcher's act. He had no great vitality. Sudden crises such as this unnerved him, by using up his forces. A crisis of this kind (a small thing in a great rebellion) was often enough to keep his brain from considering other, more important, more burning questions concerning the entire army. The end of this business was as unhappy as its beginning. Fletcher, our only soldier, was sent aboard the frigate in which the Duke had sailed from Holland. When the tide served, she set sail with him for Corunna in Spain. With him she carried all our hopes of success, together with a quantity of stores which would have been of use later in the expedition. As I left the Cobb, or pier, which makes Lyme harbour, I saw the little lame puppet−man turning away from the beach with a company of men who wore our green boughs. For a few steps I hurried towards him, so that I might overhear what he was saying; I made so sure that he was a spy. Mr. Blick, to whom I told my fears, bade me not to worry myself. "Why, boy," he said, "there are five hundred spies in Lyme; but they can't hurt us. Before they can get off to tell our enemies all about us there won't be any enemies left. We shall be marching at once. We shall drive everything before us." He spoke with such confidence that I believed him; yet the old man troubled me, for all that. When you see a face continually, at a time when you are excited, you connect the face with your excitement; it troubles your nerves.

The day wore by with all the unreality of a day of confusion. I was kept at work until the light was gone; then served at the Duke's table while he supped, then snatched a hurried supper while he talked with his officers. After supper, I had to go from billet to billet, looking for people whom the officers wished to see. Something very important was in the air. The discussion in the inn's great room was the first serious council of the war. About eleven o'clock, Lord Grey came out of the room, telling me to follow him. We went out into the street, where presently our men began to fall in, four or five abreast, about a hundred ranks of them. A few cavalry came, too, but not enough, I heard Lord Grey say, not enough to do any good with. In spite of all the efforts of those who loved us (by efforts I mean the robbing of farm–stables) we were very short of horses. Those which we had were not good; they were cart, not saddle–horses, unused to the noise of guns. Still, such as they were, they formed up in the street ahead of the foot. The force took a long time to form; for the men kept saying that they had forgotten something, their powder–horn, their cartridges, their guns, even. Then they had to run back to their billets to fetch whatever it was, while those who remained behind, puzzled at the movement so late at night, when they wished to sleep, began to get nervous. They began to ask where it was that we were going, was it to Axminster, or to Bridport

CHAPTER XVII. A VOICE AT DAWN

Word was passed about that we were going to surprise the militia at Bridport at dawn. We were told to keep quiet on the march, after passing Charmouth, as the night was so still that we should be heard far off. We did not know how near the Bridport outposts might come to us under cover of the night. "You come with us, Martin," said Lord Grey: "Take a horse. If we win Bridport you'll have to gallop back with the news." I was made a little nervous by the thought of going into battle so soon; but gulping down my fears I mounted a marsh–mare which stood near the inn door. I hoped sincerely that no militia bullet would find any part of either of us. Then the drums began to play us out of the town with their morning roll. A fife whined out, going down to our marrows with its shrillness. Lights showed at the windows. We saw dark heads framed in yellow patches. People called to us. In the door of the great inn stood Monmouth; his face seemed very white in the glare of the torches. He raised his hand to us as we passed him. The last thing I noticed of the town, for I rode in the rear with Lord Grey, were the ranks passing the lamp on the town hall. They came up to it in waves, their cloaks showing in glimmer for an instant. Then they passed on into the night, sliding forwards slowly with a steady roll, like the moving of waves to the shore.

We were a long time riding; so long that the dawn was on us by the time we were within shot of the enemy. I don't remember very much about the ride, except that it was unreal, very unreal; for the mists came down, blotting the world from us, so that we rode in a swirl of cold grey, amid a noise of dropping. When we got to the top of the long hill after Chideock I was bidden halt at a cross–roads, with a waggon full of ammunition, while the force moved on to the attack. The hills were showing up clearly above the mist; but the valley lay like a sea, a great grey formless level, like some world of the ghosts. The troops passed down in it, moving pretty briskly, lest the mist should lift before they were in position. Most of them knew the country, so that they could well walk confidently; but their quickness had something nervous in it, as though they were ill at ease. Very soon they were out of sight, out of hearing, swallowed up in the fog.

I waited a long time (as it seemed) up there at the cross–roads. After a long wait I rode a little down the hill, from sheer anxiety. I pulled up in a bank of cloud, through which I could see dimly, in the growing light, for about a dozen yards. I was leaning well forward, listening for the sound of shooting, when something made me look down. Someone was standing at my side, slipping something into my pocket. It gave me a start. I clutched at the person. It was the old lame puppet–man who had been at Lyme the day before. "Latter for ee," he said in a whisper. "Read en, unless you'm a fool." His hand pressed lightly on my bridle hand for an instant; then he ducked sideways swiftly into the wilderness of ferny gorse at the side of the road, where I could not hope to follow him, even if the mist had not hidden him. Something in the voice, something in the lightness of the touch startled me into the knowledge. As he ducked, it came over me that this old man was Aurelia disguised, come to spy upon us, but bent, also, on giving me a warning, some little kind word of advice, at the beginning of my lord's war. I ought to have recognized her before. I had been blind. She had been under my eyes the whole day, yet I had never once suspected, no one, of all that army, had suspected. She had been disguised by a master–hand. She had played her part like a great actress. It was terrible to think of the risk she was running. One man's suspicion, in a time of war, would have been enough to give her to a horrible death. I tried to follow her into the jungle into which she had vanished; but my horse would not face the furze. I tried hard to see her, but it was no use; the tangle was too thick; she had gone. I called out to her softly; but I got no answer; only, at some little distance away, I heard a twig snap under a passer's foot.

In a momentary clearing of the mist, I pulled out my letter. It was written in a fine, firm hand, with signature. It was a short, purposeful letter, which kept sharply to the point. It only contained two lines. "Your Duke's cause is hopeless. He has no possible chance. Take the Axminster road to safety." That was the whole letter. It gave me a feeling of uneasiness; but it did not tempt me to desert. I thought that if I deserted I might very well be tortured into betraying all that I knew of the Duke's plans, while I doubted very much whether the Duke's body– servant would find mercy from the merciless, frightened King. What was I to do, even if I escaped from the King's party? I was too young for any employment worthy of my station in life. I had neither the strength nor the skill for manual labour. Who would employ a boy of my age on a farm or in a factory? All that I could hope would be to get away to sea, to a life which I had already found loathsome. As to going back to my uncle's house, I doubt if I would have gone, even had I had the certainty of getting to it safely. When a boy has once taken to an adventurous life, nothing but very ill health will drive him back to home–life. Yet there was the thought of Aurelia. Somehow the thought of her was a stronger temptation than any fear of defeat. I would have liked to have seen that old enemy of mine again.

I was thinking over the letter, wondering what would come to the Duke's cause, when the valley below me began to ring with firing. A heavy fire had begun there. It thundered in a long roll, which died down, momentarily, into single sputterings through which one could hear shouting. About twenty minutes after the beginning of the shots, when all the party on the hill–top were edging nearer to the battle, taking a few steps at a time, on tenter–hooks to be engaged, we heard a great gallop of horses' hoofs coming to us at full tilt. At first we were scared by this, for the noise was tremendous, too great, we inexperienced soldiers thought, to be caused by our little troop of cavalry. We thought that it was the Bridport militia charging down on us, after destroying our friends. The mist by this time was all blowing clear, though wisps of it clung along the hedgerows in unreal rolling folds. The day above was breaking in the sultry blue summer dimness. We could see, I suppose, for a quarter of a mile, straight down the road.

We had swung round, facing towards Lyme, when the noise of the hoofs first came to us. When the turn of the road showed us a squad of cavalry coming to us at the charge, led by half a dozen riderless horses, we waited for no more. We spurred up our nags in a panic, till we, too, were going full tilt for Lyme, shouting out as we went any nonsense which came to our heads. We were in a panic fear; I believe that the horses in some way felt it too. We galloped back to Chideock as though we were chased by witches, while the gun–firing at Bridport steadily grew less, till at last it stopped altogether. At Chideock, some of the cavalry came up with us. They were our own men, our own troop of horse, not an enemy after all. The riderless horses were a few of the militia charges which had been seized from a cavalry outpost to the west of the town. We had bolted from our own crazy terror. But we were not the only fleers. Our cavalry had bolted first, at the first volley outside the town. It is unjust to say that they were afraid. Lord Grey was not a coward; our men had stout hearts enough; but they had not reckoned on the horses. The first discharge of guns scared the horses almost frantic. They swung about out of action in a couple of seconds. Another volley made them all bolt. It was when they were bolting that the men began to grow alarmed. Fear is a contagious thing; it seems to pass from spirit to spirit, like a flame along a powder train, till perhaps a whole army feels it. Our horsemen pulled up among us in Chideock in as bad a scare as you ever saw; it was twenty minutes before they dared walk back to find out what had happened to the foot at Bridport, after their retreat.

Our foot came back very angry with the horse. They had fired away a lot of powder to very little purpose, before orders reached them, bidding them retire. They had not wished to retire; but at last they had done so sullenly, vowing to duck Lord Grey for deserting them. We had taken about a dozen horses without harness, instead of the two hundred equipped chargers which we had promised ourselves.

We had killed a few of the militia, so everybody said; but in the confusion of the powder–smoke who could say how many? They were certain that none of our own men had been killed; but in a force so newly raised, who could say for certain which were our own men? As a matter of fact several of our men had been taken by the royalists, which is as much as to say that they had been killed. Altogether the affair had been a hopeless failure from the very beginning. The foot had learned to despise the horse. The horses had learned to be afraid of gun–fire. The cavalrymen had learned to despise Lord Grey. The militia had learned to despise us. The only valuable lesson that our men had learned was that a battle was not so terrible a thing. You knelt down, fired your gun, shouted, borrowed your neighbour's drinking bottle, took a long swig, then fired again, with more shouting, till somebody clapped you on the shoulder with orders to come away. But this lesson, precious as it was did not console our men for their beating. They were cross with the long night–march as well as with Lord Grey's desertion. We dragged our way back to Lyme very slowly, losing a good fifty of our number by desertion. They slipped away home, after falling out of the ranks to rest. They had had enough of fighting for the Duke; they were off home. The officers were strict at first, trying to stop these desertions; but the temper of the men was so bad that at last they gave it up, hoping that some at least would stay. That was another evil consequence of fighting for the crown with an undisciplined mob; they could sustain defeat as ill as they could use victory. We did not trail into Lyme until after noon; for we marched like snails, fearing that the militia would follow us. When we got into camp, the men flung their arms from them, careless of the officer's orders. All that they wanted was sleep (we had eaten a late breakfast at Charmouth), they were not going to do any more soldier's foolery of drill, or sentry–go. As for Lord Grey, whom everybody called a coward, the Duke could not cashier him, because he was the best officer remaining to us. Poor Fletcher, who might have made something of our cavalry, was by this time far away at sea. The other officers had shown their incapacity that morning. For my own part, I chose out a snug billet on a hearthrug in the George Inn, where I slept very soundly for several hours. While I slept, the Duke held a melancholy council to debate what could be done.

They say that he ought to have marched that morning to Exeter, where Lord Albemarle's militia (all of them ripe for rebellion) would have joined him.

Exeter or Bristol, one or the other, would have been a fine plume in his cap, a strong, fortified town, full of arms, where he could have established himself firmly. I do not know why he decided against marching to Exeter. He may have had bad reports of troops being on the road waiting for him; or he may have thought that his friends (who were plentiful on the Bristol road) would rally to him as soon as he appeared. He was deceived by those protesting gentry, his friends, who had welcomed him so warmly only a few months before. He thought that all the countryside was ready to join him. He had been deceived, as perhaps a cleverer man would have been deceived, by the warmth of his welcome on his earlier visit. An Englishman is always polite to a Duke when he meets him in a friendly gathering. But when the Duke says, "Lend me all your ready money, together with your horses, or rather give them to me, since I am the King," his politeness leaves him; he gets away to London to warn the police as fast as his horse will take him. Thus it was with the Duke's friends scattered about along the main–road from Lyme to Bristol.

I know not who persuaded the Duke to march; probably it was Grey; it may have been Venner; it may have been a momentary mad resolution caused by a glass of wine. They say that he was solemn about it, as though he expected to fail. Perhaps he would have gone back to Holland if the ship had been still in the harbour, but of course she had gone away. He would not go in La Reina; for she was sluggish from barnacles, having been long un–careened. The Channel at this time was full of ships looking for him; how he escaped them when he sailed from Holland I cannot think. He hesitated for a long time, poor man, before deciding; no man could have acted more like a Stuart, at such a time. When the decision was made he gave word to start early on the following morning. But this I did not know till one A.M, when Lord Grey routed me out from my berth on the hearth–rug, so that I might go from house to house, calling up our officers.

I suppose that all our officers were out of bed by two o'clock, yet it took them eight hours to get their men together, into some sort of order. We were hardly ready for the road at ten A.M. when the drums beat up to play us out of the town. As I was the Duke's servant, I was allowed to ride by my master; I daresay people thought that I was the young Prince. We marched up the hill gaily, with a multitude flocking all about us, but there were many of that crowd who looked doubtfully at my master's sad face, thinking that he looked over–melancholy for a conquering king.

We marched out of Lyme into a valley, through a sort of suburb called Uplyme. After that we marched steadily up hill, a long climb of two miles, having a great view of the countryside on our left hand. Our right was shut from us by a wooded hill. It was a warm, sunny June day: the grass just ripe for hay harvest; the country at its best; everything at its full flower, so that you wondered at the world's abundance. We sent out scouts, when we were about a mile from Lyme; but when we were at the top of the hill we could see for ourselves, without putting scouts abroad. We could see horsemen on the high ground away to the left, two or three hundred of them. Besides these there were some companies of foot drawn up in good order in the fields outside Axminster, at some distance from the town. When this army caught sight of us, it began to file off towards the town, as though to dispute it with us, so our advanced guard pushed on to drive them out of it. The sight of so many men in order, was a very moving one. To see them advance their colours, to see the light on the shifting steel, to hear the low beating hum of the feet was stirring to the heart. Word ran along the line that there was going to be a battle. Our foot left the road, so as to spread out into line in the open, where they could take up positions behind hedges. I was sent back to the rear at this instant, to order up the ammunition waggons, so that I missed some part of the operations; but I shall never forget how confidently our men spread out; they marched as though they were going into the fields for partridges. The drums began again, to hearten them, but there was no need for drums in that company; they began to sing of their own accord, making a noise which drowned the drums altogether. I gave my orders to the ammunition waggons, which were blocked in a jumble of sightseers, camp–followers, etc., etc., so that they could hardly move. The drivers got me to charge my horse through the mob to make a path, which I did, with a good deal of pain to myself, for the people thus thrust aside struck at me. The drivers struck out at them in return; we had a little fight of our own, while Axminster was being won.

CHAPTER XVIII. I SPEAK WITH AURELIA

The next thing which I remember was coming out of the mob with the waggons just behind me, going at a smart pace to a position on the army's right. The road was pretty full of all sorts of people; but as we shouted for them to clear the way, they made a lane for us. I saw the Duke's little clump of staff–officers on a pitch of rising ground, but there was no firing; only a noise of many voices singing. Just as we were about to turn off the road into the fields behind our right wing, I saw the little old lame puppet–man sitting on a donkey by the ditch at the side of the road. I shouted to the drivers to pass on, which they did, at full tilt, while I drew rein by the old man's side. "Aurelia," I said, "this is no place for you. Do get away from here before they find you out."

"Why," she said, very calmly, in the broad burring man's voice which she imitated so exactly. "I be come 'ere to find you out. You'm going to your death, boy. You get out of this 'ere army afore you're took. I tell ee thy Duke be a doomed man. Look at en's face. Why, boy, there be eleven thousand soldiers a–marching to put er down. You've only a got a quarter of that lot. Come out of en, boy. Do–an't ee be led wrong." I was touched by her kind thought for me; she was risking her life for me for the second time, but in the hurry of the moment I could not put words together to thank her.

"Aurelia," I said, "I can't talk to you now. Only get out of this. Don't stay here. I'm all right."

"No, Martin," she said, in her ordinary voice, "you're not all right. Come out of this. Slip away tonight to Newenham Abbey. It be over there, not more than a couple of miles. Oh, come, come. I can't bear to see you going away to certain death. I KNOW that this force cannot win."

"Yes, Aurelia," I answered. "But I'm not going to be a hang–back for all that. I'm not going to be a coward. You risk a horrible death, only to tell me not to do the same. You wouldn't give up a cause you believed in, merely because it was dangerous. I'll stick by my master, Aurelia. Don't try to tempt me."

She would have said more; she would perhaps have persuaded me from my heroics, had not the guns begun firing. That broke the spell with a vengeance; nothing could be done after that. I shook up my horse, hardly pausing to say "God bless you." In another minute she was out of sight, while I was cantering off to the extreme right wing with the Duke's orders to his officers to cut in on the road to Chard. As I rode along, behind the scattered line of our men, I could see the rolls of smoke from the firing on the left. The men on the right were not firing, but being raw troops they were edging little by little towards the firing, in which I do not doubt they longed to be, for the sake of the noise. They say now that the Duke threw away this battle at Axminster. He could have cut Albemarle's troops to pieces had he chosen to do so. They made a pretty bold front till we were within gunfire of them, when they all scattered off to the town pell–mell. While they were in the town, we could have cut them off from the Chard road, which would have penned them in while we worked round to seize the bridges. After that, one brisk assault would have made the whole batch of them surrender. Some of our officers galloped from our right wing (where I was) to see how the land lay, before leading off their men as I had brought them word. A few of them fired their pistols, when they came to the road, which was enough to make the right wing double forward to support them without orders. In a minute about a thousand of us were running fast after our officers, while the Duke's aides charged down to stop us. He had decided not to fight, probably thinking that it would do his cause no good by killing a lot of his subjects so early in his reign. We know now that had he made one bold attack that morning, the whole of Albemarle's force, with the exception of a few officers, would have declared for him. In other words we should have added to our army about a thousand drilled armed men who knew the country through which we were to pass. By not fighting, we discouraged our own army, who grumbled bitterly when they found their second battle as ineffectual as the fight at Bridport.

I remember next that I saw the whole of Albemarle's troops flying for their lives along the Chard road, flinging away their weapons as they ran. They had the start of us; but a resolute captain could have brought them to a stand, by pushing forward his cavalry. However "a bridge of gold to a flying foe" is a good saying. We let them go. When our cavalry advanced (to keep them on the move, not to fight with them) they passed the time in collecting what the militia had flung away; about four thousand pounds' worth of soldiers' stores, chiefly uniforms. I went forward with the horse on that occasion. I picked up altogether about a dozen muskets, which I gave to some of our men who were armed only with clubs. Then I rode back to report myself ready for service to my master, who was getting ready for camp, thinking that his men had done enough for one day.

It was a sad waste of time. A rough camp was formed. We went no further for that time. About half a precious day was wasted, which might have brought us nearly to Taunton under a resolute man, sworn to conquer. Some of our men went out to forage, which they did pretty roughly. It was theft with violence, coloured over by some little touch of law. The farmers who were unpopular thereabouts had their cattle driven off; their ricks carted off; their horses stolen; their hen–roosts destroyed. We were like an army of locusts, eating up everything as we passed. Our promises to pay, when the King came to his own, were really additional insult; for the people robbed knew only too well how Stuart kings kept their promises. One strange thing I saw that night. The men who were cooking their newly stolen beef at the camp–fires kept crying out for camp–kettles in which to boil the joints. We had no camp–kettles; but an old man came forward to the Duke's quarters to ask if he might show the men how to cook their meat without kettles. The Duke at once commanded him to show us how this might be done. Like most useful inventions, it was very simple. It was one of those things which are forgotten as life becomes civilised, but for want of which one may perish when one returns to barbarity, as in war. The old man began by placing stout poles in tripods over the camp–fires, lashing them firmly at the top with faggot–binders. Then he took the hide of one of the slaughtered cattle, gathering it up at the corners, so as to form a sort of bag. He cut some long narrow strips from the hide of the legs, with which to tie the four corners together. Then he lashed the four corners to the tripod, so that the bag hung over the fire.

"There," he said. "There is your kettle. Now put water into en. Boil thy victuals in er. That be a soldier's camp–kettle. You can carry your kettle on your beef till you be ready for en."

Indeed, it proved to be a very good kind of a kettle after one got used to the nastiness of it, though the smell of burning hair from the kettles was disgusting. To this day, I have only to singe a few hairs in a candle to bring back to my mind's eye that first day in camp at Axminster, the hill, the valley ringed in by combes, the noise of the horses, the sputtering of the fires of green wood, the many men passing about aimlessly, wondering at the ease of a soldier's life after the labour of spring ploughing. It was a wonderful sight, that first camp of ours; but the men for the most part grumbled at not fighting; they wanted to be pushing on, to seize the city of Bristol, instead of camping there. How did they know, they said, that the weather would keep fine? How were we to march with all our ten baggage waggons if the weather turned wet, so that the roads became muddy? The roads in those parts became deep quagmires in rainy weather. A light farmer's market cart might go in up to the axles after a day's steady rain. To march through such roads would break the men's hearts quicker than any quantity of fighting, however disastrous. Thus they grumbled about the camp–fires, while I bustled over the Duke's dinner, in the intervals of running errands for the colonel.

That evening, after the summer dusk had come, but before the army had settled to sleep, I heard an old man, one of our cavalrymen, talking to another trooper. "Ah," he said, "I was fighting in the old wars under Oliver. I've seen wars enough. You mark my words, boy, this army won't do much. We've not got enough men, for one thing. We could have had fourteen thousand or more if he'd thought to bring muskets for en. We've not got cavalry, that's another thing. When us do come face to face with all the King's men us shall be sore put to it for want of a few trusty horses. Horsemen be the very backbones of armies in the field. Then, boy, we not got any captains, that's worst of all. The Duke's no captain. If he'd been a captain her'd have fought this morning. Them others aren't captains neither, none of them. Besides, what are they doing sitting down in camp like this when we ought to be marching? Us ought to be marching. Marching all night, never setting down once, marching in two armies, one to Exeter, one to Bristol. Us'd 'ave the two towns by late tomorrow night if us was under old Oliver. It'll take us a week to get to Bristol at this rate. By that time it will be full of troops, as well as secured by ships. As for us, by that time we shall have troops all round us, not to speak of club–men."

"Ah," said the younger man. "What be club–men, gaffer?"

"You'll know soon enough what club–men are," the old man answered, "if there's any more of this drunken dirty robbery I saw this afternoon. Those thieves who stole the farmer's cattle would have been shot in Oliver's time. They'd have cast lots on a drum in sight of all on us, drawn up. The men who got the low numbers would have been shot. The captains would have pistolled them where they stood. If this robbing goes on, all the farmers will club together to defend themselves, making a sort of second army for us to fight against. That is what club–men means. It's not a nice thing to fight in a country where there are club–men all round you. No, boy. So what with all this, boy, I be going to creep out of this 'ere army. I do–an't like the look of things, nor I do–an't like the way things are done. If you take a old man's advice you'll come too."

"Noa," said the honest oaf, "I be agoin' to vight. I be a–goin' to London town to be a girt sol–dier."

"Ah," said the old man, shortly, "you be a vule, Tummas. Wish ee good day, maister." Then the old man turned sharply on his heel to leave the camp, which he did easily enough, for he knew several of the sentries. Even if he had not known them, it would have made little difference, because our sentries were so lax that the camp was always swarming with strangers. Women came to see their husbands or sweethearts. Boys came out of love of mischief. Men came out of curiosity, or out of some wish to see things before they decided which side to take. Our captains were never sure at night how many of their men would turn up at muster the next morning.

After the old man had deserted, I sat down on the high ground above the camp, in the earthen battery where our four little guns were mounted. I was oppressed with a sad feeling that we were all marching to death. The old man's words, "we shall have troops all round us," rang in my head, till I could have cried. My mind was full of terrible imaginings. I saw our army penned up in a little narrow valley where the roads were quagmires, so that our guns were stuck in the mud, our horses up to their knees, our men floundering. On the hills all round us I saw the King's armies, fifty thousand strong, marching to music under the colours, firing, then wheeling, forming with a glint of pikes, bringing up guns at a gallop, shooting us down, while we in the mud tried to form. I knew that the end of it all would be a little clump of men round the Duke, gathered together on a hillock, holding out to the last. The men would be dropping as the shot struck them. The wounded would waver, letting their pike–points drop. Then' there would come a whirling of cavalry, horses' eyes in the smoke, bright iron horse–shoes gleaming, swords crashing down on us, an eddy of battle which would end in a hush as the last of us died. I saw all these pictures in my brain, as clearly as one sees in a dream. You must not wonder that I looked over the misty fields towards Newenham Abbey with a sort of longing to be there, well out of all the war. It was only a mile from me. I could slip away so easily. I was not bound to stay where I was, to share in the misery caused by my leader's want of skill. Then I remembered how my father had believed in the right of the Duke's cause. He would have counselled me to stay, I thought. It seemed to me, in the dusk of the night, that my father was by me, urging me to stay. The thought was very blessed; it cleared away all my troubles as though they had not been. I decided to look no more towards Newenham; but to go on by the Duke's side to whatever fortune the wars might bring us. Somehow, the feeling that my father was by me, made me sure that we were marching to victory. I went to my quarters comforted, sure of sleeping contentedly.

Like the rest of us, I had to sleep in the open, without any more shelter than a horse–cloth. Even the Duke was without a tent that night. He slept in camp with us, to set an example to his men, though he might well have gone to some house in the town. I liked the notion of sleeping out in the open. In fine warm summer weather, when the dew is not too heavy, it is pleasant, until a little before the dawn, when one feels uneasy, for some reason, as though an enemy were coming. Perhaps our savage ancestors, the earliest ancient Britons, who lived in hill–camps, high up, with their cattle round them, expected the attacks of their enemies always at a little before the dawn; so that, in time, the entire race learned to be wakeful then, lest the enemy should catch the slumberers, with flint–axe heads in the skull. It may be that to this day we feel the fear felt by so many generations of our ancestors. On this first night in camp, I found that many of the men were sleeping uneasily, for they did not know the secret of sleeping in the open. They did not know that to sleep comfortably in the open one must dig a little hole in the ground, about as big as a porridge bowl, to receive one's hipbone. If you do this, you sleep at ease, feeling nothing of the hardness of the bed. If you fail to do it, you wake all bruised, after a wretched night's tumbling; you ache all the next day.

After grubbing up a hollow with my knife, I swathed myself in my blanket with a saddle for pillow. I watched the stars for a while, as they drifted slowly over me. The horses stamped, shaking their picket-ropes. The sentries walked their rounds, or came to the camp-fires to call their reliefs. The night was full of strange noises. The presence of so many sleeping men was strange. It was very beautiful, very solemn. It gave one a kind of awe to think that thus so many famous armies had slept before the battles of the world, before Pharsalia, before Chalons, before Hstings. Presently the murmuring became so slight that I fell asleep, forgetting everything, only turning uneasily from time to time, to keep the cool night wind from blowing on my cheeks so as to wake me.

It must have been two in the morning when I was wakened by some armed men, evidently our sentries, who rolled me over without ceremony.

"Wake up, young master," they said, grinning. "You'm wanted. You be to get up to go a errand. You be a soldier now. You does your sleeping in peace-times when you be a soldier," I sat up blinking my eyes, in the early light, thinking how nice t'other forty winks would be.

"Heigho," I yawned. "All right. I'm awake. What is it? What's the matter?"

"Lord Grey be a wanting you, young master," said one of the men. "Down there, where them horses be in the road." I picked myself up at that, wishing for a basin of water into which I might shove my head.

"Yes, yes," I said. "Thank you. I'll go down." I left my blanket where it was, as I expected to be back in a few minutes. I walked down hill out of the camp to the road where the horses stood; there were four horses, two of them mounted. The mounted men were regular country bumpkins, with green sprays in their hats, like the rest of our men; but their horses were pretty good, much better than most of those we had. One of them was a stocky old cob, which was no doubt to be mine. The other was a beast with handsome harness for Lord Grey. "Alas," I thought. "No more sleep for me. I've got to ride. I wonder where we are going." The men touched their hats to me; for as I was in the Duke's retinue I was much respected. Some of them no doubt thought I was a princeling or little lord.

"Where are we going?" I asked the troopers.

"Going scouting out towards Colyton yonder, sir," said one of them. "Us be to pick up his Lordship in the town."

CHAPTER XIX. I MEET THE CLUB MEN

I wondered when I was to get breakfast; but I knew Lord Grey well enough to know that he was not a man to go willingly without food for more than a few hours at a time. Breakfast I should have presently, nor would it be skin–boiled beef, smelling of singed hair. So I mounted my cob with a good will. The first trooper rode by my side, the other waited for a moment to examine the feet of Lord Grey's charger. He trotted after us, leading the riderless horse, some fifty yards behind us. We trotted smartly through Axminster, where we set the dogs barking. People sprang from their beds when they heard us, fearing that we were an army coming to fight. We cantered out of the town over the river, heading towards a hilly country, which had few houses upon it. I looked back after leaving Axminster, to see if Lord Grey wanted me. He had mounted his horse somewhere in the town; but he was now a couple of hundred yards behind us, riding' with a third man, whom I judged to be Colonel Foukes, by his broad white regimental scarf. After we had gone a few miles, we came to a cross–roads where my guide bade me halt to wait for orders. The others had pulled up, too. I could see Lord Grey examining a map, while his horse sidled about across the road. The trooper who had been riding with him, joined us after a while, telling us to take the road to our right, which would take us, he said, towards Taunton. We were to keep our eyes skinned, he said, for any sign of armed men coming on the high–road from Honiton, so as to threaten our left flank. The gentlemen were going to scout towards the sea. At eight o'clock, if we had seen no trace of any armed force coming, we were to make for Chard, where we should find the Duke's army. We were to examine the roads for any signs of troops having passed recently towards Taunton. We were to enquire of the country people, if troops were abroad in that countryside, what troops they might be, how led, how equipped, etc. If we came across any men anxious to join the Duke we were to send them on to Chard or Ilminster, on the easterly road to Taunton. We were to ride without our green boughs, he said; so before starting on our road we flung them into the ditches. Lord Grey waved his hand to us, as he turned away with his friend. We took off our hats in reply, hardly in a soldierly salute; then we set off at a walk along the Taunton road. It is a lonely road leading up to the hills, a straight Roman road, better than any roads laid in England at that time; but a road which strikes horror into one, the country through which it runs is so bleak.

Martin Hyde, The Duke's Messenger

By about six o'clock (according to one of the troopers, who judged by the height of the sun) we were in a clump of firs high up on a hill, looking over a vast piece of eastern Devon. We had scouted pretty closely all round Honiton, examining the country people, without hearing of any troops. We were now looking out for some gleam upon a road, some rising of dust over a hedge, some scattering of birds even, any sign of men advancing, which might be examined more closely. The morning was bright; but the valleys had mist upon them, which would soon turn to the quivering blue June heat–haze. The land lay below us, spread out in huge folds; the fields, all different colours, looked like the counties on a map; we could see the sea, we could see the gleam of a little river. We could see Axminster far to the east of us; but the marching army was out of sight, somewhere on the Chard high–road. After scanning pretty well all around us, I caught sight of moving figures on the top of one of the combes to south of us. We all looked hard at the place, trying to make out more of them. They were nearly a mile from us. They seemed to be standing there as sentries. At first we thought that they must be people with Lord Grey; but as we could see no horses we decided that they could not be. One of the men said that as far as:i,'l he'd heard tell like, the combe on which they stood was what they call a camp, where soldiers lived in the old time. He didn't know much more about it; but he said that he thought we ought to examine it, like, before riding on to some inn where we could breakfast.

The other man seemed to think so, too; but when we came to talk over the best way of doing our espials, we were puzzled. We should be seen at once if we went to them directly. We might be suspected if we approached them on horseback. If the men went, they might be detained, because, for all that we knew, the combe might be full of militia. So I said I had better go, since no one would suspect a boy. To this the men raised a good many objections, looking at each other suspiciously, plainly asking questions with their raised eyebrows. I thought at the time that they were afraid of sending me into a possible danger, because I was a servant attached to the Duke's person. However, when I said that I would go on foot, taking all precautions, they agreed grudgingly to let me go.

I crept along towards this combe on foot, as though I were going bird's nesting. I beat along by the hedges, keeping out of sight behind them, till I was actually on the combe's north slope, climbing up to the old earthwork on the top. I took care to climb the slope at a place where there was no sentry, which was, of course, not only the steepest bit of the hill but covered with gorse clumps, through which I could scarcely thrust my way. Up towards the top the gorse was less plentiful; there were immense foxgloves, ferns, little

128

marshy tufts where rushes grew, little spots of wet bright green moss. Yellow–hammers drawled their pretty tripping notes to me, not starting away, even when I passed close to them. All the beauty of June was on the earth that day; the beauty of everything in that intense blue haze was wonderful.

The top of the combe was very steep, steeper than any of the ascent, because it had been built up like an outer wall by the savages who once lived there with their cattle. I could see just the bare steep wall of the rampart standing up in a dull green line of short–grassed turf against the sky, now burning with the intense blue of summer. One hard quick scramble, with my fingernails dug into the ground, brought my head to the top of the rampart, beyond which I could see nothing but great ferns, a forest of great ferns, already four or five feet high, stretching away below, into the cup of the camp or citadel. I did not dare to stand up, lest I should be seen. I burrowed my way among the ferns over the wall into the hollow, worming my way towards the edge of the fern clump so that I could see. In a minute, I was gazing through the fern–stems into the camp itself; it was a curious sight.

About fifty people (some of them women) were sitting about a hollow in the ground, which I guessed to be a sort of smokeless fireplace or earth–oven. Everywhere else, all over the hollow of the camp, which must have been a full three hundred yards across, were various kinds of farm–stock, mostly cattle, though there were many picketed horses, too. At first I thought that I had climbed into a camp of gipsies, which gave me a scare; for gipsies then were a wild lot, whom wise folk avoided. Then, as I glanced about, I saw a sentry standing not thirty yards from me, but well above me, on the rampart top. He was no gipsy. tie was an ordinary farmer's lad, with the walk of a ploughman. His sleeves, which were rolled back, showed me a sun–burnt pair of arms, such as no gipsy ever had. What puzzled me about him was his heavy double–barrelled pistol, which he carried in his right hand, with something of a military cock, yet as though awed by it. He was not over sure of that same pistol. I could see that he confounded it in some way with art–magic.

Then I remembered what the old soldier had said the night before about club men. This camp must be a camp of club men, I thought. They had come there to protect their stock from the rapine of our vile pillagers, who had spread such terror amongst the farmers the day before. Perched up on the combe, with sentries always on the look–out, they could see the Duke's raiders long before they came within gunshot. If an armed force had tried to rush the camp, after learning that the beasts were shut up within it (which, by the way, no man could possibly suspect until he saw them from the rampart top), the few defenders clubbed together there could have kept them out without difficulty; for there was only one narrow entrance to the camp, so constructed that any one entering by it could be shot at from three sides, if not from all four. I looked about me carefully from my hiding–place, till I decided that I could get a better view from another part of the fern clump. I began to wriggle through the thick, sweet–scented stalks, towards the heart of the camp, going with infinite care, so as not to break down the fern into a path. I hoped to make no more stir among the fern–tops than would be made by one of the many pigs scattering about in the enclosure.

While I was crawling along in this way, I suddenly heard a curious noise from an intensely thick part of the fern in front of me. It was a clinking noise, followed by a sort of dry rasping, as though a very big person were gritting his teeth very hard. It stopped suddenly, but soon began again. I thought that it must be some one mending harness with a file, or perhaps some old sheep or cow, with the remnants of a bell about her neck, licking a stone for salt. As was in an adventure, I thought that I would see it out to the end; for I was enjoying my morning. In spite of the want of breakfast I felt very like a red Indian or a pirate, creeping through the jungle to the sack of a treasure train. So I wormed on towards the noise. As I came near to it, I went more cautiously, because in one of the pauses of the noise, I heard a muttered curse, which told me that the unseen noise–maker was a man. If I had been wise I should have stopped there; for I had learned all that I came out to learn. But I was excited now. I wished to see everything, before creeping away unseen to make my report. Perhaps I wished to see something which had nothing to do with the club men, a private main of cocks, say, or a dog, or bull–baiting, carried on with some of the squire's creatures, but without his knowledge. I had a half wish that I might have something of the kind to report; because in my heart I longed to say nothing to any of the Duke's party which might lead to the ruin of these poor people who were trying so hard to protect their property.

A few feet further on, I was wishing most heartily that I had never left my room in London. It was like this. In the very heart of the fern clump, where the ferns were tallest, a little spring bubbled out of the ground, at the rate, I suppose, of a pint of water in a minute. The ferns grew immensely thick there; but someone had thinned out a few of the roots from the ground, leaving the uprooted plant with the ferns still living, to form a rough kind of thatch above a piece of earth big enough for a man's body. In the scented shade of this thatch, with the side of his face turned towards me, a big, rough, bearded man sat, filing away some bright steel irons which were riveted on his ankles. He swore continually in a low whisper as he worked, not even pausing in his curses when he spat on to the hollow scraped in the irons by his file. He was the fiercest looking savage of a man I have ever seen. His face had a look of stern, gloomy cruelty which I shall never forget. His general appearance was terrible; for he had a face burnt almost black by the sun (some of it may have been mud) with a nasty white scar running irregularly all down his left cheek, along the throat to the shoulder. He was not what you might call naked. a naked man, such as I have seen since in the hot countries, would have looked a nobleman beside him. He wore a pair of dirty linen knickerbockers, all frayed into ribbons at the knees, a pair of strong hide slippers bound to his ankles by strips of leather, a part of a filthy red shirt without sleeves, a hat stolen from a scarecrow, nothing else whatever, except the mud of many days' gathering. His shirt was torn all down the back in a great slit which he had tried to secure by what the sailors call "Bristol buttons," i.e. pieces of string. The red flannel hung from him so as to show his back, all criss-crossed with flogging scars. I knew at once from the irons that he was a criminal escaped from gaol; but the criss-crossed scars taught me that he was a criminal of the most terrible kind, probably one who had shipped into the Navy to avoid hanging.

I took in a view of him before he saw me. His image was stamped on my brain in less than ten seconds. In the eleventh second, I was lying on my back in the gloom of the fern-growth, with this great ruffian on my chest, squeezing me by my windpipe. I cannot say that he spoke to me. It was not speech. It was the snarling wild beast gurgle which passes for speech in the slums of our great cities, as though all the filth of a low nature were choking in the throat at once. He was on me too quickly for me to cry out. I could only lie still, cackling for breath, while the fierce face glowered down on me. I understood him to say that he would have my windpipe out if I said a word. I suppose he saw that I was only a very frightened boy; for his clutch upon me relaxed, after a few awful, gasping moments. When he loosed his hold, his great hand pawed over my throat till he had me by the scruff of the neck. He drew me over towards the spring, as one would draw a puppy. Then, still crouching in the fern, he hurried me to a single stunted sloe-bush which grew there. "Go down, you," he said, giving me a shove towards the bush. "Down th' 'ole."

Just behind the sloe-bush, under a fringe of immense ferns, was an opening in the earth, about eighteen inches high, by two feet across. It was like a large rabbit or fox earth, except that the mouth of it was not worn bare. I did not like the thought of going down th' 'ole; but with this great griping fist on my nape there was not much sense in saying so. I wormed my way in, helped on by prods from the file. It was a melancholy moment when my head passed beyond the last filtering of light into the tomb's blackness, where not even insects lived. After a moment of scrambling I found that the passage was big enough for me to go on all fours. It was a dry passage, too, which seemed strange to me; but on reaching out with my hand I felt that the walls were lined with well laid stones, unmortared. The roof above me was also of stone. You may wonder why I did not shoot this ruffian with my pistol. You boys think that if you had a pistol you would shoot any one who threatened you. You would not. When the moment comes, it is not so easily disposed of. Besides, a filthy, cursing pirate on your throat checks your natural calm most strangely.

The passage led into the swell of the rampart for about twenty yards, where it opened into a dimly lighted chamber about four feet high. A little blink of light came through a rabbit hole, at the end of which I saw a spray of gorse with the sunlight on it. I could see by the dim light that the chamber was built of unmortared stones, very cleverly laid. The floor of it was greasier than the passage had been, but still it was not damp. On one side it had a bed of heather stalks, on the other there was something dark which felt like cold meat. The man came grunting in behind me, clinking his leg–irons. After groping about in a corner of the room he lighted a stinking rushlight by means of a tinder box.

CHAPTER XX. THE SQUIRE'S HOUSE

"There," he said, not unkindly, "there's a nice little 'ome for yer. Now you, tell me wot you were doing spying on me. First of all, 'ave you any money?" He did not wait for me to answer, but dug his hands into my pockets at once, taking every penny I had, except a few shillings which were hidden in my belt. He did not see my belt, as I had taken to wearing it next my skin, since I began to follow the wars. I feared from the greed which showed in all his movements that he vas going to strip me; but he did not do so, thinking, no doubt, that none of my clothes would fit his body.

"Well," he said, in his snarling beast voice, "wot's up 'ere, with all these folk brought their beasts 'ere?"

Martin Hyde, The Duke's Messenger

I told him that the Duke had come co fight for the crown of England, with the result, as I supposed, that the country people dared not trust their live–stock at home, for fear of having them pillaged. He seemed pleased at the news; but being an utter wild beast, far less civilized than the lowest savage ever known to me, he showed his pleasure by hoping that the rich (whom he cursed fluently) might have their heads pulled off in the war, while as for the poor (the farmers close by us) he hoped that they might lose every beast they owned. "Do 'era good," he said. "Now," he went on, "are you come spying 'ere along of the farmers?"

"No," I said, "I am a servant of the Duke's, riding out to look for the militia."

"Ah," he said. "Are yer, cocky? 'Ow'm I to know that?"

"Well," I said, "Look at my hands. Are they the hands of a farmer?"

"No," he said. "No, Mister stuck–up flunkey, they ain't. I s'pose yet proud of yet 'ands. I'll 'ave yer wait at table on me." He seemed to like the notion: for he repeated it many times, while he dug out hunks of cold ham with his file, from the meat which I had felt as I crawled in

"'Ow proud I dig A'unk a cold pig"

he sang, as he gulped the pieces down. It was partly a nightmare, partly very funny. I was not sure if he was mad, probably he was mad, but being down in the burrow there, in the half darkness, hearing that song, made me feel that I was mad; it was all a very terrible joke; perhaps madness affects people like that. At last I spoke to him again.

"Sir," I said, "I've been up since two this morning. Give me a hunk of cold pig, too. I'm half–starved."

"'Elp yourself, can't yer?" he snarled. "Oo'm I to wait on yer?" Then, very cunningly, he put in, "'Ave you got a knife on yer?"

"No," I said cautiously, "I've got no knife," which was a lie; I did not wish my knife to go the same way as the money. He gave me some cold pig, very excellent ham it was, too, for which I was very thankful. He watched my greediness with satisfaction. I ate heartily when I saw that my confident way with him had made him more tender towards me.

"Yes," he snorted. "Per'aps you ain't been lying to me after all. Now 'ow long will these blokes be up the 'ill 'ere?" I did not know that; but I supposed that they would go home directly the Duke's army had got as far, say, as Taunton. "But," I added, "the Duke may be beaten. If he's beaten, all this part will be full of troops beating every bush for the rebels." He swore at this; but his curses were only designed to hide his terror.

"Could a fellow get to sea," he said in a whining tone. "Could a poor fellow in trouble slip away to sea, now, at one of these seaport towns? Boy, I been livin' like a wild beast all the way from Bristol, this two months. I didn't kill the feller; not dead. The knife only went into 'im a very little way, not more'n a inch. I was raised near 'ere at a farm. So I knowed of this 'ere burrow. I got 'ere two days ago, pretty near dead. Now I been penned up from the sea by these farmers comin' 'ere, doin' swottin' sentry–go all round me. I tell yer, I'll cut up sour, if they pen me in, now I'm so near got away. I been with Avery. They call Avery a pirate. They said I was a pirate. It's 'anging if. they ketch me. Do yer think I could get away to Lyme or some place, to get took into a ship?" I told him, no; because I knew from what Lord Grey had told me, that the Channel was full of men–of–war searching every ship which hove in sight; besides, he did not look to me to be a very promising hand for a captain to take aboard.

"All the same," he said, "I got to risk it. You say there may be troops coming?"

"As for that," I answered, "the troops may be here at any moment from Exeter or Honiton. They've arrested hundreds of people everywhere around. You'd better stay in the burrow here." He did not pay much attention to what I said. He cursed violently, as though he were a bag–pipe full of foul words being slowly squeezed by some player. At last he crawled to the passage, foaming out incoherently that he would show them, he would, let them just wait.

"You stay 'ere, he said. "If I find you follerin' me, I'll mash your 'ed into that much slobber." He showed me a short piece of rope which he had twisted, sailor fashion, so as to form a handle for a jagged piece of flint, which, as I could see, had been used on some one or something quite recently.

Martin Hyde, The Duke's Messenger

"Mogador Jack," he said, "'e don't like people follerin' 'im." With that he left me alone in the burrow, wondering, now that it was over, why he had not killed me. He left me quite stunned; his sudden coming into my life had been so strange. It was unreal, like a dream, to have been in an ancient Briton's burial–chamber with a mad old pirate who had committed murder. But now that he had gone, I was eager to go, too, if it could be managed. I would not stay there till the brute came back, in spite of that flint club. After waiting some little time, during which, I felt sure, he was waiting for me at the door of the burrow, I took out my pistol. I examined the charge to see that all was well; then very cautiously, I began to crawl up the passage, with my pistol in my hand.

I waited for some minutes near the door, trying to convince myself by the lie of the shadows outside that he was crouched there, ready for me. But it seemed safe. I could see no shadow at all except the tremulous fern–shadows. At last I took off my coat as a blind. I flung it through the doorway, with some force, to see if it would draw him from his hiding. Nothing happened. The ruffian did not pounce upon it. I took a few long breaths to hearten me; it was now or never. I shut my eyes, praying that the first two blows might miss my head, so that I should have time to fire. Then, on my back, with my pistol raised over my head, I forced myself out with every muscle in my body. I leaped to my feet on the instant, quickly glancing round for the madman, swinging my pistol about with my finger hard on the trigger. He was not there, after all. I might have spared myself the trouble. I was alone there in the fern, within earshot of a murmur of voices, talking excitedly. I was not going to spy into any more secrets. I was going to get out of that camp cost what it might. I made one rush through the fern in the direction of the rampart, shoving the stalks aside, as a bull knocks through jungle in Campeachy. In thirty steps I was clear of the fern, charging slap into a group of people who were giving brandy to the sentry, whom I had passed but a little while before. He was bleeding from a broken wound on his pretty hard Saxon skull. He was not badly hurt, for he was swearing lustily; but he had been stunned just long enough for my pirate man to strip him. He was dressed now in a pair of leather gaiters, all the rest of his things had been taken, the pistol with them, I saw all this at a glance, as I charged in among them. I took it all in, guessing in one swift gleam of comprehension, exactly what had happened there, as my pirate made his rush for freedom. There was no time to ask if my guess were right or not.

"Out of my way," I shouted, shoving my pistol towards the nearest of the group. "Out of my way, or I shall fire." They made way for me. I charged down hill by the way I had come. Some one cried "Stop en." Another shouted "Shoot en, maister." There came a great bang of a gun over my head. But I was going down hill like a rabbit, into the gorse, into the bracken, into the close cover of the heath. Glancing back, I saw a dozen excited people rushing down the rampart after me. Some flung stones; some ran to catch horses to chase me. But I had the start of them. I was down the hill, over the hedge, in the lane, in no time. There, a hundred yards away, I saw my friends the troopers leading my cob. I shouted to them. They heard me. They came up to me at a gallop. In ten seconds more we were sailing away together.

"You been getting into scrapes, master," said one of the troopers. "You doan't want to meddle with the folk in these parts."

"No," said the other, with a touch of insolence in his voice. "So your master may find, one of these fine days." Being mindful of the Duke's honour, I told the man to mind his own business, which he said he meant to do, without asking my opinion. After that we rode on together a little heated, till we were out of sight of the combe, where I had had such a startling adventure.

After another hour of riding, we pulled up at the garden gate of an old grey handsome house which stood at some distance from the road. I asked one of the troopers who lived in this house. He said that it was an old Abbey, which belonged to Squire; but that we were to leave word there of the Duke's movements, "for Squire be very 'tached to the Protestants; besides he'll give us a breakfast. Sure to." We left our horses at the gate while we walked up to the house. A pretty girl, who seemed to know one of the men, told us to come in, while she got breakfast for us. "Squire," she said, "would be glad to hear what was going on; for he was that given up to the soldiers we couldn't hardly believe." We were shown down a long flagged corridor to a little cool room which looked as though it had once been the abbot's cell. It had a window in it, looking out upon a garden in full flower, a little rose garden, covered with those lovely bushes of old English red single roses, the most beautiful flower in the world. The window was large, but the space of it was broken up by stone piers, so that no pane of glass was more than six inches wide. I mention this now, because of what happened later. There was not much furniture in the room; but what there was was very good. There was an old Dutch pewter jug, full of sweet–williams, on the table. On the wall' there was a picture of a Spanish gentleman on a cream–coloured, fat handsome little horse. Together they looked very like Don Quixote out for a ride with his squire. The two troopers left me in this room, while they went off to the kitchen. Presently the servant came in again, bringing me a noble dish of breakfast, a pigeon pie, a ham, a jar of preserved quince, a honeycomb, a great household loaf, newly baked, a big quart jug full of small beer. I made a very honest meal. After eating, I examined the room. There was tapestry over one part of the wall. It concealed a little low door which led to what had once been the abbot's fishpond, now a roofed–in bath–house, where one could plunge into eight feet or so of (bitterly cold) spring water. This bath–house was some steps lower than the little dining room. It was lighted by a skylight directly over the bath. It had no other window whatever. After examining the bath, wishing that I had known of it before eating, I went back to the dining room, where the servant was clearing away the food.

"I hope you enjoyed your breakfast, sir," she said.

"Yes, thank you, very much indeed," I answered.

"Squire will be down d'reckly, sir," she said. "If you will please to make yourself at home." I made myself at home, as she desired, while she, after a few minutes, took away the soiled plates, leaving all the other things on the side–board, ready for dinner. I noticed that she smiled in a rather strange way as she drew to the door behind her.

I loitered away about half an hour, waiting for the squire to come. As he did not come, I turned over the books on the shelves, mostly volumes of plays, the Spanish Tragedy, the Laws of Candy, Love Lies a Bleeding, etc., four plays to a volume in buckram covers. I was just getting tired of All for Love, when I heard a footstep in the passage outside. I thought that I would ask the passenger, whoever it might be, for how much longer the squire would keep me waiting. I was anxious about getting back to the army. It was dangerous to straggle too far from the Duke's camps when unbeaten armies followed on both his wings. So I went to the door to learn my fate at once. To my great surprise I found that I could not open it. It was locked on the outside. The great heavy iron lock had been turned upon me. I was a prisoner in the room there. Thinking that it had been done carelessly, I beat upon the door to attract the man who passed down the passage, calling to him to turn the key for me so that I might get out. The footsteps did not pause. They passed on, down the corridor, as though the man were deaf. After that a fury came upon me. I beat upon the door for five minutes on end, till the house must have rung with the clatter; but no one paid any attention to me, only, far away, I heard a woman giggling, in an interval when I had paused for breath. The door was a heavy, thick oak door, bound with iron. The lock was a bar of steel at least two inches thick; there was no chance of getting it open. Even firing into the lock with my little pistol would not have helped me; it would only have jammed the tongue of steel in its bed. I soon saw the folly of trying to get out by the door; so I turned to the window, which was more difficult still, or, if not more difficult, more tantalizing, since it showed me the free garden into which one little jump would suffice to carry me. But the closely placed piers of stone made it impossible for me to get through the window. It was no use trying to do so. I should only have stuck fast, midway. I began at once to pick out the mortar of the pier stones with my knife point. It was hopeless work, though, for the old monks had used some cement a good deal harder than the stones which it bound together. I could only dig away a little dust from its surface. That way also was barred to me. Then I went down to the bathing–chamber, hoping that there would be some way of escape for me there. I hoped that the escape pipe of the bath might be a great stone conduit leading to a fish–pond in the garden. It was nothing of the sort. It was a little miserable leaden pipe. I beat all round the walls, praying for some secret door, but there was nothing of any use to me, only a little iron ventilator high up, big enough to take my head, but nothing more. As for the skylight over the bath, it was beyond my reach, high up. For the moment I could see no means of getting to it. I went back to the dining room to give another useless pounding to the door. My head was full of miserable forebodings; but as yet I suspected merely that I had been caught by some sudden advance of militia. Or perhaps the squire had laid plans to get information from one who knew the Duke. Perhaps I had been lured away specially by one hungry for the King's good opinion. Or could it be Aurelia? Whatever it was, I was trapped, that was the terrible thing. I was shut up there till my enemy, whoever it was, chose to deal with me. I was in arms against the ruling King of England; everybody's hand would be against me, unless my own hands helped me before my enemies came. My first thought was to get the table down the steps, to make a bridge across the bath, from which I could reach the skylight. This I could not do at first; for being much flustered, I did not put the table–leaves down. Until I knocked them down in my hurry they kept me from dragging the table from the dining room. When I got it at last into the bath–room, I found that it would not stretch across the water: the legs were too close together, as I might have seen had I kept my wits about me. I could think of no other way of getting out.

I went back disheartened to the dining room, dragging my coat behind me. The first thing which I saw was a letter addressed to me in a hand already known to me. The letter lay on the floor on the space once covered by the table. As it had not been there when I dragged the table downstairs, someone must have entered the room while I was away. I opened the letter in a good deal of flurry. It ran as follows:

"Dear Martin Hyde:—As you will not take a sincere friend's advice, you have to make the best of a sincere adviser's friendship. You did me a great service. Let me do you one. I hope to keep you an amused prisoner until your captain is a beaten man. By about three weeks from this 26th of June we shall hope to have made you so much our friend that you will not think of leaving us. May I make a compact with you? Please do not shoot me with that pistol of yours when I bring you some supper tonight. That is one part of it. The other is this. Let us be friends. We know all about you. I have even talked to Ephraim about you. So let us make it up. We have been two little spit fires. At any rate you have. Let us be friends. What sorts of books do you like to read? I shall bring you some story−books about ghosts, or about red Indians. Which do you like best? I like red Indians myself. I suppose you, being a man, like ghosts best. Your sincere friend Aurelia Carew. Who by the by thinks it best to warn you that you had not better try to get up the chimney, as it is barred across. She hopes that the table did not fall into the bath."

CHAPTER XXI. MY FRIEND AURELIA AND HER UNCLE

It was a friendly letter, which relieved me a good deal from my anxieties; but what I could not bear was the thought that the Duke would think me a deserter. I made up my mind that I would get away from that house at the first opportunity, so as to rejoin the Duke, to whom I felt myself pledged. But in the meantime, until I could get away, I resolved to make the best of my imprisonment. I was nettled by Aurelia's tone of superiority. I would show her, as I had shown her before, that my wits were just as nimble as hers. A few minutes after the letter had been read, she held a parley with me through the keyhole.

"Mr. Martin Hyde. Are you going to shoot me?"

"No, Miss Carew, though I think you deserve it."

"You won't try to get away if I open the door?"

"I mean to get away as soon as ever I get half a chance."

"I've got three men with me at the door here."

"Oh. Very well. But you just wait till I get a chance."

"Don't be so bloodthirsty, Mr. Martin Hyde. Now, I'm coming in to talk with you. No pistols, mind. Not one."

"I've promised I won't shoot. You might believe a fellow. But I mean to get away, remember. Just to show you."

She opened the door after that, a brown, merry Aurelia, behind whom I could see three men, ready to stop any rush. They closed the door behind her after she had entered.

"Well," she said, smiling. "Will you not shake hands with me, Martin Hyde?"

"Yes," I said, "I will shake hands. But you played a very mean trick, I think. There."

"You mustn't think me mean," she answered. "I don't like mean people. Now promise me one thing. You say you are going to run away from us. You won't run away from me when I am with you, will you?"

"No," I said, after thinking this over, to see if it could be twisted into any sort of trap, likely to stop my escape. "I will not. Not while I am with you."

"That's right," she said. "We can go out together, then. Now you've promised, suppose we go out into the garden."

We went into the garden together, talking of every subject under the sun but the subject nearest to our hearts at the moment. I would not speak of her capture of me; she would not speak of the Duke's march towards Taunton. There was some constraint whenever we came near those subjects. She was a very merry, charming companion; but the effect of her talk that morning was to make me angry at being trapped by her. I looked over the countryside for guiding points in case I should be able to get away. Axminster lay to the southeast, distant about six miles; so much I could reckon from the course of our morning's ride. I could not see Axminster for I was shut from it by rolling combes, pretty high, which made a narrow valley for the river. To the west the combes were very high, strung along towards Taunton in heaps. Due east, as I suspected, quite near to us, was Chard, where by this time the Duke must have been taking up his position. Taunton I judged (from a mile–stone which we had passed) to be not much more than a dozen miles from where I was. I have always had a pretty keen sense of position. I do not get lost. Even in the lonely parts of the world I have never been lost. I can figure out the way home by a sort of instinct helped by a glimpse at the sun. When I go over a hill I have a sort of picture–memory of what lies behind, to help me home again, however tortuous my path is on the other side. So the few glimpses which I could get of the surrounding country were real helps to me. I made more use of them than Aurelia suspected.

We were much together that day. Certainly she did her best to make my imprisonment happy. In the evening she was kinder; we were more at ease together; I was able to speak freely to her.

"Aurelia," I said, "you risked your life twice to warn me."

"That's not quite true, Martin," she said. "I am a government spy, trusted with many people's lives. I had other work to do than to warn a naughty boy who wanted to see what the ghosts were." I was startled at her knowing so much about me; she laughed.

"Well," she said, "I like you for it. I should have wanted to see them myself. But the ghost–makers are scattered far enough now."

"All the same, Aurelia," I said, "I thank you for what you did for me. I wish I could do something in return." She laughed.

"Well," she said, "you were very kind in the ship. You were a good enemy to me then. Weren't you?"

"Yes," I said, "I beat you properly on the ship. I carried the Duke's letters in my pistol cartridges, where you never suspected them. The letters which were in the satchel I forged myself after I got on board. If you'd not been a silly you'd have seen that they were forged."

"So that was why," she said. "Those letters gave everybody more anxious work than you've any notion of. Oh, Martin, though, I helped to drug you to get those letters. It was terrible. Terrible. Will you ever forgive me?"

"Why, yes, Aurelia," I said. "After all, it was done for your King. Just as I mean to run away from here to serve mine. All is fair in the King's service. Let us shake hands on that." We shook hands heartily, looking into each other's eyes.

"By the way," I said, "where did you get to that day in Holland, when I got the letters from you?"

"Ah," she answered, "you made me like a wildcat that day. I nearly killed you, twice. You remember that low parapet on the roof? I was behind that, waiting for you with a loaded pistol. You were all very near your deaths that morning. In the King's service, of course. For just a minute, I thought that you would climb up to examine that parapet. What a crazy lot you all were not to know at once that I was there! Where else could I have been?"

"Well," I answered, "I beat you in the ride, didn't I? You thought yourself awfully clever about that horse at the inn. Well, I beat you there. I beat you in the race. I beat you with my letters to the Dutchman. I beat you over those forgeries."

"Yes, indeed," she said. "I can beat all the men in your Duke's service. Every one. Even clever Colonel Lane. Even Fletcher of Saltoun. But a boy is so unexpected, there's no beating a boy, except with a good birch rod. You beat me so often, Martin, that I think you can afford to forgive me for tricking you once in bringing you here."

"I shall beat you in that, too, Miss Carew," I said; "for I mean to get away from you as soon as I can."

"So you say," she said. "But we have club men walking all round this house all night, as well as sentries by day, guarding the stock. Your gang of marauders will find a rough welcome if they come for refreshments here."

Even as she spoke, there came a sudden crash of fire-arms from the meadows outside the garden. About a dozen men came hurrying out of the house with weapons in their hands, among them a big, fierce-looking handsome man, who drew his sword as he ran.

"That is my uncle, Travers Carew," said Aurelia. "He owns this property. He wants to meet you." There came another splutter of fire-arms from the meadows. "Come," she said. "We'll see what it is. It is the Duke's men come pillaging."

We ran through a gate in the wall into an apple–orchard, where the Carew men were already dodging among the trees towards the enemy. There was a good deal of shouting, but the tide of battle, as they call it, the noise of shots, the trampling of horses, had already set away to the left, where the enemy were retreating, with news, as I heard later, that the militia held the Abbey in force. The Carew men came back in a few minutes with a prisoner. He had been captured while holding the horses of two friends, who had dismounted to drive off some of the Carew cattle. He said that the attack had been made by a party of twenty of the Duke's horse, sent out to bring in food for the march. They had scattered at the first discharge of fire–arms, which had frightened them horribly, for they had not expected any opposition. The frightened men never drew rein till they galloped their exhausted horses into Chard camp, where they gave another touch of dejection to the melancholy Duke. As for the prisoner, he was sent off under guard to Honiton gaol; I don't know what became of him. He was one of more than three thousand who came to death or misery in that war. They said that he was a young farmer, in a small way, from somewhere out beyond Chideock. The war had been a kind of high–spirited frolic for him; he had entered into it thoughtlessly, in the belief that it would be a sort of pleasant ride to London, with his expenses paid. Now he was ended. When he rode out with bound hands from the Carew house that evening, between two armed riders, he rode out of life. He never saw Chideock again, except in the grey light of dawn, after a long ride upon a hurdle, going to be hanged outside his home. Or perhaps he was bundled into one of the terrible convict ships bound for Barbadoes, with other rebels, to die of small–pox on the way, or under the whip in the plantations.

After this little brush, with its pitiful accompaniment, which filled me full of a blind anger against the royal party, so much stronger, yet with so much less right than ours, I was taken in to see Sir Travers Carew. He had just sent off the prisoner to Honkon, much as he would have brushed a fly from his hand. He had that satisfaction with himself, that feeling of having supported the right, which comes to all those who do cruel things in the name of that code of unjust cruelty, the criminal law. He looked at me with rather a grim smile, which made me squirm.

"So," he said, "this is the young rebel, is it? Do you know that I could send you off to Honiton gaol with that poor fellow there?" This made my heart die; but something prompted me to put a good face on it.

"Sir," I said, "I have done what my father thought right. I don't wish to be treated better than any other prisoner. Send me to Honiton, sir."

"No," he said, looking at me kindly. "I shall not send you to Honiton. You are not in arms against the King's peace, nor did you come over from Holland with the Duke. I can't send you to Honiton. Besides, I knew your father, Martin. I was at college with him. He was a good friend of mine, poor fellow. No, sir, I shall keep you here till the Duke's crazy attempt is knocked on the head. I think I can find something better for you to do than that fussy old maid, your uncle, could. But, remember, sir. You have a reputation for being a slippery young eel. I shall take particular pains to keep you from slipping out of my hands. But I do not wish to use force to your father's son. Will you give me your word not to try to escape?"

"No," I answered, sullenly. "I won't. I mean to get away directly I can."

"Come," he said kindly, "we tricked you rather nastily. But do you suppose, Martin, that your father, if he were here, would encourage your present resolutions? The Duke is coming (nearly unprepared) to bring a lot of silly yokels into collision with fully trained soldiers ten times more numerous. If the countryside, the gentry, the educated, intelligent men, were ready for the Duke, or believed in his cause, they would join him. They do not join him. His only adherents are the idle, ignorant, ill–conditioned rogues of this county, who will neither fight nor obey, when it comes to the pinch. I do not love the present King, Martin, but he is a better man than this Duke. The Duke will never make a king. He may be very fit for court–life; but there is not an ounce of king in him. If the Duke succeeds, in a year or two he will show himself so foolish that we shall have to send for the Prince of Orange, who is a man of real, strong wisdom. We count on that same prince to deliver us from James, when the time is ripe. It is not ripe, yet. I am telling you bitter, stern truth, Martin. Now then. Let me have your promise not to continue in the service of this doomed princeling, your master. Eh? What shall it be?"

"No," I said, "that's desertion."

"Not at all," he answered. "It is a custom of war. Come now. As a prisoner of war, give me your parole."

"You said just now that I was not a prisoner of war," I answered.

"Very well, then," he said. "I am a magistrate. I commit you add suspected person. Hart! Hart!" (Here he called in a man–servant.) "Just see that this young sprig keeps out of mischief. Think it over, Mr. Martin. Think it over."

In a couple of minutes I was back in my prison cells, locked in for the night, with neither lamp nor candle. A cot had been made up for me in a corner of the room. Supper was laid for me on the table, which had been brought back to its place. There was nothing for it but to grope to bed in the twilight, wondering how soon I could get away to what I still believed to be a righteous cause in which my father wished me to fight. I slept soundly after my day of adventure. I dreamed that I rode into London behind the Duke, amid all the glory of victory, with the people flinging flowers at us. But dreams go by contraries, the wise women say.

I was a full fortnight, or a little more, a prisoner in that house. They treated me very kindly. Aurelia was like an elder sister. Old Sir Travers used to jest at my being a rebel. But I was a prisoner, shut in, watched, kept close. The kindness jarred upon me. It was treating me like a child, when I was no longer a child. I had for some wild weeks been doing things which few men have the chance of doing. Perhaps, if I had confided all that I felt to Aurelia, she would have cleared away my troubles, made me see that the Duke's cause was wrong, that my father would wish his son well out of civil broils, however just, that I had better give the promise that they asked from me. But I never confided really fully in her. I moped a good deal, much worried in my mind. I began to get a lot of unworthy fancies into my head, silly fancies, which an honest talk would have scattered at once. I began to think from their silence about the Duke's doings that his affairs were prospering, that he was conquering, or had conquered, that I was being held by this loyalist family as a hostage. It was silly of me; but although in many ways I was a skilled man of affairs, I had only the brain of a child, I could not see the absurdity of what I came to believe. It worried me so much that at the end of my imprisonment I became very feverish; really ill from anxiety, as prisoners often are. I refused food for the latter part of one day, hoping to frighten my captors. They did not notice it, so I had my pains for nothing.

I went to bed very early; but I could not sleep. I fidgeted about till I was unusually wakeful. Then I got out of bed to try if there was a way of escape by the old–fashioned chimney, barred across as it was, at intervals, by strong old iron bars. I had never thought the chimney possible, having examined it before, when I first came to that house; but my fever made me think all things possible; so up I got, hoping that I should have light enough to work by.

CHAPTER XXII. THE PRIEST'S HOLE

It was too dark to do much that night, but I spent an hour in picking mortar from the bricks into which the lowest iron bar had been let. After a brief sleep I woke in the first of the light (at about one o'clock) ready to go at it again. My fever was hot upon me. I don't think that I was quite sane that day; but all my reason seemed to burn up into one bright point, escape, escape at all costs, then, at the instant. I must tell you that the chimney, like most old chimneys, was big enough for a big boy to scramble up, in order to sweep it. For some reason, the owners of the house had barred the chimney across so that this could not be done. They swept it, probably, in the effective old-fashioned way by shooting a blank charge of powder from a blunderbuss straight up the opening. The first two iron bars were so placed that it was only necessary to remove one to make room for my body. Further up there were others, more close together. The fire had not been lighted for many years; there was no soot in the passage. There was a jackdaw's nest high up. I could see the old jackdaw looking down at me. Up above her head was a little square of sky. I did not doubt that when I got to the top I should be able to scramble out of that square on to the leads, then down by a water–spout, evading the sentries, over the garden wall to freedom. After half an hour of mortar picking I got one end of the lowest iron bar out of its socket. Then I picked out the mortar from the other end, working the bar about like a lever, to grind the fulcrum into dust. Soon I had the bar so loose that I was able to thrust it to one side, leaving a passage big enough for my body.

I was very happy when this was done. I went back to the room to make up a packet of food to take with me. This I thrust into an inner pocket, before launching out up the hole. When I had cleaned up the mess of mortar, I started up the chimney, carefully replacing the bar behind me. Soon I was seven or eight feet above the room, trying to get at the upper bars. I was scrambling about for a foothold, when I noticed, to my left, an iron bar or handle, well concealed from below by projecting bricks. I seized hold of it with my left hand, very glad of the support it offered, when, with a dull grating noise, it slid downwards under my weight, drawing with it the iron panel to which it was clamped. I had come upon a secret chamber in the chimney; there at my side was an opening big enough for a man's body. I was pretty well startled by it, not only by the suddenness of the discovery, but from the fear I had lest it should lead to some inhabited room, where my journey would be brought to an end. I peered into it well, before I ventured to enter. It was a little low room, about five feet square, lit by two loopholes, which were concealed from outside by the great growth of ivy on the side of the house. I clambered into it with pleasure, keeping as quiet as I could. It was a dirty little room, with part of its floor rotten from rain which had beaten in through the loopholes. It had not been used for a great while. The pallet bed against the wall was covered with rotten rags, dry as tinder. There were traces of food, who could say how ancient, in a dish by the bed. There was a little crucifix, with a broken neck–chain, lying close to the platter. Some priest who had used this priest–hole years before had left it there in his hurry; I wondered how. Something of the awe which had been upon him then seemed to linger in the place. Many men had lain with beating hearts in that room; the room seemed to remember. I have never been in a place which made one's heart move like that room. Well. The priest's fears were dead as the priest by this time. Nothing but the wreck of his dinner, perhaps the last he ever ate, remained to tell of him, beside the broken symbol of his belief. I shut–to the little panel–door by which I had entered, so that I might not have the horrible fancy that the old priest's shaven head was peering up the chimney at me, to see what I was doing in his old room, long since given over to the birds.

As I expected, there was a way of escape from the hiding–place. A big stone in the wall seemed to project unnecessarily; the last comer to that room had shut the door carelessly; otherwise I might never have found it. Seeing the projecting stone, I took it for a clue feeling all round it, till I found that underneath it there was a groove for finger tips. The stone was nothing more than a large, cunningly fashioned drawer, which pulled out, showing a passage leading down, down, along narrow winding steps, just broad enough for one man to creep down at a time. The stairs were more awesome than the room, for they were dark. I could not see where they led; but I meant to go through this adventure, now that I had begun it. So down I crept cautiously, clinging to the wall, feeling with my feet as I went, lest there should be no step, suddenly, but a black pit, far down, into which a man might fall headlong, on to who knows what horrors. I counted the steps. I thought that they would never end. There were thirty–seven altogether. They brought me to a dark sort of room, with damp earth for its floor, upon which water slowly dropped from some unseen stalactite. I judged that I must be somewhere under the bath–chamber, not more than ten feet from the abbot's old fish–pond. If there was a way out I felt that it must be to my left, under the garden; not to my right, which would lead back under the body of the house.

Very cautiously I felt along to my left, till I found that there was indeed a passage; but one so low that I had to stoop to get along it. A few steps further brought me with a shock against a wall, a sad surprise to me, for I thought that I was on the road to safety. When I recovered from my fear I felt along the wall till I found that the passage zigzagged like a badger's earth. It turned once sharply to the right, going up a couple of steps, then again sharply to the left, going up a few more steps, then again to the right up one step more, to a broader open stretch, lit by one or two tiny chinks, more cheering to me than you can imagine. I guessed that I was passing at last under the garden, having gone right below the house's foundations. The chinks of light seemed to me to come from holes worn in the roof by rabbits or rats. They were pleasant things to see after all that groping in the blackness of night. On I went cautiously, feeling my way before me, till suddenly I stopped dead, frightened terribly, for close to me, almost within touch as it seemed, some men were talking to each other. They were evidently sitting just above my head, in the cool morning, watching for me to come through my window, as I suppose. They were some of Sir Travers's sentries. A moment's thought told me that I had little to fear from them, if I moved quietly in my burrow. However, as my walk was often noisy, through stumblings on stones, I waited till they moved off, which was not for some minutes. One of the men was asking the other what was the truth about the Duke.

"Why," his mate answered, "they say as he got beat back coming towards London. They say he be going to Bridgewater, now, to make it a castle, like; or perhaps he be a coming to Taunton. They say he have only a mob, like, left to en, what with all this rain. But I do—an't know. He be very like to come here agen; so as us'll have to watch for our stock."

"Ah?" said the first. "They did say as there was soldiers come to Evilminster. So as to shut en off, like. I seed fires out that way, myself, like camp—fires, afore it grew light. They do say the soldiers be all for the Duke."

"Yes," the other answered, "he be very like to win if it come to a battle. He'd a got on to London, I dare—say, if the roads had but been dry."

"What do ee say to a bit of tobaccy, master?" said the first, after a pause.

"Why, very well," said the other. At this instant, without any warning, something in the wall of my passage gave way, some bit of rotten mortar which held up a stone, or something of the sort. At any rate, a stone fell out, with a little rush of rotten plaster, making a good deal of noise, though of course it seemed more to me than to the men outside.

"What ever in the world was that?" said one of them.

"I dunno," said the other. "It seemed to come from down below somewhere, under the earth, like. Do you think as it could be a rabbit?"

"It did sound like a stone falling out of a wall," came the answer. "I dunno. Where could it a come from?"

They seemed to search about for some trace of a rabbit; but not finding any, they listened for another stone to fall.

"I tell you what I think," said the first man. "I believe as there be underground passages all over these here gardens. Some of them walks sound just as hollow as logs if you do stamp on 'em. There was very queer doings here in the old monks' time; very queer. Some day I mean to grub about a bit, master. For my old grandmother used always to say as the monks buried a lot of treasure hereabouts in the old time."

"Ah?" said the other. "Then shall us get a spade quiet like, to see if it be beneath." The other hesitated, while my heart sank. I very nearly went back to my prison, thinking that all was over.

"No," said his comrade. "Us'll ask Sir Travers first. He do—an't like people grubbing about. Some of his forefathers as they call them weren't very good, I do hear, neither. He do—an't want none of their little games brought to light, like."

After this, the men moved off, to some other part of their beat. I went on along the passage quickly, till suddenly I fell with a crash down three or four steps into a dirty puddle, knocking my head as I fell. I could see no glimmer of light from this place; but I groped my way out, up a few more steps further on into a smaller, dirtier passage than the one which I had just left. After this I had to crawl like a badger in his earth, with my back brushing against the roof, over many masses of broken brickwork most rough to the palms of my hands. All of a sudden I smelt a pleasant stable-smell. I heard the rattle of a halter drawn across manger bars. I heard a horse paw upon the ground quite close to me.

Martin Hyde, The Duke's Messenger

A dim, but regular chink of light showed in front of me, level with my head as crawled. Peering through it, I saw that I was looking into a stable, almost level with the floor; the passage had come to an end.

By getting my fingers into the crack through which I peered, I found that I could swing round some half a dozen stones, which were mortared together, so as to form a revolving door. It worked with difficulty, as though no one had passed through by that way for many years; but it worked for me, after a little hard pushing. I scrambled through the narrow opening into a roomy old stable, where some cart–horses peered at me with wonder, as I rose to my feet. After getting out, I shut to my door behind me, so firmly that I could not open it again; there must have been some spring or catch which I could not set to work. Two steps more took me out of the horses' stalls into the space behind, where, on a mass of hay, lay a carter, fast asleep, with the door–key in his hand. By his side lay a pitchfork. He was keeping guard there, prepared to resist Monmouth's pillagers.

He slept so heavily that I was tempted to take the key from his hand. Twice I made little half steps forward to take it; but each time something in the man's look daunted me. He was a surly–looking man who, if roused suddenly, in a locked stable, might lay about him without waiting to see who roused him. He stirred in his sleep as I drew near him for the second time; so I gave up the key as a bad job. The loft seemed to be my only chance; as there was only this one big locked double door upon the lower floor, I clambered up the steep ladder to the loft, hoping that my luck there might be better, but resolved, if the worst came, to hide there in the hay until the carter took the horses to work, leaving the doors open.

I had hardly set my foot upon the loft floor, when one of the horses, hearing some noise outside, or being moved by some evil spirit, whinnied loudly, rattling his halter. The noise was enough to arouse an army. It startled the carter from his bed. I heard him leap to his feet with an oath; I heard him pad round the stable, talking to the horses in turn; I heard him unlock the door to see what was stirring. I stood stock–still in my tracks, not daring to stir towards the cover of the hay at the farther end of the loft. I heard him walk slowly, grunting heavily, to the foot of the ladder, where he stopped to listen for any further signal. If he had come up he must have caught me. I could not have escaped. But though he seemed suspicious he did not venture further. He walked slowly back to his bed, grunting discontentedly. In a few minutes he was sound asleep again; for farming people sleep like sailors, as though sleep were a sort of spirit muffling them suddenly in a thick felt blanket. After he had gone off to sleep, I took off my boots, in order to put them on under my stockings, for the greater quiet which that muffling gives to the tread. Then I peered about the loft for a way of escape.

There were big double doors to this upper loft, through which the hay could be passed from a waggon standing near the wall. These doors were padlocked on the inside; there was no opening them; the staples were much too firm for me to remove without a crowbar. The other openings in the walls were mere loophole slits, about four feet long but only a few inches broad. There were enough of these to make the place light. By their light I could see that there was no way of escape for me except by the main door. I was almost despairing of escape from this prison of mine, when I saw that the loft had a hayshoot, leading downwards. When I saw it I fondly hoped that it led to some outer stable or cart–shed, separated from that in which the carter slept. A glance down its smooth shaft showed me that it led to the main stable. I could see the heads of the meditative horses, bent over the empty mangers exactly as if they were saying grace. Beyond them I saw the boots of the carter dangling over the edge of the trusses of hay on which he slept. I stepped back from this shaft quickly because I thought that I might be seen from below. My foot went into the nest of a sitting hen, right on to the creature's back. Up she started, giving me such a fright that I nearly screamed. She flew with a cackling shriek which set all the blackbirds chippering in the countryside. Round the loft she scattered, calling her hideous noise. Up jumped the carter, down came his pitchfork with a thud. His great boots clattered over the stable to the ladder. Clump, clump, he came upstairs, with his pitchfork prongs gleaming over his head like lanceheads. I saw his head show over the opening of the loft. There was not a second to lose. His back of course was still towards me, as the ladder was mercifully nailed to the wall. Before he turned I slid over the mouth of the shaft down into the hayrack of the old brute who had whinnied. I lit softly; but I certainly shocked that old mare's feelings. In a second, before she had time to kick, I was outside her stall, darting across the stable to the key, which lay on the truss of hay, mercifully left there by its guardian. In another second the lock had turned. I was outside, in the glorious open fields again. Swiftly but silently I drew the key out of the lock. One second more sufficed to lock that door from without. The carter was a prisoner there, locked safely in with his horses. I was free. The key was in my pocket. Yonder lay the great combes which hid Taunton from me. I waved my hat towards them; then, with a wild joyous rush, I scrambled behind the cover of the nearest hedge, along which I ran hard for nearly a quarter of a mile.

I stopped for a few minutes to rest among some ferns, while I debated how to proceed. I changed the arrangement of my stockings; I also dusted my very dirty clothes, all filthy from that horrid passage underground. "Now," I said to myself, "there must be many ways to Taunton. One way, I know, leads along this valley, past Chard there, where the houses are. The other way must lie across these combes, high up. Which way shall I choose, I wonder?" A moment's thought showed me that the combes would be unfrequented, while the valley road, being the easy road, which (as I knew) the Duke's army had chosen, would no doubt be full of people, some of them (perhaps) the King's soldiers, coming up from Bridport. If I went by that road my pursuers would soon hear of me, even if I managed to get past the watchers on the road. On the other hand, Aurelia would probably know that I should choose the combe road. Still, even if she sent out mounted men, she would find me hard to track, since the combes were lonely, so lonely that for hours together you can walk there without meeting anybody. There would be plentiful cover among the combes in case I wished to lie low. Besides, I had a famous start, a five hours' start; for I should not be missed until eight o'clock. It could not then have been much more than half-past two. In five hours an active boy, even if he knew not the road, might put some half a dozen miles behind him. I say only half a dozen miles, because the roads were the roughest of rough mud-tracks, still soft from the rains. As I did not know the way, I knew that I might count on going wrong, taking wrong turns, etc. As I wished to avoid people, I counted on travelling most of the way across country, trusting to luck to find my way among the fields. So that, although in five hours I should travel perhaps ten or twelve miles, I could not count on getting more than six miles towards Taunton.

CHAPTER XXIII. FREE

For the first hour or two, as no one would be about so early, I thought it safe to use the road. I put my best foot foremost, going up the great steep combe, with Chard at my back.

The road was one of the loneliest I have ever trodden. It went winding up among barren-looking combes which seemed little better than waste land. There were few houses, so few that sometimes, on a bit of rising ground, when the road lifted clear of the hedges, one had to look about to see any dwelling of men. There was little cultivation, either. It was nearly all waste, or scanty pasture. A few cows cropped by the wayside near the lonely cottages. A few sheep wandered among the ferns. It was a very desolate land to lie within so few miles of England's richest valleys. I walked through it hurriedly, for I wished to get far from my prison before my escape was discovered. No one was there to see me; the lie of the valley below gave me my direction, roughly, but closely enough. After about an hour of steady, fairly good walking, I pulled up by a little tiny brook for breakfast. I ate quickly, then hurried on, for I dared not waste time. I turned out of the narrow cart–tracks into what seemed to be a highroad.

I dipped down a hollow, past a pond where geese were feeding, then turned to a stiff steep hill, which never seemed to end for miles. The country grew lonelier at every step; there were no houses there; only a few rabbits tamely playing in the outskirts of the coverts. A jay screamed in the clump of trees at the hill–top; it seemed the proper kind of voice for a waste like that. Still further on, I sat down to rest at the brink of the great descent, which led, as I guessed, as I could almost see, to the plain where Taunton lay, waiting for the Duke's army to garrison her. There were thick woods to my right at this point, making cover so dense that no hounds would have tried to break through it, no matter how strong a scent might lead them. It was here, as I sat for a few minutes to rest, that a strange thing happened.

I was sitting at the moment with my back to the wood, looking over the desolate country towards a tiny cottage far off on the side of the combe. A big dog–fox came out of the cover from behind me, so quietly that I did not hear him. He trotted past me in the road; I do not think that he saw me till he was just opposite. Then he stopped to examine me, as though he had never seen such a thing before. He was puzzled by me, but he soon decided that I was not worth bothering about, for he made no stay. He padded slowly on towards Chard, evidently well–pleased with himself. Suddenly he stopped dead, with one pad lifted, a living image of alert tension. He was alarmed by something coming along the road by which I had come. He turned his head slightly, as though to make sure with his best ear. Then with a single beautiful lollopping bound he was over the hedge to safety, going in that exquisite curving rhythm of movement which the fox has above all English animals. For a second, I wondered what it was that had startled him. Then, with a quickness of wit which would have done credit to an older mind, I realized that there was danger coming on the road towards me, danger of men or of dogs, since nothing else in this country frightens a fox. It flashed in upon me that I must get out of sight at once; before that danger hove in view of me. I gave a quick rush over the fence into the tangle, through which I drove my way till I was snug in an open space under some yew trees, surrounded on all sides by brambles. I shinned up one of the great yew trees, till I could command a sight of the road, while lying hidden myself in the profuse darkness of the foliage. Here I drew out my pistol, ready for what might come. I suppose I had not been in my hiding–place for more than thirty seconds, when over the brow of the hill came Sir Travers Carew, at a full gallop, cheering on a couple of hounds, who were hot on my scent. Aurelia rode after him, on her famous chestnut mare. Behind her galloped two men, whom I had not seen before. In an instant, they were swooped down to the place where the dog–fox had passed. The hounds gave tongue when they smelt the rank scent of their proper game; they were unused to boy–hunting. They did not hesitate an instant, but swung off as wild as puppies over the hedge, after the fox. The horsemen paused for a second, surprised at the sudden sharp turn; but they followed the hounds' lead, popping over the fence most nimbly, not waiting to look for my tracks in the banks of the hedge. They streamed away after the fox, to whom I wished strong legs. I knew that with two young hounds they would never catch him, but I hoped that he would give them a good run before the sun killed the scent. I looked at the sun, now gloriously bright over all the world, putting a bluish glitter on to the shaking oak leaves of the wood. How came it that they had discovered my flight so soon since it could not be more than six o'clock, if as much? I wondered if it had been the old carter, who had never really seen me. It might have been the old carter; but doubtless he drummed for a good while on the door of the stable before anybody heard him. Or it might have been one of the garden sentries. One of the sentries might well have peeped in at the window of my room to make sure that I was up to no pranks. He could have seen from the window that my bed was empty. If he had noticed that, he could have unlocked my door to make sure, after which it would not have taken more than a few minutes to start after me. I learned afterwards that the sentry had alarmed the house at a little before five o'clock. The carter, being only half–awake when he came after me, suspected nothing till the other farm–hands came for the horses, at about six o'clock, when, the key being gone, he had to break the lock, vowing that the rattens had took his key from him in the night. My disappearance puzzled everybody, because I had hidden my tracks so carefully that no one noticed at first how the chimney bars had been loosened. No one in that house knew of the secret room, so that the general impression was that I had either squeezed myself through the window, or blown myself out through the keyhole by art–magic. The hounds had been laid along the road to Chard, with the result that they had hit my trail after a few minutes of casting about.

Now that they were after me, I did not know what to do. I dared not go on towards Taunton; for who knew how soon the squire would find his error, by viewing the fox? He was too old a huntsman not to cast back to where he had left the road, as soon as he learned that his hounds had changed foxes. I concluded that I had better stay where I was, throughout that day, carefully hidden in the yew−tree. In the evening I might venture further if the coast seemed clear. It was easy to make such a resolution; but not so easy to keep to it; for fifteen hours is a long time for a boy to wait. I stayed quiet for some hours, but I heard no more of my hunters. I learned later that they had gone from me, in a wide circuit, to cut round upon the Taunton roads, so as to intercept me, or to cause me to be intercepted in case I passed by those ways. The hounds gave up after chasing the fox for three miles. The old squire thought that they stopped because the sun had destroyed the scent. With a little help from an animal I had beaten Aurelia once more. When I grew weary of sitting up in the yew tree, clambered down, intending to push on through the wood until I came to the end of it. It was mighty thick cover to push through for the first half mile; then I came to a cart−track, made by wood−cutters, which I followed till it took me out of the wood into a wild kind of sheep−pasture. It was now fully nine in the evening, but the country was so desolate it might have been undiscovered land. I might have been its first settler, newly come there from the seas. It taught me something of the terrors of war that day's wandering towards Taunton. I realized all the men of these parts had wandered away after the Duke, for the sake of the excitement, after living lonely up there in the wilds. Their wives had followed the army also. The while population (scanty as it was) had moved off to look for something more stirring than had hitherto come to them. I wandered on slowly, taking my time, getting my direction fairly clear from the glimpses which I sometimes caught of the line of the highway. At a little after noon I ate the last of my victuals near a spring. I rested after my dinner, then pushed on again, till I had won to a little spinney only four miles from Taunton, where my legs began to fail under me.

I crept into the spinney, wondering if it contained some good shelter in which I could sleep for the night. I found a sort of dry, high pitched bank, with the grass all worn off it, which I thought would serve my turn, if the rain held off. As for supper, I determined to shoot a rabbit with my pistol. For drink, there was a plenty of small brooks within half a mile of the little enclosure. After I had chosen my camp, I was not very satisfied with it. The cover near by was none too thick. So I moved off to another part where the bushes grew more closely together. As I was walking leisurely along, I smelt a smell of something cooking, I heard voices, I heard something clink, as though two tin cups were being jangled. Before I could draw back, a man thrust through the undergrowth, challenging me with a pistol. Two other men followed him, talking in low, angry tones.

They came all round me with very murderous looks. They were the filthiest looking scarecrows ever seen out of a wheat–field.

"Why," said one of them, lowering his pistol, "it be the Duke's young man, as we seed at Lyme." They became more friendly at that; but still they seemed uneasy, not very sure of my intentions.

"Where is the Duke?" I asked after a long awkward pause. "Is he at Taunton?" They looked from one to the other with strange looks which I did not understand.

"The Duke be at Bridgewater," said one of them in a curious tone. "What be you doing away from the Duke?"

"Why," I said, "I was taken prisoner. I escaped this morning."

"Yes?" they said with some show of eagerness. "Be there many soldiers hereaway, after us?"

"No. Not many," I said. "Are you coming from the Duke?"

"Yes," said one of them, "we left en at Bridgewater. We have been having enough of fighting for the crown. We been marching in mud up to our knees. We been fighting behind hedges. We been retreating for the last week. So now us be going home, if us can get there. Glad if we never sees a fight again."

"Well," I said, "I must get to the Duke if I can. How far is it to Bridgewater?"

"Matter of fifteen mile," they said, after a short debate. "You'll never get there tonight. Nor perhaps tomorrow, since we hear the soldiers be a coming."

"I'll get some of the way tonight," I said; but my heart sank at the thought; for I was tired out.

"No, young master," said one of the men kindly, "you stop with us for tonight. Come to supper with us. Us 'ave rabbits on the fire." Their fortnight of war had given them a touch of that comradeship which camp–life always gives. They took me with them to their camp–fire, where they fed me on a wonderful mess of rabbits boiled with herbs. The men had bread. One of them had cider. Our feast there was most pleasant; or would have been, had not the talk of these deserters been so melancholy. They were flying to their homes like hunted animals, after a fortnight of misery which had altered their faces forever. They had been in battle; they had retreated through mud; they had seen all the ill–fortune of war. They did all that they could to keep me from my purpose; but I had made up my mind to rejoin my master; I was not to be moved. Before settling down to sleep for the night I helped the men to set wires for rabbits, an art which I had not understood till then, but highly useful to a lad so fated to adventurous living as myself. We slept in various parts of the spinney, wherever there was good shelter; but we were all so full of jangling nerves that our sleep was most uneasy. We woke very early, visited our wires, then breakfasted heartily on the night's take. The men insisted on giving me a day's provision to take with me, which I took, though grudgingly, for they had none too much for themselves, poor fellows. Just before we parted I wrote a note to Sir Travers, on a leaf of my pocketbook. "Dear Sir Travers," I wrote, "These men are well–known to me as honest subjects. They have had great troubles on their road. I hope that you will help them to get home. Please remember me very kindly to your niece." After folding this very neatly I gave the precious piece of impudence to one of the men. "There," I said, "if you are stopped, insist on being carried before Sir Travers. He knows me. I am sure that he will help you as far as he can." For this the men thanked me humbly. I learned, too, that it was of service to them. It saved them all from arrest later in the same day.

Having bidden my hosts farewell, I wandered on, keeping pretty well in cover. I saw a patrol of the King's dragoons in one of the roads near which I walked. The nets were fast closing in on my master: there were soldiers coming upon him from every quarter save the west, which was blocked too, as it happened, by ships of war in the Channel. This particular patrol of dragoons caught sight of me. I saw a soldier looking over a gate at me; but as I was only a boy, seemingly out for birdsnests, he did not challenge me, so that by noon I was safe in Taunton. I have no clear memory of Taunton, except that it was full of people, mostly women. There were little crowds in the streets, little crowds of women, surrounding muddy, tired men who had come in from the Duke. People were going about in a hurried, aimless way which showed that they were scared. Many houses were shut up. Many men were working on the city walls, trying to make the place defensible. If ever a town had the fear of death upon it that town was Taunton, then. As far as I could make out it was not the actual war that it feared; though that it feared pretty strongly, as the looks on the women's faces showed. It feared that the Duke's army would come back to camp there, to eat them all up, every penny, every blade of corn, like an army of locusts. Sometimes, while I was there, men galloped in with news, generally false, like most warmews, but eagerly sought for by those who even now saw their husbands shot dead in ranks by the fierce red-coats under their drunken Dutch general. Sometimes the news was that the army was pressing in to cut off the Duke from Taunton; that the dragoons were shooting people on the road; that they were going to root out the whole population without mercy. At another time news came that Monmouth was marching in to music, determined to hold Taunton till the town was a heap of cinders. Then one, bloody with his spurred horse's gore, cried aloud that the King was dead, shot in the heart by one of his brother's servants. Then another came calling all to prayer. All this uproar caused a hurrying from one crowd to another. Here a man preached fervently to a crowd of enthusiasts. Here men ran from a prayer-meeting to crowd about a messenger. Bells jangled from the churches; the noise of the picks never ceased in the trenches; the taverns were full; the streets swarmed; the public places were now thronged, now suddenly empty. Here came the aldermen in their robes, scared faces among the scarlet, followed by a mob praying for news, asking in frenzy for something certain, however terrible. There several in a body clamoured at a citizen's door in the like fever of doubt. There was enough agony of mind in Taunton that day to furnish out any company of tragedians. We English, an emotional people by nature, are best when the blow has fallen. We bear neither doubt nor rapture wisely. Our strength is shown in troublous times in which other people give way to despair.

CHAPTER XXIV. THE END

Among all the confusion, I learned certainly from some deserters that the Duke was at Bridgewater, waiting till his men had rested, before trying to break through to the north, to his friends in Chester. He had won a bad name for himself among his friends. Nobody praised him. The Taunton people, who had given him such a splendid welcome ten days before, now cursed him for having failed; they knew too well what sort of punishment was sure to fall upon them, directly the fighting came to an end. Somehow all their despairing talk failed to frighten me. I was not scared by all the signs of panic in the streets. I was too young to understand fully; but besides that I was buoyed up by the belief that I had done a fine thing in escaping from prison in order to serve the cause dear to my heart. My heart told me that I was going to a glorious victory in the right cause. I cannot explain it. I felt my father in my heart urging me to go forward. I would not have drawn back for all the King's captains in a company riding out against me together. I felt that these people were behaving absurdly; they should keep a brave patient face against their troubles. Tomorrow or the next day would see us in triumph, beating our enemies back to London, to the usurper's den in Whitehall.

It drew towards sunset before I had found a means to get to Bridgewater. The innkeepers who in times of peace sent daily carriers thither, with whom a man could travel in comfort for a few pence, had now either lost their horses, or feared to risk them. No carriers had gone either to Bridgewater or to Bristol since the Duke marched in on the fourth day of his journey; nor had the carriers come in as usual from those places; the business of the town was at a standstill. I asked at several inns, but that was the account given to me. There was no safety on the roads. The country was overrun by thieves, who stole horses in the name of the Duke or of the King; nothing was safe anywhere. The general hope of the people was for Monmouth to be beaten soon, or to be victorious soon. They had lost quite enough by him; they wanted the rebellion over.

At last, just when I had begun to think the thing hopeless, I found an honest Quaker about to ride to Bridgewater with a basket of Bibles for the Duke's men. He did not ask me what my business at Bridgewater might be; but he knew that no one would want to go there at such a time without good cause. "Well," he said, "if you can ride small, you shall ride behind me, but it will be slow riding, as the horse will be heavily laden." He was going to start at eight o'clock, so as to travel all night, when the marauders, whether deserters from the Duke or ill-conditioned country people, were always less busy. I had time to get some supper for myself in the tavern-bar before starting. Just as we were about to ride off together, when we were in the saddle, waiting only till some carts rolled past the yard-door, I had a fright, for there, coming into the inn yard, was one of the troopers who had beguiled me from the Duke's army that day at Axminster. I had no doubt that he was going from inn to inn, asking for news of me. We began to move through the yard as he came towards us; the clack of the horse's feet upon the cobbles made him look up; but though he stared at me hard, he did so with an occupied mind; he was in such a brown study (as it is called) that he never recognized me. A minute later, we were riding out of town past the trench-labourers, my heart going pit-a-pat from the excitement of my narrow escape. I dared not ask the Quaker to go fast, lest he should worm my story from me, but for the first three miles I assure you I found it hard not to prod that old nag with my knife to make him quicken his two mile an hour crawl. Often during the first hours of the ride I heard horses coming after us at a gallop. It was all fancy; we were left to our own devices. My pursuers, I found, afterwards, were misled by the lies of the landlord at the inn we had left. We were being searched for in Taunton all that fatal night, by half a dozen of the Carew servants.

Bridgewater had not gone to bed when we got there. The people were out in the streets, talking in frightened clumps, expecting something. After thanking the Quaker for his kindness in giving me a lift I asked at one of these clumps where I could find the Duke. I was feeling so happy at the thought of rejoining my master, after all my adventures, that I think I never felt so happy.

"Where can I find the Duke?" I asked. "I'm his servant, I must find him."

"Find him?" said one of the talkers. "He's not here. He's marched out, sir, with all his army, over to Sedgemoor to fight the King's army. It's a night attack, sir."

I was bitterly disappointed at not having reached my journey's end; but there was a stir in the thought of battle. I asked by which road I could get to the place where the battle would be. The man told me to turn to the right after crossing the river. "But," said he, "you don't want to get mixed up in the fighting, master. There be thousands out there on the moor. A boy would be nowhere among all them."

"Yes," said another. "Better stay here, sir. If the Duke wins he'll be back afore breakfast. If he gets beat, you'd be best out of the way."

This was sound advice; but I was not in a mood to profit by it. Something told me that the battle was to be a victory for us; so I thanked the men, telling them that I would go out over the moor by the road they had mentioned. As I moved away, they called out to me to mind myself, for the King's dragoons were on the moor, as a sort of screen in front of their camp. By the road they had mentioned I might very well get into the King's camp without seeing anything of my master. One of them added that the battle would begin, or might begin, long before I got there, "if the mist don't lead en astray, like."

It took me some few minutes to get out of the gates across the river; for there was a press of people crowded there. It was as dark as a summer night ever is, that is, a sort of twilight, when I passed through, but just at the gates were two great torches stuck into rings in the wall. The wind made their flames waver about uncertainly, so that sometimes you could see particular faces in the crowd, all lit in muddy gold light for an instant, before the wavering made them dark again. Several mounted men were there, trying to pass. Among them, in one sudden glare, I saw Aurelia on her Arab, reined in beside Sir Travers, whose horse was kicking out behind him. I passed them by so close that I touched Aurelia's riding habit as I crept out of the press. They were talking together, just behind me, as I crept from the town over the bridge above which the summer mists clung, almost hiding the stream. Aurelia was saying "I only hope we may be in time." "Yes, poor boy," said Sir Travers. "It will be terrible if we are too late." It gave me a pang to hear them, for I knew that they were talking about me.

I crept into the shelter of the bridge parapet while they rode on past me. The mist hid them from me. The town was dark above the mist like a city in the clouds. The stars were dim now with the coming of day. A sheep–bell on the moor made a noise like a nightbird. A few ponies pastured on the moor trotted away, lightly padding, scared, I suppose, by the two riders. Then, far away, but sounding very near at hand, for sound travels very strangely in mist, so strangely that often a very distant noise will strike loudly, while it is scarcely heard close to, there came a shot. Almost instantly, the air seemed full of the roar of battle. The gun–fire broke out into a long irregular roar, a fury of noise which roused up the city behind me, as though all the citizens were slamming their doors to get away from it. I hurried along the road towards the battle, praying, as I went, that my master might conquer, that the King's troops had been caught asleep, that when I got there, in the glory of dawn, I might find the Duke's army returning thanks in their enemy's camp. I pressed on along the rough moor road until the dawn came over the far horizon, driving the mists away, so that I could see what was doing there.

I saw a great sweep of moorland to my left, with a confused crowd of horsemen scattering away towards a line of low hills some miles beyond. They were riding from the firing, which filled all the nearer part of the moor with smoke, among which I saw moving figures, sudden glimpses of men in rank, sudden men on horseback, struggling with their horses. The noise was worse than I had expected; it came on me with repeated deafening shocks. I could hear cries in the lulls when the firing slackened; then the uproar grew worse again, sounds of desperate thuds, marking cannon shot. I heard balls going over my head with a shrill "wheep, wheep," which made me duck. A small iron cannon ball spun into the road like a spinning top, scattering the dust. It wormed slowly past me for a second, then rose up irregularly in a bound, to thud into the ditch, where it lay still. I saw cannon coming up at a gallop, with many horses, on the bare right flank of the battle.

Martin Hyde, The Duke's Messenger

Another ball came just over my head, with a scream which made my heart quite sick. I sat down cowering under a ruined thorn–tree by the road, crying like a little child. It must have been a moment after that when I saw a man staggering down the road towards me, holding his side with both hands. He fell into the road, dead, not far from me. Then others came past, some so fearfully hurt that it was a miracle that they should walk. They came past in a long horrible procession, men without weapons, without hands, shot in the head, in the body, lacerated, bleeding, limping, with white drawn faces, tottering to the town which they would never see again. I shut my eyes, crouching well under the tree, while this fight went on. It was nothing but a time of pain, a roaring, booming horror with shrieks in it. I don't know how long it lasted. I only know that the shooting seemed suddenly to pass into a thunder of horse–hoofs as the King's dragoons came past in a charge. Right in front of me they galloped, hacking at the fleers, leaning out from their saddles to cut at them, leaning down to stab them, rising up to reach at those who climbed the banks. Under that tide of cavalry the Duke's army melted. They fought in clumps desperately. They flung away their weapons. They fled. They rushed down desperately to meet death. It was all a medley of broken noises, oaths, stray shots, cries, wounded men whimpering, hurt horses screaming. The horses were the worst part of it. Perhaps you never heard a horse scream.

That morning's work is all very confused to me. I remember seeing men cut down as they ran. I remember a fine horse coming past me lurching, clattering his stirrups, before leaping into the river. I remember the stink of powder over all the field; the strange look on the faces of the dead; the body of a trumpeter, kneeling against a gorse–bush, shot through the heart, with his trumpet raised to his lips, the litter everywhere, burnt cartridges, clothes, belts, shot, all the waste of war. They are in my mind, those memories, like scattered pictures. The next clear memory in my mind, is of a company of cavalry in red coats, under a fierce, white–faced man, bringing in a string of prisoners to the King's camp. A couple of troopers jumped down to examine me. One had the face of a savage; the other was half drunk. "You're one of them," they said. "Bring him on." They twisted string about my thumbs. I was their prisoner. They dragged me into the King's camp, where the white–faced man sat down at a table to judge us.

I will not talk of that butchery. The white–faced man has been judged now, in his turn; I will say no more of him. When it came to my turn, he would hear no words from me; I was a rebel, fit for nothing but death. "Pistol him" was all the sentence passed on me. The soldiers laid hands on me to drag me away, to add my little corpse to the heap outside.

One of the officers spoke up for me. "He's only a boy," he said. "Go easy with the boy. Don't have the poor child killed." It was kindly spoken; but quite carelessly. The man would have pleaded for a cat with just as much passion. It was useless, anyway, for the colonel merely repeated "Pistol him," just as one would have ordered a wine at dinner. "Burgundy." "No, the Burgundy here is all so expensive." "Never mind, Burgundy." So I was led away to stand with the next batch of prisoners lined against a wall to be shot. My place was at the end of a line, next to a young sullen–looking man black with powder. I did not feel frightened, only hopeless, quite hopeless, a sort of dead feeling. I remember looking at the soldiers getting ready to shoot us. I wondered which would shoot me. They seemed so slow about it. There was some hitch, I think, in filling up the line; a man had proved his innocence or something.

Then, the next instant, there was Aurelia dragging the white–faced man from his table. I dimly remember him ordering me to be released, while Sir Travers Carew gave me brandy. I remember the young sullen–looking man's face; for he looked at me, a look of dull wonder, with a sort of hopeless envy in it, which has wrung my heart daily, ever since. "Mount," said Aurelia. "Mount, Martin. For God's sake, Uncle Travers, let us get out of this." They were on both sides of me each giving me an arm in the saddle, as we rode out of that field of death through Zoyland village towards the old Abbey near Chard.

I shall say little more, except that I never saw my master again. When they led him to the scaffold on Tower Hill I was outward bound to the West Indies, as private secretary to Sir Travers, newly appointed Governor of St. Eulalie. We had many of Monmouth's men in St. Eulalie after the Bloody Assizes; but their tale is too horrible to tell here. You will want to know whether I ever saw Aurelia again. Not for some years, not very often for nine years; but since then our lives have been so mingled that when we die it will be hard to say which soul is which, so much our spirits are each other's. So now, I have written a long story. May we all tell our tales to the end before the pen is taken from us.

Printed in the United Kingdom
by Lightning Source UK Ltd.
103058UKS00002B/25

9 781419 132919